The

Cake Café

Sue Watson

The
Christmas
Cake Café

Bookouture

Published by Bookouture, an imprint of StoryFire Ltd.
23 Sussex Road, Ickenham, UB10 8PN
United Kingdom

www.bookouture.com

ISBN: 978-1-78681-087-8

This book is dedicated to you.

Thank you for reading, have yourself a merry little Christmas – and whatever you do, please don't skimp on the cake!

Prologue

The Christmas Proposal

It was Christmas Eve, the champagne was cold and sparkly, the tree was twinkling, and Bing Crosby was tinkling across the restaurant, filling the air with festive warmth and glitter. It was also the eve of my fortieth birthday, so it was extra special, and I was feeling particularly emotional looking at Tim across the table. The time was right. At last. He looked gorgeous. Not only was the candlelight warming his face, softening his big brown eyes, it was also rekindling our love. Despite the sparkle of the season I had to admit we'd been a little lacklustre on the love front recently.

'This is just what we need,' I sighed. 'I know things haven't been easy for us – you've been working so hard I've hardly seen you – but I'm glad we made this time for each other, Tim.'

'Yes, I wanted us to spend tonight together,' he said. 'It's been ten years now, and I think it's time we talked about the future.'

A frisson of excitement bubbled up in my chest – though it may have been the champagne.

'Yes, ten wonderful years,' I said, smiling, gazing into his eyes and thinking of the good times. It had taken a while, and there'd been doubts along the way. It hadn't been a bed of roses, and Tim had a tendency to put work before our relationship, coming home and burying his head in the computer, and often forgetting our anniversaries because he was so busy. But here, by the glittering light of candles, it seemed Tim was finally ready to put us first. He knew Christmas was my favourite time of year, and I'd often talked of a wedding in December, so perhaps we could organise it in time for next year? It was my childhood dream to be a winter bride, dressed in icy white, crystals and fur. I'd imagined being delivered to my soul mate by horse and carriage, cutting through a white landscape of snowy mountains and shimmering fir trees. And it looked like that dream was just about to come true, so I sat back and waited for the confetti to fall.

Tim lifted the champagne bottle from the ice bucket, tutting slightly at the drips on the table. I wiped them away with my napkin then folded it again, pushing the creases with my fingers, desperately trying to make it smooth.

'The waitress should have brought a cloth,' he sighed. 'I wasn't sure about buying this fizz anyway... it's an inferior brand.' He scrutinised the label then screwed up his face in that way he often did.

I smiled indulgently. How like Tim to want everything about the 'surprise proposal' to be perfect. We were quite alike really – both wanted a nice home, clean, tidy with a perfectly manicured lawn and a kitchen stuffed with high-end white goods. My friend Storm said we were in a rut, but as I pointed out to her, one girl's rut was another girl's life of domestic bliss. We both knew where we were and what the other was doing at any given time, nothing wrong with that – and we were both in bed by 9.30 p.m. every night, asleep by 9.35 p.m. I was happy; I felt safe with Tim. He wasn't what you'd call spontaneous, but if spontaneity meant he'd run off with the first good-looking woman he saw, then give me predictable. Given our routine and the fact I knew him inside out, the proposal wasn't going to be a surprise because I'd seen all the signs. There was mistletoe above the table, champagne in the ice bucket and deliberately vague references to it being time to 'talk about our future'.

He'd also insisted I meet him at 6.30 p.m., which meant I had to miss taking part in the annual carol service at the hospital. My half-sister Jody was a nurse there, and I'd felt really torn about backing out – and Jody hadn't helped with her emotional black-mail. 'Don't worry about the hospital charity, Jen. I mean if Tim wants an early dinner then sick patients will have to come second,' she'd said sarcastically. For God's sake, this was my Christmas pro-posal. It was everything I'd ever wanted and still she didn't get it. I put Jody and her anger from my mind. It was my birthday tomorrow, and I was having a special Christmas Eve birthday din-ner with my future husband. I looked round at the glittery lights, the mistletoe, the sparkling champagne and the man with twinkly blue eyes. I was a lucky girl.

As Tim lifted the bottle to pour our drinks, I discreetly checked the bottom of my glass flute to see if he'd popped the engagement ring in when I wasn't looking. Tim wasn't really a romantic – he always said grand gestures were just a desperate attempt for at-tention, or a cover-up for infidelity. I suppose that's why he never bought me flowers and didn't want to get engaged, until now. If I ever made vague suggestions about getting married (which I did, sometimes once a week) he'd always reject them quite strenuously: 'Isn't it enough that I come back to our shared home every evening?' he'd say. But I knew if I waited long enough it would happen. And here we were, champagne on the table, Bing Crosby in the air – my moment had arrived.

'So... to us,' I said, raising my glass, looking into his eyes, offering him the moment. 'And to love,' I added, for good measure.

'Whatever love is,' he said in his best Prince Charles voice, which stung a little, but now wasn't the time to compare our love to that of the doomed prince and princess, so I pushed forward.

'I wonder what our future holds?' I said, with a questioning but coquettish look, along with another rather blatant cue.

'I don't know.'

'Oh.' I put down my glass, still smiling. Was he teasing me? It wasn't like Tim to tease – he was usually very serious.

'I've been thinking a lot lately and tonight I want to share my thoughts with you,' he started.

I shimmered with excitement and, taking another gulp, I waited as he took a sip of his champagne. Now would be good, I thought – this would be the perfect memory with the candles and the musical accompaniment. Bing was reaching a climax – a few more festive lyrics and he'd be gone, leaving only cutlery clatter and murmured conversations. The Christmas proposal had to have a backdrop of good Christmas music, and I was worried about what would be piped through next, because I didn't want this moment drowned by a shrieking Mariah Carey wailing about what she wanted for Christmas. I felt like a film director, longing to shout 'Action!' so it would all fall into place here and now – everything perfect, even the timing. You had to grab these perfectly framed moments so you could hold on to them forever.

And then he spoke. 'We've had ten good years together... and the thing is... tonight I wanted to say... thank you...'

'You're welcome.'

'But... but I think we've reached the end of the road.'

And my Christmas world stood still. Baubles stopped sparkling, candles went out – and Bing Crosby left abruptly, taking his white Christmas with him.

This wasn't in the script. Tim was now supposed to be on one knee placing the ring on my finger as the restaurant erupted around us in applause. My mouth was suddenly very dry, and I took a large gulp of champagne before asking, 'What do you mean?'

'I'm not happy.'

'Happy? Not happy?'

'No... I don't want this life... with you.'

My throat closed up and I couldn't speak, breathe or swallow – my whole world had crashed, taking my past and future with it. No sparkly ring in my glass, no flower-framed wedding photos of the two of us smiling, my bouquet thrown in the air, my life fused with his.

I looked into his cold eyes, a tiny cell in my body still hoping against hope this might be an elaborate joke. But Tim didn't do jokes.

'How long have you felt like this?' I asked.

'Years.'

'Years? YEARS?'

'Yes... don't shout, Jennifer.' He looked over at the couple on the next table, giving them an embarrassed smile.

'Oh I'm sorry, you've just thrown a bomb into my life, forgive me if I embarrass you by shouting,' I snapped. 'Tim, what the hell...?'

'I'm sorry. I just haven't felt... love... for you for a while now.'

This was a final stab to the heart. 'But it's Christmas... and it's my birthday...' I said, desperately searching for reasons for him not to do this, like it was illegal to dump someone at Christmas or on their birthday.

'Why this... now?' I asked, gesturing towards the champagne, the glittering candles, the perfect bloody setting for a perfect bloody proposal.

'It's your birthday. We always go out for your birthday. I wanted it to be pleasant...'

'Pleasant? PLEASANT?' I raised my voice again.

'Ssshhh, you're making a scene,' he said, looking round furtively.

'A scene? A SCENE? I yelled, aware I was simply repeating key words and saying them more loudly, but it was involuntary. 'You dump me after ten years... my best years... We were on the cusp of marriage.' He was shaking his head, but I wasn't taking this on.

'You've taken my youth, my fertile years – I wanted a baby, Tim.'

'I'm sure you'll meet someone...' he started.

'I WON'T. No one will want me. You've had the best years, the childbearing...'

'Please stop shouting about fertility and childbearing in here.' He was hissing, more concerned about how we looked to the rest of the diners than the fact my heart was splattered all over the table.

'You've taken away my future, you bastard!' I shouted this and in my rising fury picked up the bottle of champagne and hurled the rest of the contents at him. He yelped like a dog, and then the manager came over and asked if he could help.

'Yes, kick him in the balls for me,' I shouted, and grabbing my bag, I rushed out in a flurry of tears and heartbreak – just as Bing Crosby suggested we have ourselves a merry little Christmas.

Chapter 1

The Most Wonderful Time of the Year

Ten months later

I'd always assumed I'd be married with children in a perfect home in a perfect life by now, and my Decembers would be filled with advent calendars, nativity plays and children's excited laughter. But of course that wasn't the case. It was now October and this Christmas I would decorate my tree alone and wrap what few presents I'd need to buy, including one for myself and for Mrs Christmas, my cat. She liked to tear the paper off with her claws and I'd convinced myself she knew it was Christmas. It didn't take a psychologist to work out she was my child substitute.

I'd bought her as a gift for Tim three Christmases before he dumped me, but she'd never really taken to him, nor he to her. And when she clawed at his best cashmere jumper, he threatened to send her back to the cat-rescue centre. But I had refused. I loved Mrs Christmas, and I knew how it felt to be abandoned; my own father had walked out on me and my mum when I was just ten, and the very idea of doing the same to Mrs Christmas appalled me.

So Mrs Christmas was extra special. I loved the way she'd purr and swish her tail when I came home from work, and when I settled down on the sofa she'd push her head into my neck, happy to have me back.

Tim said cats didn't have feelings, but Mrs Christmas and I knew differently. We'd both been hurt and I loved her. Though I'd never planned to be a cat mother, it seemed like I was a natural.

With Tim now gone, Mrs Christmas was my family; both my parents were dead, and the only person who shared my gene pool was my half-sister Jody, and that was only half a pool because we had different mothers.

'I know it's stupid but I miss Tim... I even miss him telling me I'm silly,' I'd said to Jody.

'You are silly if you miss that – bloody silly,' she'd sniped.

'You know what I mean. My life is all over the place. Somehow he kept it in order, and I feel like I've nothing to hold on to. Everything's falling apart. I didn't make my bed this morning – I am seriously going insane.'

'Well, if not making your bed is insane then I should be locked up,' she said, bored with my whingeing about being single and childless.

During that first difficult year, Jody and I spent many evenings drinking wine together and talking into the night like 'real' sisters, and if nothing else my terrible break-up with Tim had certainly brought us closer together. I'd talk while she listened, which was a revelation, because young, irritating, fast-living Jody could be quite insightful at times, and she had become a great support to me.

'Tim had everything,' she'd said. 'Good job, lovely home and, yes, on paper he was perfect – but that's all you saw – this perfect man with this perfect flat in this perfect life. If they were casting for the next series of *The Bachelor*, Tim would be it. But real life isn't like that, Jen. He was as cold as his bare brick walls.

'I remember going round there once when you cooked dinner for us,' she said, 'and instead of saying "This is lovely", which it was, he said it needed more spice and you should have cooked the chicken for a shorter time. He gave you a bloody cookery lesson in front of everyone at the table. It was embarrassing.'

'I know, I know. I feel stupid that I let that happen,' I said, 'but if I'd challenged him, the evening would have been ruined.'

'It *was* ruined – *for you* – and me for that matter,' Jody sighed. 'He undermined you, he was a bully,' she said. 'What did you ever see in him, Jen?'

'Oh, I don't know now. I feel like I was under a spell and it's only recently I've emerged into the light,' I replied. 'At first he was kind and I was so scared of being abandoned again that I clung hard. I suppose he lulled me into a false sense of security.'

We both knew that my dad had started me on that particular drug when he'd walked out when I was little. I'd loved him so much, and the very idea of him not being in my life wasn't one I'd ever considered. He was 'Dad' and Mum was 'Mum' and I was me... and that's how it would always be – or so I thought. Dad would always give me extra presents at Christmas, saying, 'Everyone else has birthday *and* Christmas, but you will have one special day all rolled into one – let's make it twice as good!'

And he did. He would buy me double the amount of presents and make two piles – one for Christmas and one for birthday. He and Mum also made sure I always had a birthday cake and we also had a Christmas cake... until he left, and nothing was quite the same ever again. The shock of his departure left me very vulnerable and needy, and when I grew older and looked for a partner, my priority was someone I was certain wouldn't leave me. Looking back now, I'm not even sure I ever loved Tim – I just thought he'd always stay.

'I think my neediness fed Tim's ego...' I'd said to Jody when we talked this through. 'The writing was on the wall if only I'd realised it at the time – but I loved living in his beautiful, organised flat with the neat venetian blinds, the perfect lighting, the perfectly matched sofas and cushions. I'd try so hard to be the perfect girlfriend and be there in the evenings waiting for him, wine chilling, dinner ready. I'd change and put on more make-up so that when he walked in I'd be there standing in the kitchen, like a scene from a romantic film.' The thought of me doing this now makes me feel slightly ill...

'God – all that effort. It was a relationship not a bloody three-act play, Jen – you always love the *idea* of something rather than the actual reality of it.'

'What do you mean?'

'Well, it's like Christmas. You search for the perfect tree, the perfect decorations, the tastiest bloody turkey – and for what? I've never spent Christmas with you, but I know when I've met up with you in January you're down because it didn't turn out how you expected. And I'm not surprised. You have such big expectations of yourself and of life – how can you ever be happy?'

I shrugged, but what she said made a kind of sense – perhaps perfect didn't exist? And that made me feel sad.

'When I was with Tim, I always had this lovely vision of us sitting together by candlelight at the end of the working day,' I said.

'You know, like people do in films and books – and I'd imagine big glasses of wine, lovely food and gentle chatter segueing into mind-blowing sex...'

Jody guffawed.

'And sometimes I'd leave work early in an attempt to achieve this,' I continued, refusing to be put off by her laughter at the prospect of Tim and me in flagrante. 'But after shopping, and preening and cleaning, I'd be bloody exhausted by the time he came home. I'd be totally frazzled, my hair would be limp, the pasta overcooked and I'd end up gulping the wine like lemonade I'd be so stressed. Then Tim would find something wrong with the sodding pasta so I'd drink more wine to block out his voice and he'd start on about how much I was drinking. On those "perfect" nights we'd either have a row or I'd give in and go to bed early – alone.'

'But your pasta and your hair was probably fine, and the right guy would have told you that. And even if your pasta was a little soggy, you'd have laughed about it – but you couldn't laugh about anything with that miserable sod.'

'You say that, but he seems to have found someone else to put up with him. I've heard he's met a young blonde who loves the gym.'

'He's still going for the same type then?' she said and laughed, looking me up and down.

'Very funny, Jody,' I said, aware I wasn't young, blonde or gym obsessed. 'Tim had women chasing him all the time. We'd go to a dinner party and they'd be all over him... and sometimes, when I wondered if we should stay together, I'd think, "Someone else will have him if I don't."'

'That's not a reason to stay.'

'I know that now. If I'm honest I was flattered that he let me share his life. We had some wonderful holidays, dined in lovely restaurants, and when things changed and he became irritated by me, I just wanted the good times back.'

'No one should be "flattered" to be with another person. How dare he be "irritated" by you. He was the lucky one! You are pretty and intelligent and kind and...'

'I wasn't enough for him.'

'No one would *ever* be enough for Tim. He encouraged you to move into his flat, lose touch with all your friends and become swallowed up in his life. You were living in his life – but he wasn't living in yours, Jen – and the woman he left you for will be doing exactly the same now. Men like Tim are controlling. You may not have realised it at the time, but that's what he looks for in a woman: someone with low self-esteem, someone needy he can manipulate.'

'God it sounds awful, doesn't it?' I sighed. I'd known this deep in my heart, but hearing it spoken out loud made me feel stupid, and at the same time angry with myself for allowing it to happen.

'If you two had married you'd have had the most amazing wedding and a beautiful home, but it wouldn't have made him love you more or treat you any better.'

'I know – you don't have to tell me, Jody.'

I was aware I had to move on, but Christmas was just round the corner and all I could think of was the devastation of the previous year. Everything reminded me of our Christmases together – and just walking down supermarket aisles I was bombarded with memories. Bottles of Harvey's Bristol Cream sherry in blue glass all lined up on shelves made me think how we always had a little glass when we decorated the tree. The first year together we'd almost drunk a whole bottle and we'd made love under the tree – but the pine needles were a nuisance and Tim was itching for days, so we didn't do that again. Actually, thinking about it, Tim didn't even decorate the tree again after that first year. I did it on my own, a solitary glass of sherry at my side, mince pies warming in the oven for when he came home late after work. Even my memories were fraudulent, it seemed.

Talking to Jody was like therapy for me. But as great as Jody was for being there, her brand of consolation left much to be desired. 'You can't spend Christmas as a spinster' and 'He was a dick' were her go-to lines of comfort. Her observation that 'They have old people like you on Matchmaker.com too', which was apparently meant to make me feel better, was typical. Oh yes, Jody was always very honest with me, but we don't always want to hear the truth. I know I certainly didn't. It wasn't her fault – she was just trying to help me, but when she said I needed to start seriously looking for someone I laughed.

'If only it were that easy. You're twenty-eight – it's okay for you to talk about finding someone else, but I'm older, less of a catch,' I'd sighed.

'Yes, I know you're old and dried-up, but there are men who like that kind of thing, I saw it on a documentary once,' she'd said, laughing. I think she was joking.

'I feel like I have no future! I'm going to be that aunt who drinks vodka straight out of the bottle and ruins Christmas,' I'd said.

'No you aren't, because you don't drink vodka,' was her response.

We were worlds apart, Jody and I, and until my mum died four years previously, we had barely known each other. To Jody's credit, she'd reached out after Mum's death, coming to the funeral and trying to offer an olive branch. As our father and her own mother were both now dead, we realised we were the only family either of us had and so had begun a very basic, very vague friendship based on the odd phone call, a rare coffee or a drink after work. Now we stayed over at each other's homes and spoke most days on the phone. And when it all kicked off with Tim, Jody looked after me, and as annoying and childish and drunk as she sometimes gets, I don't know what I'd do without her.

Now, over a bottle of wine, she began telling me all about her planned trip to Switzerland. Having heard about this since she first considered a working holiday 'on the piste', as she put it, I felt I already knew everything. I'd seen the photos of the ski resort and seen most of the younger ski instructors' profiles on her phone, along with pictures of every outfit she was planning to wear.

'But you don't need cropped tops in Switzerland. Apart from the fact you'll be freezing, you're going out there to work,' I'd said. 'Not to party.'

'Ooh that's cruel, Jen.' She rolled her eyes. 'I am so going to party! You see everything in little boxes – just because you're at work, doesn't mean you can't enjoy yourself too. Anyway, I now have this delicious hiatus between finishing my nursing degree and finding a job in hospital making beds and washing old men's bits – so I'm going to have one last fling.'

I had to laugh at the phrase. 'Last fling? At your age I don't think I'd even had my *first* fling,' I said, shaking my head and smiling.

'Jen, you so need a fling. You've worked in that dusty old library since you were about twelve...'

'Twenty-one actually – I was one of the first graduates on my course to walk straight into a job,' I said.

'Oh whoopee doo! So while everyone else was travelling the world, drinking too much and sleeping with everyone in sight you were stamping books in the local library. Wow, your mates must have been dead jealous.'

This stung a little, and I think she saw the look on my face because she backtracked slightly.

'Look, Jen, I'm not putting you down, or the fact that you've reached the lofty heights of Head Librarian at South Manchester Libraries. I just think it's a shame you haven't experienced anything other than here.'

Then she did something she often did, which was extremely annoying – she said, 'OH MY GOD!' and did a sort of collapse on the sofa that often accompanied these proclamations for dramatic effect.

'What?' I asked in a monotone. I wasn't buying in to her drama.

'I just had an AMAZING idea.'

'Oh, I assumed you'd just been shot.'

'You know how you've been thinking of going on a six-month sabbatical?'

'Yes, to take a course in cataloguing history books.'

'Ooh cataloguing history books, that's a wild ride, you really must spend six precious months of your life face down in old tomes – said no one EVER! Sod that – come with me to Switzer-land!'

'No.'

'Oh, it would so do you good, Jen. All that fresh air, exercise, hunky ski instructors. The resort I'm going to is looking for more staff for the season... Jen, we'd be there for Christmas. Together. Can you imagine?'

'Yes, I can, and I'm not wasting my sabbatical, my sanity or my Christmas snowbound in a ski lodge with you.'

'Think about it – really, really think about it. You love Christmas and you'll just be on your own here, moping around, thinking about that dickhead.'

'You mean Tim, the man who broke my heart into a million pieces.'

'Yes – but forget about Tim the tosser – just think about that sparkly white Christmas in Switzerland. The girls would love you to come along. There are three of us so you'd round it off nicely.'

Jody was good. She could often make me see things differently, and this sounded like a way for me to forget about last Christmas, forge new festive memories and move on.

I'd always longed for the perfect Christmas, and Jody was right – I'd never quite managed it. It always seemed as though obstacles got in the way. It could have been something as simple as overcooked sprouts, or the wrong shade of bauble, but I was a perfectionist and had to have everything just so – especially at Christmas. But I realised now that, despite all this effort trying to attain perfection, I wasn't happy.

I thought now about how I would have felt if, instead of finishing our relationship, Tim had asked me to marry him, and it occurred to me with a jolt that I'd never wanted to marry Tim. I'd wanted marriage and children and the perfect home, but in truth, I didn't want it with Tim, which was why everything else around us had to be perfect – because we weren't. I was overcompensating, framing the picture of our relationship, always adding flowers and candles and twinkly lights. I had to dress it up to make it pretty and acceptable, because deep down perhaps I knew it wasn't. I recalled a moment even before Tim announced his departure from my life when I'd been sitting at my dressing table applying the most perfect red Chanel lipstick, and it hadn't mattered how many times I'd layered on that classy shine, I hadn't been able to cover the emptiness I felt inside. Being me, I'd pretended it was all good and just kept on painting pictures over the truth, adding pretty accessories, creating a beautiful setting. And now it just made me very sad to realise that I'd wasted ten years lying to myself.

I hadn't realised this properly until now. There were niggles in the back of my mind – there always had been with Tim – but I'd been scared of losing everything and being left alone. And during this time I didn't look too closely – I couldn't take our relationship apart and look at it – because deep down I knew it might not fit back together again.

Jody's plans for a perfect and snow-filled Christmas in Switzerland, without a hint of Tim, suddenly began to feel like the cure I needed.

'Switzerland sounds lovely, but you and me... we're so different,' I sighed, trying to be realistic about this wonderful idea of a Christmas of glittering snow and crackling log fires.

'Yes, but that doesn't mean we can't have fun. And besides, this is about a six-month rehab. You can forget about Tim, the dusty old library, that crazy woman who's obsessed with ghosts...'

'Storm. My gifted colleague, who penetrates the sixth dimension, is called Storm,' I said.

'She can penetrate whatever she likes, but the fact is, you need a bloody break from everyone and everything. Go on, why not just run away with me, Jen?'

'Because it's Christmas. I've always been at home for Christmas.'

'Just because you've always done it this way, doesn't make it right.'

'That's true.'

'So try something different this year. Jen, think of the snow-covered mountains, the steaming hot chocolate... we *have* to spend Christmas together. We're family – we're sisters.'

'I know, and I really appreciate what you're saying and – a few years ago I might have taken you up on it.'

'And in a few years you'll say the same. You always say it: "When I was younger I'd have done that... if I was twenty-five I'd do that." No you wouldn't and you won't and you'll go to your bloody grave saying it. In fact I'll have it written on your grave. "Here lies Jennifer Barker. She would have done such a lot if she'd been younger."'

I stood up and went into the kitchen, her words ringing in my ears. She was right. I'd been talking about taking a six-month sabbatical for years, and I'd flirted with a course (as much as anyone can flirt with cataloguing history books), but I hadn't really decided what I wanted to do. The library expected me to take an academic course, but I'd recently been thinking less about cataloguing books and more about doing something I enjoyed. There were several courses I could take, but the one I thought about most was a cake-baking course. I loved baking cakes and spending hours icing them – it was what had kept me sane over the years with Tim.

When I was very young, my mum had given me a book called *The Christmas Cake Café*, about a girl who loves to bake. She meets the man of her dreams, gets married and opens a beautiful café serving fabulous cakes. It was a children's book, and the illustrations were quite beautiful: sugar-spun cakes, falling white snow all around the cosy glow of the café. I showed it to Tim once and I recall him saying the whole narrative was ludicrous.

He just didn't seem to understand that this wasn't about critiquing a child's book – it was an idea, a concept that had stayed with me since childhood. I couldn't let go of the café – I saw it so clearly in my head. It was always winter and frosty outside, but the café glowed on a dark, cobbled street, like a little star twinkling in the cold darkness. The cakes melted in your mouth and tasted of marzipan and cinnamon, the ceiling was covered in mistletoe and young couples sat holding each other's hearts and hands in the warmth as snow tumbled past the little lead windows. I'd always longed to spend my days baking and creating. I once thought I'd run away to London and find work as a pastry chef in a top hotel. But I couldn't leave Mum in Manchester on her own, so after finishing my degree I'd applied to the local library to become a librarian. 'A dream job,' my mum described it as on my first day – but I wasn't convinced, and there were dark days when I could be found sobbing in the 'Cakes and Bakery Books' section, poring over recipes, dreaming of piped cream and rosettes of sugary icing instead of dusty books.

I opened the oven now, and a hot blast of fruity cinnamon hit me in the face. I placed the dark, rich cake onto the countertop and it was weighed down with Christmas goodness. I licked my lips – what a shame I had to wait until December. At this point I felt a soft, swishing around my legs as Mrs Christmas demanded supper, and after a cuddle and a packet of cat food she wandered off, her tail high.

'I couldn't leave Mrs Christmas for three months,' I said, wandering back into the living room where Jody was now downloading pictures of the resort to tempt me with.

'Oh someone will look after the cat – she'll be fine. Stop looking for excuses to live your life,' she said absently. Then, whooping at each picture, she kept thrusting her phone into my face, each shot white with snow, blue skies, hot men and dangerous sports.

I loved the idea of all that snow, learning to ski, meeting new people. But there was still a part of me that longed to stay safe, stay working at the library and spend Christmas locked up in the house...

'Come on, Jenny, it will be the picture-perfect setting... it's what Christmas is all about. You can come out with us at the end of November, and if you don't like it you could be home by Christmas... but I know you'll LOVE it. Imagine it – a cabin in the Swiss Alps – a log fire, a hot tub and all the gorgeous ski instructors you can handle.'

'I've given up on men, and... as for a hot tub, ew!'

'Is that because Tim said they were full of germs?'

'No,' I lied.

'So ski instructors, hunky, on ice, sliding all over you... don't tell me you're not interested in that?'

'I'm not.'

'Is that because Tim said you'd never get another man?'

'No!' Damn, I wish I'd never told her he'd said that – it was quite different in context. 'He'd said it in the heat of the moment, in a fit of pique when we'd argued about the best way to flambé pork,' I said, attempting a superior tone.

'Flambé pork? I'd have flambéed his balls,' she said, then whooped at the sight of another snow scene/dangerous sport/dangerous man on her phone. 'So you're rejecting my white winter-wonderland Christmas, casting me aside like I'm nothing to you...' She was a complete drama queen.

'No, I'm not *rejecting* your white Christmas *or* casting you aside. I just happen to know that there's a *Downton Abbey* special on TV on Christmas Day, and I will be watching it with a bottle of sherry.'

'But you hate *Downton Abbey*.'

'Exactly, which is why I will be drinking a bottle of sherry – it's the only way I'll get through it. Anyway, drunk *Downton* aside, I'd be no use working at a ski resort. For a start I can't ski!'

'Excuse after excuse.'

'I'd have thought it was pretty fundamental to be able to ski in a ski resort.'

'No, there are jobs in the coffee shop and the hotel. And you can learn to ski.'

'I have to say I always fancied skiing, but hurling myself up and down slopes in clothes that make me look fatter than I am is another thing.'

After a rather prolonged period of relationship mourning with Mr Krispy Kreme, where I'd periodically locked myself in the library toilets (with a half-dozen box on a bad day), I'd come through that early phase and moved on to loss of appetite. Consequently I was now looking slimmer than I had in years – I'd rejected sugar and carbs and embraced a life of lettuce and longing.

'You look fab. It's time to premiere that new body on the slopes – you'd look fantastic in a ski suit.'

'Yeah after liposuction and a facelift. I'm not exactly Elle Macpherson.'

'You're not doing that weird doughnut thing again are you?' She looked up from her phone a little concerned.

'No, I'm fine now.' I didn't meet her eyes. I'd licked the window of the Krispy Kreme shop a couple of days ago – these things don't go away overnight.

'Think about it, Jen! Horse-drawn carriages through a winter landscape, glittering snow, Glühwein... Sachertorte...' She was giving a running commentary while flicking through more pictures on her phone.

'Sacher who?' I joked, but it was lost on Jody.

'The cake... chocolate and yummy toppings. You could seek out new cake recipes for that café you're going to open one day.'

'Yeah, who knows? I suppose one of the positives of being single is that anything's possible, and there's only me to think of.'

'Yep, it's up to you – café owner, librarian, wife and mother...'

'I don't think I'll ever be a mum, Jody, not now. My periods are sporadic to say the least... so on top of being single I'm also about to be menopausal and barren, ooh what a catch!' I half laughed.

'You're young to be having the menopause, but if you are then embrace it. Perhaps it's your body's way of telling you time's running out?'

'I wish you'd stop trying to cheer me up,' I snapped.

'Oh, stop feeling sorry for yourself. And, stop banging on about your dying eggs. You aren't defined by your womb. You can live the life you want to – it's up to you. There's adoption, IVF, surrogacy, more than one way to skin a cat or have a baby. But the key word here is "live" – stop putting everything off and blaming your bloody ovaries for everything.'

'I'm not.'

'So come to Switzerland with me and the girls. We'll work hard, but we'll also eat delicious rich chocolate cake and watch the world go by... downhill on skis.'

I hated to admit it, but it sounded fun and the very prospect of Swiss chocolate cake made me salivate. Damn, the appetite-loss stage of my relationship grief hadn't lasted long – it was coming back with a vengeance.

'At night the landscape glows, the stars twinkle, the sky is so velvety black...'

'You're reading from the brochure, aren't you?' I said, knowing this poetic description was beyond Jody. She was a nurse, not Noel Coward.

'Yeah, but it's just gorgeous. Even if I did want to go away, I told you there's no one to look after Mrs Christmas.'

'What about supernatural Susie? She loves cats, dead or alive.'

'You mean Storm. I can't leave my cat with Storm – she'd have her contacting the dead before I got back.'

'And talking of dead – Switzerland is on the list of things to do before I die... life's short, Jen.'

This made me think. It seemed a mere handful of years since I'd been in my twenties, young, free and single, life ahead of me and a future filled with possibilities. It was like I just turned round and suddenly here I was on the cusp of forty-one, and overnight my future and all those possibilities had shrunk. A year of being single had brought no suitors, so even without my suspected menopause, the lack of bedroom action meant I couldn't get pregnant anyway in the last dying days. Jody said she knew a student doctor who might oblige with a turkey baster of sperm, but I'd declined her kind offer. 'Thanks, but I'll pass on that romantic encounter,' I'd said, deciding to face the fact that I may have a different future than I'd planned.

When Jody had gone I spiked my lovely Christmas cake with a prong and poured brandy in, trying to put thoughts of a white Christmas and sleigh rides through fir trees out of my head. I tried not to think about snow and Sachertorte as I turned on the TV to watch *Midsomer Murders*, but I couldn't settle. I couldn't work out who the murderer was, distracted by the early ads for Christmas hampers and families sitting down to Christmas dinner. But the perfume ads really got me – always the beautiful, flawless six-foot woman, usually ending up dancing round the Eiffel Tower at dawn with some gorgeous hunk, a painful reminder I wasn't anywhere near Paris, and I was on my own.

Christmas would be difficult but remembering Tim taking down my tinsel and criticising my 'tacky tree' made me realise I was happier without him. I was happier without anyone – because people only come into your life to leave you, and I should know. The Christmas I'd turned ten my dad had taken me out for tea and given me two beautifully wrapped gifts – one for my birthday and one for Christmas. I'd been delighted and still remembered the moment through a glittery gauze framed by fairy lights.

The first gift was wrapped in Christmas paper and I tore it off to discover a small radio with headphones, which in those days was the ultimate in music technology. 'You can listen to that any time – and if you ever feel lonely you can put those earphones in any time, day or night, and listen to the music and imagine us singing along together,' he'd said.

Dad and I often sang along to his radio so it was perfectly natural that I should have my own now I was 'grown up', and I'd squealed with excitement at the prospect of us singing the top twenty in the kitchen. 'I'll let you listen too, Dad,' I'd said, open-ing the birthday gift and reading the card attached, which said, 'Happy birthday to the most important girl in the world.'

Opening the box I'd been delighted to see the most beautiful doll but surprised because this was a 'little-girl' gift. Yet as I'd touched her long, silky hair I hadn't been able to articulate my feelings but some-how knew it was permission to continue being a little girl, Dad's little girl. The doll had real eyelashes that blinked slowly when you moved her and I remember such happiness at receiving this wonderful gift from my father. After tea he'd driven us home and, walking with me to the front door, unlocked it before saying, 'I'm not coming in, Jenny.' I'd been shocked, horrified. 'Where are you going, Daddy?' I'd heard myself say, but he'd just kissed me on the forehead; 'I have to go away for a while. I'll phone you.' He'd smiled sadly, touched my fringe with his fingers then walked slowly down the path and climbed into his car. I didn't see him again for two years.

Later, I learned that he'd walked out on me and my mum for another woman. My parents had decided it would be less painful for me if he stayed away, and I never really understood the logic – I still don't. After that day, my only comfort was the doll – and the card that told me I was 'the most important girl in the world'. But after a while, I began to question this – if I was the most important girl in the world, how come he'd walked out on me?

As an adult I've always found it hard to trust men, and I'm so desperate for them to stay I'm aware I can be a bit needy. With Tim I thought I'd finally found someone who'd stick around, but now I knew that wasn't possible and, as much as I'd have loved a partner, I'd given up on that dream because I always ended up with men like my father – who leave.

The next day I was discussing Jody's idea for Switzerland with my friend and colleague, Storm. She said a working holiday away sounded like a great idea because I needed to let go of the past. As we talked she brewed a calming pot of her peppermint tea and was, as always, a sympathetic friend.

'Ten bloody Christmases I waited for him to get on one knee under that Christmas tree,' I said.

'Yes, like I say, you need to let go,' she said and smiled. Storm had been through it all with me – when I received the letter from Tim's solicitor telling me we had to sell the house, I'd wept openly during the morning session of Toddlers' Story Time. Much to the dismay of the children and their mothers who'd come to hear me read *Horrid Henry's Cannibal Curse*, Storm arrived to find me in the middle of a protest from rampaging four-year-old boys and continued with the story before escorting me into the staff room. But being psychic she said she wasn't surprised about Tim. 'I saw the colour of that man's chakras and I can tell you it gave me a few sleepless nights,' she'd said, handing me a steaming mug of bracing mint tea. Having worked together for over twelve years we'd shared the last of our youth with each other among those dusty old library shelves. When I'd had to move out of Tim's house I'd ended up lodging in Storm's big old Victorian villa just south of Manchester.

Storm was desperately looking for meaning in life like the rest of us. Some people find meaning in music or shopping, but Storm found it in Uncle Albert, her spirit guide who'd apparently 'passed through' in 1972, choking on a chip butty and a Woodbine on a day out in Southport.

Her style was less Gypsy Rose Lee and more Psychic Sally with her northern accent and conversations with Uncle Albert about who would win the 15 to 1 at Aintree. But Storm's kindness and apparent contacts gave me comfort, and as I now had to take a belt and braces approach to the future I agreed to let her read my cards. After all, if there was wisdom to be had from any other dimension I wasn't going to turn it away at this stage in the game – I needed all the help I could get.

'Let's see what the future really holds,' she said, setting herself up on a small table and asking me to hold the cards and think only of myself. After about two minutes I handed them back to her but when she turned round my first card I saw it was a skeleton.

'Oh God, I'm going to die.'

'It doesn't mean death – it means change,' she said calmly.

I nodded as she turned over another card, this time with a broken-down building on it, which I immediately interpreted to be my womb.

'I see a man. He's waiting for you,' she was saying quietly under her breath. 'He's tall and handsome and...'

'But where is he and when will he reveal himself?' I said, wanting a time, date and telephone number, something the Tarot wasn't apparently prepared to yield.

'Have patience, dear,' she muttered. 'Ah... I see... snow, I see a glittering frost, a Christmas tree... a white Christmas... pure and oh dear...'

I thought of Switzerland, of snowy peaks and Christmas in the mountains and a thrill of excitement ran through me. 'What? What?'

'I see you standing outside a big, beautiful church – it is here on hallowed ground that your future will unfurl before you... like a cloak.'

'Great, I'm going to be a nun,' I said and we both laughed, but the mere mention of my future unfurling before me did provide a tingle. All my friends were married with kids and living different lives. I looked at Storm, realising that I now had more in common with this childless older woman with wild hair and pierced nipples, who sought answers from dead people and a deck of cards. And despite this I was feeling quite positive. Perhaps I was finally recovering from Tim? He'd moved on. Perhaps it was now time for me to do the same?

Chapter 2

A Mistletoe Ménage with Mrs Scrooge

I wasn't living in a fairy tale. There was no such place as The Christmas Cake Café and there never would be – only in my mind. I wasn't going to find my romantic hero among the library bookshelves – not unless you count the weirdos and nerds who hung around the 'Vampire' section. But I was a grown woman with a career and a life, and I wasn't going to let myself be hurt by anyone again. I had to start with me – and stop fantasising about things I'd never have.

Jody was slowly but surely wearing me down about going to Switzerland with her and I had to admit, there were worse things than a white Christmas in Switzerland. I had been thinking a lot about my future recently and how it might have to change – no white picket fence or babies but something else perhaps? A new career doing something I'd always wanted to do? I had the time off, the money for the flight and enough to keep me going if the short-term job worked out. I could do a lot of thinking somewhere like Switzerland – all that pure white snow, like a blank canvas to write a new life on. What did I have to lose?

It also occurred to me that going to Switzerland would give Jody and I the chance to develop a much stronger relationship. She was now my only living relative, but the twelve-year age gap had always made me feel more like an estranged aunt than a big half-sister. It didn't help that we hadn't actually grown up together either. When I was twelve, my dad had finally got in touch and asked if I'd like to spend the day with him. I was elated. Despite Mum telling me I didn't have to go if I didn't want to, I gently told her that I did want to see him. I sensed that I was being asked to choose between them, but my twelve-year-old head managed to bat this away temporarily and, in spite of still feeling hurt at his departure, I think I still harboured some hope that I could convince him to come home.

'We're going to my new house,' he said, once I was in the car. I was delighted at this prospect, imagining Dad and I playing Scrabble and drinking hot chocolate together like we used to – and perhaps moving Mum in at some stage once they started talking again. It hadn't occurred to me that anyone else would be there, but when we arrived at his new house there was a welcome committee. Maureen, the woman my mother could only ever refer to as 'her', was standing on the doorstep – and to my abject horror she was holding a baby.

'This is Jody, your new baby sister,' Dad said, proudly plucking the cooing baby from Maureen's arms.

I was devastated. The one thing I'd clung to while we'd been apart was what had been written on that gift card. But as Dad and 'her' oohed and ahhed over the tiny little scrap in their arms I felt nothing but betrayal. I wasn't the most important girl in the world any more. Mum had told me he didn't want us, but I'd refused to believe her until now – but I could see how he looked at that baby and I knew I'd finally lost my father.

Consequently, I never became part of his second family as he'd perhaps hoped. There was always too much hurt, and the adults were too wrapped up in their own feelings to try and assuage mine. As a result of all this I never bonded with Jody when we were young and had secretly spied on her Facebook page out of nosiness rather than any concern. I had felt the sting of resentment when I saw a page filled with photos of her with 'Mum and Dad' – my dad. I was also slightly bitter about her university life of clever friends and long hot summers – a life Mum said we could never afford for me. Dad died when I was twenty, and although we'd been estranged for several years by then, I was surprised to feel such grief for him.

But as time went on I'd begun to wonder about my sister and how she'd turned out. We'd spent the last few years building up a tentative friendship and making up for lost time, but we were an odd couple really – she had her rowdy friends and a life of late nights and early mornings and a different boyfriend every week – and I'd had Tim. But we got on quite well, and lately she'd been a wonderful support, a good friend... a sister really.

'Let's meet up for a drink and talk properly about this trip,' I said when she asked again about me going with her to Switzerland. 'I agree we need to bond, the two of us. After all, you're the only family member I have. I'll be leaving you all my Wham! records when I die, and I need to make sure they're going to a good home.'

'Ahhh, I suppose at your age you have to think about stuff like that,' she sighed. She wasn't joking. 'I'm SO excited about Switzerland. You will LOVE it. Oh I can't wait to go skiing with my big sis.'

I was now as excited as she was. This could be a wonderful opportunity to finally become the sisters we should be in a lovely Christmassy setting with the world locked out.

❅ ❅ ❅

Jody and I met in her local wine bar where it seemed Christmas had come early. The bar staff were dressed as Santa Claus, the tree was flashing like crazy, all the drinks had Christmassy names and there was noise and tinsel everywhere.

'It's only November,' I said, sipping on my Christmastini, a lurid red drink that glowed like nuclear waste. It was probably toxic, but it tasted okay.

'Yeah but the guy who owns the bar is going to Australia for Christmas so he wants a British one here first.'

It made perfect sense to Jody.

'How stupid,' I replied. 'You can't have Christmas before December.'

'You can have Christmas whenever you want – there's no local bylaw that says you can't celebrate Christmas in July if you want to.' She rolled her eyes at what she probably saw as my pedantry.

'It's idiotic,' I said. 'And don't kid yourself – he just wants to make money out of Christmas before he leaves the country!'

She lifted her head from a large Mistletoe Ménage cocktail and gave me a stern look. 'I hope you aren't going to be this scratchy in Switzerland, Mrs Scrooge.'

'I am not "Mrs" anything. And please don't rub it in.'

'Okay, *Miss* Scrooge,' she said, wide-eyed and innocent.

'So... me and you spending the next few months – including Christmas – together – I worry we may not want to do the same things.' I had to shout over Noddy Holder screaming, 'It's Christmaaaaas!' which was very annoying but certainly supported my concerns.

'We will. We both LOVE Christmas – well Dad said you always loved Christmas.'

'Did he? Well, he was right... I did, I still do... I just don't like *that* Christmas,' I said, gesturing at a group of lads in Santa hats, drinking shots and dropping their trousers – with gusto. I was always surprised when Jody talked about Dad and how he'd sometimes spoken about me like I was there, part of their family. It made me irrationally happy to think I was on his mind and that he'd wanted to share memories of me with Jody. At the same time it made me feel such regret that I couldn't share some of that family life and special times with my sister when we were younger. I hoped Dad could see us from wherever he was and that he knew we had become friends after all – it would have made him very happy, I was sure of that.

I was momentarily distracted from my thoughts by the obscene antics of the Santas on the next table and pulled a disapproving face.

'They're only having fun,' Jody sighed, winking at one of the boys in the Santa hats.

'If what they're doing with their fake beards is your idea of "fun", then you must be mad.' I averted my eyes once more from the circus going on at the next table, hoping to unsee the spectacle – suffice to say the beards weren't being worn on their faces.

'Boring... that's what you are now.'

'No, I'm not, I've just matured...'

'Old. Old and boring.'

'I'm forty-one... almost. I'm not old and...'

'Oh, Jenny, chillax, you are old – you're over forty for God's sake. But you don't look it.'

'Thanks.' I had to smile – I remember when I'd been twenty-eight and being forty had been akin to being an old-age pensioner.

'You sound old though,' she added as an afterthought, before sipping on her drink. 'Storm was telling me you used to be different, that you were great fun and always got really drunk at the library Christmas party. What happened to fun Jen who used to do shots and photocopy her arse...'

'Storm told you about that?' I said, horrified.

'Yeah, she said you were a real laugh. What happened to that Jen?'

I didn't know what to say. I'd been asking myself the same question recently, but grief and work and disappointment can have that effect on you.

I shrugged and we continued to drink our ludicrous cocktails in silence, but Jody wasn't letting it lie for long.

'So Switzerland. Roaring log fires, swirling down crisp white nursery slopes, shopping in bustling, vibrant Christmas markets and drinking Glühwein as the snow falls outside. Sounds good, doesn't it? Are you excited?'

It did sound good. I had to move on and stop bursting into tears every time I saw a commercial for wedding dresses or disposable nappies. Working in another town in another country with

Jody would provide a fresh horizon, an opportunity to meet new people and contemplate a different future than the one I'd hoped for. It was now time to take the next step, so in the middle of a tacky wine bar in Manchester, with loud music in my ears and a naked Santa with a strategically placed beard assaulting my eyes, we planned our Christmas escape.

A week later, I'd bought two padded ski suits (in shades of pink and blue as, according to *Vogue*, the ski catwalks were all about ice-cream pastels that winter). I did my research in true, thorough librarian style, reading every ski manual possible and trawling through guidebooks and language discs. By the end of November, I'd paid for my flight, filled in a million forms and visas and we were set to go. Jody came over for dinner the night before we left and we looked through the online photos of the rather fabulous snow-covered cabins in the resort. We were both named as 'resort staff' on the forms, but Jody would be working in the ski lodge and I would be safely ensconced in the ski café. But just looking through all the photos it didn't seem like a place of work – even the staff cabins had log fires, hot tubs and huge, open-plan living rooms with kitchens.

'It all looks so – sophisticated, elegant... European,' she sighed.

'You'll fit in then,' I said sarcastically and laughed.

She stuck out her tongue, and I saw the little girl she probably once was. I hoped we hadn't left it too late to become sisters.

'So you said some of your friends are coming to Switzerland too... do I know them?'

'Not sure. There's Kate, she's divorced, disillusioned but lovely, and there's Lola – she's a firecracker. She's still having sex and she's as old as you.'

'Wow, as old as me – that's amazing,' I said sarcastically.

'Yeah, she sexted George Clooney last week.'

'Did he respond?'

'No, but there's time… and while she's waiting she's keeping in practice. I introduced her to Dr Delicious who works in my department. He's absolutely gorgeous and rich… she says she's done stuff with him she's never done with anyone else.'

'Oh God. Really?'

'Oh nothing sexual – she's done everything there is to do in *that* department.' She laughed. 'No, they have meals out, cinema, theatre, that sort of thing. Until Dr Delicious, Lola had only slept with men, never been out as such… nothing outside the bedroom. She said she'd never wanted to actually go out on a date with a man.'

'Even George Clooney?'

'Well, it's a long story, of which there are many. She lived in LA for a while, had her fill of film stars. I'll get her to tell you all about it. You should hear about the time Lola was naked, at this pool party… and there was this actor…'

'I look forward to it, but not just now. I'll hear it from the horse's mouth I think,' I said, hoping it would be forgotten; I didn't want a detailed account of any evening that began with 'Lola was naked'.

'Suit yourself.' She shrugged.

I didn't know Lola that well, but according to Jody, Lola had a 'voracious appetite' that had nothing to do with doughnuts. I'd met Kate once and after trying, and failing, to have a conversation with her, I assumed she was on drugs, but Jody said she was always like that – which didn't augur well for a great Christmas. Oh, and there was also the small fact that all three women drank too much, danced on tables and existed in a permanent state of loud and raucous.

'You won't all be bringing men back to our staff chalet, dancing on tables and...'

'And having fun? Yes we might,' she said. 'And so might you.'

'You must be joking, Jody.' I was still filled with doubts about this, but it was too late for me to back out now.

'I just wanted it to be a little more Christmassy, sisters going shopping together, learning to ski, getting to know each other in the evenings after a day at work.'

'Well, we will. Just because there are four of us doesn't mean you and I won't have quality time.'

Jody and her mates all wanted to party, get plastered and bed the first ski instructor who was naïve enough to reveal his ski pole. It looked like I was hurtling downhill towards my sister's idea of fun – unable to stop. But then again, why should I stop? Perhaps it was time I relearned to table dance, drink too much and sing along to the music... time to leap out of my fur-lined comfort zone. And as I ordered two 'Thank God it's Christmas' cocktails I felt a little scared about what was to come – and a little excited too!

Chapter 3

DJs, Dancing, and Sex in the Snow

I invited Jody to stay the night before we went away. Storm was away at a Shamanic-dancing workshop in Milton Keynes but would be back the following day to look after Mrs Christmas for me.

'Have you told her Mummy's going on an adventure?' Jody asked the following morning as we left. She was staggering through the hall with about four suitcases and wearing a full-length fake fur coat, looking not unlike a Rolling Stones groupie from the seventies, while Mrs Christmas was getting caught up in the action and making alarming noises as she tried to escape 'the yeti' in her hall. My sister really was quite chaotic.

'I feel guilty leaving her,' I said, rescuing Mrs C from Jody's suitcase wheels and cuddling her tightly. 'I just told her Auntie Storm would be giving cuddles and Katomeat for the next few months.' It sounded like a long time away from home and my tummy twisted into a tight little knot, until I thought of white slopes and real Christmas trees and it smoothed slightly. I think Jody could see the flicker of doubt pass over my face, and she bustled me out of the house before I could change my mind.

'Now, Mrs C – you know the rules,' she called as we left. 'No boy cats, no drugs... no pussy parties, don't post anything dodgy on the internet and no sex in the garden.'

My heart was in my mouth. 'Oh don't, I feel like I'm leaving my teenage daughter here all alone,' I sighed as we shut the door.

❄ ❄ ❄

Meeting 'the girls' at the airport was an experience in itself. Kate, the nursery nurse and Jody's oldest friend, was already tipsy. 'It's only two o'clock,' I whispered to Jody as she tangoed towards us.

'You sound just like bloody Tim,' she sighed, kicking up her legs and joining Kate in an impromptu performance that looked like some sort of lap dance and grabbed the attention of everyone in the departure lounge.

'Where's Lola?' Jody gasped, breathless as she finally extricated herself from an enthusiastic Kate. 'I hope she turns up.' The fact that my sister could even wonder if a friend would turn up for a planned working holiday gives you some idea of Lola, who lived by nobody's rules.

'I'll call her. She was working until late last night,' Kate explained as she dialled her number. 'She'll be dog-tired and hungover. She'll probably be limping too – that pole is unforgivable.'

I looked at Jody.

'I thought she sold advertising space?'

'She does, but times are hard and a girl's gotta make a crust. She can't drive that Porsche on ad space alone, so she does a bit of... dancing,' she answered, clearly not wishing to elaborate.

I didn't want to judge, but one had to wonder what the hell this working holiday was going to be like. A wild student nurse, a nursery nurse with the mental age of her pupils, an entrepreneurial, serial-sexting pole dancer and me – a pent-up, single librarian with man issues.

Eventually our flight was called and the three of us headed off to begin the journey. We were just getting seated when there was a commotion at the back of the plane.

'That'll be Lola,' Jody said, unable to stop herself smiling and turning round to greet her friend.

And sure enough, the fabulous forty-something blonde dressed in a bright pink jumpsuit with fur trim was trooping down the aisle shouting, 'Where are my girls?'

'Here!' they were calling and Kate started a 'Lola' chant, which Jody joined in on, the whole thing becoming louder and more unnecessary as it went on.

I hid behind my copy of *Ski Monthly* until they stopped and Lola landed on the seat next to me in a fug of alcohol and French perfume.

'OH. MY GOD,' she sighed loudly. 'You won't believe the morning I've had.'

She went on to detail aspects of her morning that I felt she should really have kept to herself, but involved a 'hunk of a man', a festive bra and too much sex and tinsel before noon for my liking.

'But... tinsel handcuffs? It's only November...' was all I could muster.

'It's always Christmas in my bed,' she guffawed, then leaned in and whispered conspiratorially, 'S & M isn't what it used to be,

Jen.' She said this like she was talking about the decline of the family in the twenty-first century. 'I blame shoddy workmanship. One
hard tug and the stitching just falls apart.' She was gesticulating
wildly and I couldn't imagine, nor did I want to know, what the
hell she was referring to.

'Ooh, it's going to be a long journey in this underwear,' she
said, suddenly hitching her trousers before announcing to everyone in the vicinity that 'lacy thongs are killers on economy seats'.

❄ ❄ ❄

The wood cabin at the ski resort was lovely – everything Jody
had said it would be, sitting halfway up a snowy hill with a holly
wreath on the door. Inside, a big fur rug lay in front of a huge,
crackling open fire and a big Christmas tree stood in the middle
of the open-plan living area. It was covered in twinkling fairy
lights, and the fire, the snow and a glass of wine soon softened
my spiky edges. It wasn't for long though – within an hour the
huge white sofas were covered in the contents of the girls' cases,
as were the bedroom and kitchen floors. Jody's definition of a
'working holiday' was quite different from mine, and as she and
the girls unpacked their litre bottles of vodka, fur G-strings and
loud music, I followed them round tidying up. This was not going to be the traditional Bing Crosby 'White Christmas' I had
in mind, and as Jody rode Kate through the living room and
Lola sexted a stranger, I could only imagine what the next few
months would bring.

We had to be at work the following day, so I was keen to
unpack my case and go straight to bed. I'd explained over the

phone and in all of the many forms I had to fill in that I didn't ski, and to my relief I'd received an email to say I would be working in the resort's coffee shop, The Ski Bunny. I was really quite excited about this – making coffee and serving snacks and cakes in a snowy setting couldn't have been more different from life in a concrete library where everyone had to 'shush'.

I was just contemplating what to wear for my first day and beginning to feel a little nervous, when I was rudely awoken from my thoughts.

'OH MY GOD,' Jody was screaming from the balcony. My heart was in my mouth.

'What on earth...' I said, rushing across the room and whipping back the curtain to the balcony. She was jumping up and down, open-mouthed and pointing out across the mountains, and the sheer volume of her screech indicated she was either about to fall or had at least been shot.

'What? What?' I said, wanting to protect her from whatever had caused such apparent anguish.

'That... that over there.' She was pointing to the breathtaking view of the mountains, and I realised it must be the spectacular whiteness in the blueish dusk.

'Yes, it's quite amazing, isn't it?' I sighed. 'It's just like a Christmas card.' Perhaps my sister did have a soul after all?

'Yeah, yeah the view's alright, but I'm talking about that over there. Can you see it?' she said, as she began pushing clumps of snow into a large glass of something. 'Look over there.' She pointed again, out beyond the white infinity, and there it was, glowing in the snowy darkness like an alien spaceship. 'On the Piste Nightclub and Bar'.

'I told you they have everything,' she said, looking out long-ingly across the dark snow. 'We will work hard and play hard, sis... that nightclub will be just sick.'

I smiled. This wasn't really my idea of sick...or perhaps it was, in the original sense.

'It's the kind of place I've dreamed of, you know...' she was say-ing. 'And according to the forums the DJs are bloody mental... in a good way,' she added, like this would reassure me.

My heart sank. This was a nightclub, but not as I knew it. The building was huge and spiky and neon, and when I looked more closely I could see the front was plastered with posters offering ice parties and DJs with weird-sounding names. And. A. Luge.

'Am I reading this right? Are they offering a luge?' I said, screw-ing up my eyes to read it more clearly from the distance. 'Isn't that a chute for people to go down... usually outside?'

'I know, but this is inside – don't get too excited...'

'I wasn't.'

'Because at your age your heart just might not take it, and you might die and not be able to join in.'

'Let's hope so,' I said.

'Jen, you will LOVE it!'

'I won't. And stop telling me I'll love things when I know I'll hate them.'

'You're being boring again. Open yourself up, Jen. You don't know you'll hate it because you've never been on a luge before.'

'How do you know?'

She gave me a look.

'Okay, I haven't been down a luge, but I've lived. I've been covered in foam and jumped into a swimming pool fully dressed...' I smiled at the memory. It seemed so long ago.

'Foam parties!' she rolled her eyes. 'They were around with the dinosaurs. Oh you do make me laugh with your retro life,' she said, gazing back out onto her own personal Xanadu. I giggled at this, and we both stood together, the navy blue night descending around us, dotted with stars.

'Just look out there,' I said, taking it all in. 'You don't get that at home.'

'Fabulous, isn't it?' She smiled. 'I read about it online. The luge starts at the top of the roof and just swirls down.'

I rolled my eyes. 'I meant the unpolluted night sky.'

'And I meant the luge. You come down it at about a hundred miles an hour – apparently it's bloody scary, in a good way. Just awesome, isn't it?'

'And stop adding "in a good way", to everything in a vain attempt to make something awful sound better. Are you like that with your patients? "I'm sorry, Mr Peters, but you are dying...in a good way", or "when you wake up, your leg will have been amputated... in a good way".'

'No, I'm not like that at all. Besides I don't work in limbs. Hey but how bloody awesome is that luge, babe?' She really thought I was impressed and couldn't wait to climb on.

'Awesome,' I repeated. 'With any luck I'll be dead by morning... in a good way.'

'Ooh, don't be such a party pooper, Jen. You'll have a blast, and you know it. There's an ice party tonight – you'll LOVE that. Bloody hell, chill out.'

Instead of moving me forwards, this working holiday with Jody and the girls was in danger of dragging me back. The prospect of drunken nights at On The Piste where I held the girls' coats to the tune of deafening music and screaming luge divers made me feel rather out of my depth. I wanted candlelit dinners, trips to museums, evenings at home reading a good book... but indoor luges? An ice party? Mental DJs?

'I mean, who wants an ice party?' I said. 'More importantly, what *is* an ice party?'

'I've no idea, but it'll probably be so cold we'll scream our tits off.'

'In a good way,' I said and laughed, and we leaned on the balcony, gazing out onto a perfect Christmas scene of fir trees and glittering snow. Perhaps this was going to be fun after all?

I looked at Jody, about to say something positive about how lovely things were going to be, but she was now taking a large swig of whatever she'd just snowed up in the glass.

'What if someone's urinated in that snow?' I asked, watching her try and suck the alcohol through the dense clod of snow she'd packed in.

'Well if some guy has whipped it out two floors up in this cold I want his number – who needs Dating.com?' And she laughed, continuing to slurp. 'Want a swig?'

'Eugh, no thank you.'

'I bet you would have when you were my age.'

'I hope you're not trying to say you learned your vile behaviour from me.' I laughed.

'Well not exactly, but I remember how I used to want to be you when I was little. You'd always be fun and usually wearing something outrageous. I remember you coming over one day in really tiny shorts and you had a massive argument with Dad...'

'God, I'd forgotten about that – I remember buying those tiny shorts just to wind him up. I knew it would annoy him.' I sighed, pretending to be amused, but sad for the teenager I'd once been, desperately craving Dad's attention, even if it meant him being angry with me.

'Yeah, Dad told you off, and you shouted back, and it ended up with you telling him to sod off.'

'Mmm and reminding him he gave up any right to tell me what to wear when he walked out on me to live with "that slag", your mum. I'm... sorry Jody,' I added, feeling awful. I'd tried to forget about my difficult teens and how horrible I'd been.

'It's okay, she knew you were hurt. She wanted to help but your mum didn't want you having anything to do with us.'

'Well, Mum was hurt,' I sighed. 'And I wouldn't have listened to your mum. To me she was the reason we were in that situation... I've realised as I've got older that it's not quite as black and white as it all seemed.'

'No, it was all about the grown-ups' resentments, misunderstandings and simply falling out of love – it happens. But Mum tried with you, Jen, she really did.'

I nodded. I couldn't look at Jody. I found it hard to face the past and the way I'd behaved. I'd ignored her mum and at times resented my little half-sister too – but I was just a kid.

We continued to stand in silence, gazing out over the snow scene, neither of us speaking, then she turned to look at me.

'I miss the old Jen, the one who shouted and wore unsuitable clothes and drank too much.'

'I don't miss her. She was very angry.'

'Well, she probably should have shown some of that anger to bloody Tim – he walked all over you.'

'I think my anger was still there with Tim, but I just suppressed it. I wanted him to think I was the perfect girlfriend, never angry, never a hair out of place... I wanted him never to have an excuse or a reason to leave me.'

'And ironically, that made you even angrier,' she sighed.

'Yeah, if I'm honest there were times I wanted to strangle him, especially when he was being pompous. He once tried to show me how to make Christmas trifle, my bloody signature dish... I wanted to push his face in it.'

'But I bet you just smiled and said, "What a good idea, Tim!" You weren't yourself when you were with him.'

'You're right,' I said, and it was painful to think I'd smothered my personality for ten years. 'I should have challenged him more,' I conceded.

I could see that being with Tim had changed me, but I'd also grown up in that time, and he wasn't completely responsible for my change in behaviour. Yes I'd stopped drinking and dancing on tables, but wasn't that also about growing up? Then again, he said he hated seeing people drunk... and by that I knew he meant me, so I was always careful never to get even tipsy. I recall a Christmas a few years back when someone bought me a bottle of champagne for my birthday. We had some friends round for dinner and I'd only drunk one glass when one of the guests went to pour me a second one, and Tim put his hand over it. 'She's had enough,' he said. There was a definite murmur of surprise around the table, but I just laughed along and pretended to agree with him. Going along with Tim was easier than rebelling then having to suffer his sulking all through Christmas.

'Anyway, forget boring old Tim. This is the beginning of a new life for you,' she said. 'I have a good feeling about this trip.'

'Me too.' I pushed my arm through hers and continued to try and read from the distant posters lit by spotlights around the dreaded nightclub. 'What's an... après ski... sexy?' I asked, hating myself for even saying those words together and out loud.

'Who knows? But tonight we are going to find out,' she said, slugging down the last of her snow-drenched drink.

I felt like I was already on that luge as my heart dipped at a hundred miles an hour. 'Tonight? But we haven't unpacked our cases yet.'

'Oh love, never mind that now. Just grab something to wear and we can worry about unpacking tomorrow... or the next day even.'

'We all start work tomorrow, Jody – we can't be out late.'

'Okay, Tim.'

'No, I'll just stay here tonight while you girls party,' I said, ignoring the Tim jibe. 'I can unpack your bags for you too while you're out?'

'We've got days to unpack, months even – hell we don't ever have to unpack if we don't want to,' she said, a defiant twinkle in her eye. 'You have to live for the moment, Jen. When was the last time you had the chance to get pissed and go down a luge with the girls?'

'You're so right – and being pissed on a luge? Oh it was at least a week ago,' I agreed sarcastically.

But she wasn't listening – she was heading back into the room, holding her arms in the air and singing 'PARTAY!' loudly. This was immediately repeated in the same sing-song voice by the other girls, like a tribal cry through the twenty-something jungle. I continued to look out onto the spectacular snow scene – it was a perfect, winter setting and with Christmas around the corner there was an added sparkle in the air. I was looking out at this from our fairy-tale, snow-covered chalet – we'd arrived, and I'd made my first leap of faith. Now I just needed to 'chillax' and stop living a 'retro' life – apparently.

✳ ✳ ✳

Inside the girls began rifling madly through cases, holding up tiny pieces of material shaped like skirts and tops only to abandon them seconds later to the brightly coloured plumage emerging from their cases. Shoes were already on the floor with cast-aside T-shirts and a leopard-skin bra, which had to be Lola's. I thought about Tim and how, on our first holiday together, he'd shown me a 'system' to pack and unpack a case. 'It takes minutes and makes the world of difference,' he'd said, folding shirts and towels and lowering them slowly into his case like a priest giving communion. He always packed life into little boxes, everything neat and tidy on its shelf and in its place – but spontaneity? Love? I don't think he knew the box where those were kept.

Looking out of the window I could see the snow coming down heavily; I'd need my special clothing for tonight and was glad I'd bought myself a couple of lovely jumpers, as it was quite cold. I'd also gone mad and bought some nice new jeans, waterproof trousers and a jacket. I was pleased with my stylish but sensible purchases – good for work and play – and I put my case carefully on my bed, subconsciously planning to unpack properly like Tim had taught me. I hadn't come out of that relationship with nothing after all, I thought to myself as I opened my case and reached in. I was anticipating my pristinely pressed wardrobe all placed in sections, socks rolled in the side pockets, underwear to the left of outerwear and thick, outdoor clothing on the top. But as I peered in, expecting a neat matrix of shades and fabrics, my eyes were greeted with alien colours and textures that I simply couldn't process. At first I assumed this was because my clothes were new, but as I delved further into the case I found nothing familiar and, lifting out a pair of child's dinosaur pyjamas, it dawned on me there'd been a mix-up. I had someone else's case. And the owner of these dinosaur pyjamas with 'age 8' in the label was probably at this very minute looking at a pink size-twelve thermal nightie.

'Has anybody got my case by mistake?' I called out, hoping against hope that the M&S pyjamas meant for an eight-year-old boy were Kate's idea of fashionable irony. It was a last-ditch attempt to make everything right, but within seconds it was established that everyone had their own cases and their own clothes. And it didn't take Sherlock Holmes to work out by now what had happened... although it did take Kate a little while – as usual.

'Jenny, what are you doing with dino jamas?' she asked, smiling and wandering into my room. She picked them up and looked at me. 'Oh I get it...'

I nodded. She wasn't so daft after all.

'You were hoping to slim down in time and get into these?'

I smiled. Was she joking?

'Well don't you worry, missy, we'll keep an eye on you over this week.' She wasn't joking.

'NO CAKE FOR JEN,' she suddenly yelled, then gave me a wink. 'We've got your back. I know how it is, as my mum's getting on and it's tough – your hormones shrink, don't they?'

'Do they?' I said, still holding up the pyjamas in vague horror.

'Yeah. My mum's hormones have shrunk right down, but her tummy hasn't... just like yours,' she teased, patting my stomach playfully.

I was too concerned about my case to be offended or try to defend my figure.

'So keep the jamas in your case and trust me – you'll be wearing them in a few weeks.'

'Oh for God's sake, do you really think I'd bring a pair of bloody dinosaur pyjamas on holiday?' I asked, feeling extremely stressed.

She nodded, and as Jody walked into the room, I saw Kate roll her eyes in my direction, like I was the crazy one.

Once we'd established what had apparently happened with my case, I'd called down to reception, who said they would chase it up at the airport. It seemed things like this happened a lot here, and I was assured my case would be with me by morning.

Meanwhile, I had no choice but to take up the girls' offer to help myself to the contents of their cases. It was a tough one. Jody and Kate were both a size smaller than me and twelve years younger. Lola, on the other hand, was nearer my size and age but had treated herself to a rather extravagant boob job and dressed more like a drag queen than a woman in her forties. Consequently, my breasts couldn't begin to meet the majestic cleavage-revealing low-cut tops, but she insisted I try her favourite lime-green lamé jumpsuit with feather trim, and as I squeezed it on she shook her head. 'Totally drains you of colour, my love.'

'What a shame,' I said, trying not to smile with relief. Whatever I wore I was going to look ridiculous, so I chose the least noticeable outfit, a short black skirt and snug white shirt from Jody's case, which appeared to be the least offensive option.

Arriving inside the nightclub the girls ran to the bar shouting 'drinks' like it was a mirage in the dry desert. And as they screamed for 'Orgasms in the Snow', a cocktail apparently – well hopefully – I knew it wouldn't be the log fires that were roaring – it would be the girls.

Once our Orgasms were delivered we sipped and stared as the first frosty revellers began their descent into the nightclub via the luge. They were hurtling down at quite a pace, thrashing and screaming down the long helter-skelter that snaked its way from the roof down to the middle of the dance floor.

While looking for the exit I spotted the musical accompaniment for the evening was provided by DJ Spinladen and DJ Vinyl Richie, who were shouting over their 'tunes' for everyone to 'sign up for the hard ride'. I assured the girls and anyone else who cared to listen that I would not be hard-riding tonight or any other night, but as usual no one was listening.

Having downed her drink, Jody ordered everyone a 'Sexy Snowman', a white chocolate and rum cocktail, but as I reached for mine she smacked my hand gently.

'This is yours,' she said, handing me a glass containing bright green liquid with a funny little plastic glass ornament clinging to the side. 'It's a Grinch,' she said, pursing her lips and giving me a look.

'Okay, I get it, but I feel like I was... dragged here under false pretences,' I started. 'I didn't expect to be in the snowy equivalent of bloody Ibiza! I thought it would all be lovely and white and Christmassy and everyone would be singing "Silent Night" in the snow.'

'God, Jenny, how much "white" do you want for your Christmas. There's a blizzard starting out there. And I'm sure Spinladen has a version of "Silent Night".'

'I'm sure he does, but I don't want to hear it,' I said.

'Oh drink your Grinch... Grinch.' She rolled her eyes and within a couple of slurps she was ordering more cocktails.

Unlike the rest of the party I stopped after the first two cocktails; we all had work in the morning, even if it was a holiday job, and I intended to turn up at The Ski Bunny coffee shop bright and breezy, without a hangover. So as the girls came screaming and swearing down the luge, I stood firmly at the bottom, minding their bags and taking their photos. As they screeched and hurtled, I smiled and snapped. Jody bought another round of Christmas cocktails, but I insisted on lemonade and as the ice became mushier and the girls' landings soaked me to the skin, even home and the library were looking good.

'Well, Jenny, you're certainly advertising *all* your goods tonight,' Lola said, handing me another lemonade as the last of the lugers landed. I looked down at myself in Jody's 'office' shirt to see the water from the luge had caused the shirt to become completely see-through, premiering my new black bra for the whole nightclub.

At first I was horrified, but the girls and the music were infectious and as everyone was demanding I get on the dance floor, I suddenly let go and joined them. I was quite tipsy and didn't care that my top was see-through and my dancing terrible – I just joined the girls, throwing myself into various shapes. I roared, laughing as loudly as they did, and was amazed at my own flexibility as I joined them in one of their impromptu cancans. But when Lola started using a random ski rod as a pole, I decided I was out of my depth. And not used to the drink or exertion, I was also feeling rather nauseous, which was compounded when I spotted myself in a shard of mirror on the wall (meant to look like ice) and saw my still-wet shirt and clear view of my bra. I suddenly felt naked.

It seemed I wasn't the only one who'd spotted my fashion faux pas, because DJ Vinyl Richie was shouting, 'Wet T-shirt competition,' and making his way over to where I was leaning against the bar along with Kate, who was laughing and lunging at my chest.

'No way,' I called back, emboldened by the icy cold water – or perhaps it was the two cocktails I'd had earlier?

In the middle of this madness Lola quickly took me aside and asked if she could borrow the shirt the following evening. 'That's quite something,' she said admiringly before Vinyl Richie embraced me like a long-lost friend.

I extricated myself immediately. My shirt was wetter than ever and I was concerned Spinladen might appear at any moment and get me in a pincer movement on stage with his mate Vinyl.

Refusing to take part in any competition, I eventually managed to escape from Kate, the DJ and the throng and took a stool at the other side of the bar. I was feeling extremely woozy now and keen to get away from the thumping noise, the slushing luge and the rampant DJs. 'Ooh, Jen, who are you making eyes at?' Jody appeared next to me and sat on the next bar stool. 'He's making eyes back at you since your shirt got wet,' she said, nodding her head in the direction of a man who must have been sixty.

'I've nothing against older men,' I said, 'but I draw the line at an OAP just yet.'

'He's not an OAP, he's about your age,' she said. I think she was joking.

'Thank you, Jody, but age aside I really would rather not. It's not that I'm fussy, I'll do bald, fat, old and short – just not all at once.'

'You're such a misery guts,' she said and laughed, ordering another round and insisting I have another lemonade.

I felt an urge to escape from this dark place filled with loud people and melting ice. It was like being inside a giant slush puppy. I'd wanted to come to Switzerland for the Christmas snow, but not like this – I had dreamed of beautiful glacial landscapes, Christmas markets and cinnamon-scented coffee shops filled with Christmas cake and gingerbread. I wanted to feel like Heidi skipping through snowy mountains – or a singing Julie Andrews at the very least. I didn't expect the first night of my working holiday to be spent holding handbags as my sister and her friends hurled themselves at rampant DJs. I was momentarily distracted by Lola 'lassoing' some poor guy on the dance floor with her scarf and pulling him towards her until their bodies met and writhed together.

Dirty dancing had got a whole lot dirtier since I was in my twenties.

But Jody was used to Lola's 'dancing' and was more concerned about finding me a man, any man, and continued to suggest various suitors dotted around the dance floor. I knew she wouldn't stop so I told her I was about to vomit any second, which was an exaggeration, but also a strong possibility. The idea of me staying single wasn't half as bad as the thought of my sick down her new cropped top, so she reluctantly but quickly released me from her clutches. 'I'm going outside for some fresh air,' I said, and she readily agreed, both arms in a protective gesture over herself lest the nausea took a quick hold.

I staggered out into the cold, neon-white evening to take a break and once outside the minty cool air filled my nostrils and my lungs. Invigorated and at the same time calmed after the damp, warm club, I leaned back against the brickwork, taking deep breaths and absorbing the grainy mountains in the dark distance, watching over us like guardians in the night.

I needed carbs and thinking space and, in the absence of a disabled toilet and a box of Krispy Kremes, the chalet and Christmas cake would have to do. I was about to head off into the night when I heard a foreign man's voice behind me. 'Where are you going... miss?'

I turned to see a tall, dark-haired man in a resort ski suit – obviously he was staff too.

'I'm going back to my chalet,' I said. 'It's a bit rowdy in there for me.'

'You don't like the luge?'

I shook my head.

'Me neither.' He smiled and I smiled back. 'You aren't wearing the clothes for the weather?' he asked, and I looked down at my miniscule outfit, perfectly ridiculous for the cold night air.

'No. It's a long story. I'm heading back to my chalet now before this snow sets in.' I looked all around me and thought what a ludicrous thing to say. It probably 'set in' thousands of years ago here.

'I don't think you should be walking through the snow like this, she is too cold – tourists have died here.'

I shivered slightly at the thought. 'Oh it's not far, really – it's just over there.' I pointed randomly in the distance. I didn't want anyone else telling me what to do. Jody had tried to stop me coming out for a breath of fresh air, and now some stranger was telling me I couldn't walk home on my own.

In my desperation to leave the club I'd forgotten to grab Jody's big fur coat, but I daren't go back in for fear Kate and Vinyl Richie were still planning a wet T-shirt on the luge competition – with me as the star attraction.

'Here, take my coat,' he was saying in what I now realised was probably a Swiss or German accent.

He was looking at me and I shook my head and smiled – I couldn't take his coat from him. But I felt the electricity of connection, that moment when you catch someone's eye and realise there's something between you. He made my heart flutter and my face burn, and whatever it was between us, I hadn't felt this in a long, long time. I tried not to look at him and told myself not to read too much into those big blue eyes and that sexy German accent. And when he looked over and I caught him giving me an appreciative glance my insides turned to slush. There in the white, white snow, I was completely helpless, unable to speak or move, just mesmerised by this gorgeous man.

'I start work here tomorrow so I want to head back and try to get some sleep,' I explained. He seemed nice and I didn't want to be rude, so I smiled and explained that I was working and would be serving all kinds of goodies the following morning in The Ski Bunny Café.

'I'm not much of a ski bunny myself,' I said.

'You can be the ski bunny if you would like.'

I laughed. 'Yes, I would like. I won't be doing the luge though.'

'Oh you don't know what she is missing,' he said in broken English. 'Why don't you go down there now? You'll see it is great, and you'll be sliding down her every night.'

'No thanks, I...'

'Come with me now – I will take you.' And he gently tugged at my scarf.

I giggled. 'No, no, no,' I said, pretending to pull my scarf back but actually quite liking the fact that he was holding on to it. He had kind eyes, a gentle voice and I suppose it was the cocktails, but I just let him keep tugging at my scarf until I was almost next to him. I felt his warm breath as our faces came close and, still pretending to pull away, I noticed he might just have the bluest eyes I'd ever seen.

'You want to, don't you?' he said, suddenly seeming quite serious – and I looked up into those eyes and nodded, unsure exactly what I was agreeing to. What was happening to me? I felt abandoned, relaxed, like life could take me anywhere tonight and I wouldn't resist.

To my surprise, he suddenly lifted me up and, kicking open the door of the nightclub, we arrived back in, bringing a flurry of snow and several surprised looks from the girls.

They were all standing by the bar enjoying their cocktails, and Kate put her hand over her mouth as my handsome stranger put me gently on the ground.

I suspect it was the sudden temperature change combined with the Grinch cocktail earlier – but as my feet touched the floor, they gave way. I yelped, tried to get my balance, doing a very good Bambi impression, and thankfully just before I landed on my face, I felt big strong arms around my waist.

'Oh God, are you okay, love?' Jody and the girls rushed towards me as the stranger lifted me again. (I had regained my composure by now and could probably have stood on my own feet – but why do that when I was being 'rescued' by a rather handsome hero type?) I felt like a woman in a Jane Austen novel, the back of my hand to my forehead as he carried me through the throng of people shouting, 'First aid.' He literally swept me off my feet and took me into the back of the club to a small room with a couple of chairs, some boxes and a first-aid kit.

'You feel cold?' he asked in a concerned way that warmed me up immediately.

'Yes... I am a little cold,' I answered shyly as he took off his padded jacket and wrapped it around my still-wet blouse. 'Thank you... I'm not quite sure what happened...' I said once I'd begun to thaw.

'You young girls come here from UK, you wear the next to nothings and then you drink so much.' All I'd heard was 'you young girls' in a lovely German accent and, despite the fact that I was freezing in a cheap see-through blouse, I attempted to smile back at him in a coquettish way.

'Are you a doctor?' I asked breathlessly, trying not to think where my mascara must be by now.

'No, I'm a ski instructor.' He flashed a smile as he opened up a first-aid box and produced what looked like a large blanket of tinfoil. As he wrapped it around me I was unable to take my eyes off him. One of the bar girls came in with a glass of water and a sort of hot-water bottle that he handed to me. 'You must get warm,' he said.

'Yes, please,' I heard myself murmur. Oh God, I was definitely tipsy. I was now completely relaxed and leaning on him, which felt very comforting, but in my hypothermic state I wasn't sure if it would be considered sweet or desperate.

He said something in German to the girl who'd brought the drink and she laughed, leaving us alone together. I felt my face burn with embarrassment. Oh God, were they laughing at me? Did he think I was some sad, middle-aged woman coming on to him? He was probably a similar age to me – but that's the problem when you're a forty-something single woman: the forty-something single men want thirty-somethings. I tried not to look at him as, on discovering a graze on my cheek, he was now gently dabbing antiseptic onto it. I'd had no physical contact with a man for nearly a year and – it's all relative – what he was doing to my cheek felt something like foreplay.

Fortunately, at this point the door opened and in walked Jody and the girls.

'Thank God you're okay,' Jody screeched, running towards me, arms outstretched. 'One minute you're saying you've had enough and want some fresh air and next you walk back in with a tall, dark, handsome stranger.' She nodded at said stranger.

'She's a fast worker,' Lola said, with an admiring whistle. I only heard them in the distance – I was too absorbed by this lovely man wrapping me in tinfoil. I bet even Lola had never experienced this avenue of pleasure.

'Now you should be okay, but you need transport back to your accommodation—' he started.

'Oooh, if you're offering a piggyback, can I come too?' Lola asked, all marabou feathers and Marilyn breathlessness. She was only half-joking, but he smiled politely and asked where we were staying.

'I will call reception and ask them to send a snow vehicle,' he said.

'Thank you so much,' Jody said as she tried to help me up, but I wanted him to do it, so I feigned a little more weakness than perhaps was honest... but only a little.

The stranger immediately rallied. 'Let me,' he said and slid one arm around my waist. I put my arm up around his shoulder and we staggered through the nightclub to greet the vehicle to take me back to the chalet. All I could think of was warmth and cake... and if I'd ever see this knight in shining armour again.

'I don't even know your name?' I whispered, unable to take my eyes off his face. 'I'm Jen...'

'I'm Jon,' he whispered back without taking his eyes from mine, and I felt the ice beginning to crack around my heart.

Chapter 4

A Cold Night, A Hunky Man and Other People's Clothes

I was still so cold I doubted I'd ever get warm again as I sat by the fire in Jody's fur coat with a cup of cocoa, just trying to thaw.

'Well you're a dark horse,' Kate said, wandering over and inspecting my drink. 'I hope that's a skinny hot chocolate. You want to get into those little jammies, don't you?'

'No. I don't. I want to get into my own pyjamas, if they ever arrive.'

'He was quite a looker, the guy you hooked up with tonight,' she said, sitting on the sofa next to me, dipping a digestive into her hot chocolate and slurping loudly.

'Oh I didn't cop off... I just met him outside, and we were walking back in together and...'

'Where I come from that's a date, hon,' Lola piped up as she wandered in to join us. She was drinking whisky straight from a large tumbler.

'So are you seeing him again?' she said.

'Well yes, he's taking me to Gstaad for the weekend where we'll spend the days skiing and the nights wrapped in each other's arms, licking ice-cold champagne off each other's naked bodies.'

'That sounds a bit like a weekend I once spent with...' Lola started.

'I was joking,' I monotoned. 'Knowing my luck he's leaving the resort tomorrow and I'll never see him again. I'm destined to spend the rest of my time here coming straight back after work, eating fattening food, drinking hot chocolate and becoming the size of a small car.'

'Why?' Kate said.

'Why what?'

'Why would you abuse yourself like that? It's stupid.' For someone so slow on the uptake, Kate could sometimes be scarily profound, and she had a point, even if was a different one to the one she was making. Why did I think that the only alternative to being in a relationship was becoming a fat spinster?

'You're right, Kate – that would be stupid, and there are other options. But forgive me – tonight isn't the night to explore possibilities. I've no clothes, I'm freezing, I just made a complete fool of myself in front of a really nice man, and I don't know where I'm going or what I'm doing... I'm not even excited about Christmas.'

Then I burst into tears and Jody tried to hug me until I stopped.

'Now then, missy, what's all this about you not being excited about Christmas? You had a great time tonight – admit it! You were dancing on the tables and knocking back the drinks. And I'm sorry, I know you asked for lemonade, but I asked them to put just a teensy leetle beet of vodka in.'

'I knew it,' I said through my tears. 'Jody, you can't go through life like this.'

'What, making sure my family and friends have a good time? I think that vodka gave us a little glimpse of the old Jen tonight – the one before bloody Tim and his rules and regulations. You don't have to think your life is over, Jen. You can still find someone new – even in your forties. You proved that tonight, copping off with a good-looking guy outside.'

'No, I didn't.'

'Oh I think you did, Jen,' Kate started. 'You went out for a breath of air and came back clinging to a stranger!'

'It wasn't like that – he rescued me... I was just a little tipsy. And now I'm going to bed,' I said, getting up off the floor, only to be faced with the sight of Jody dressed as a cow. Yes, a cow. In my upset I'd clearly not realised, or perhaps I was hallucinating?

'Are you dressed as a cow?' I asked.

She nodded, and unable to contain her delight, she gave me a twirl.

'*Why* are you dressed as a cow?' I monotoned, dreading the answer from her parallel universe.

'Oh LOL, Jen, it's my onesie... I wear it for bed.'

'But it's so... *real*,' I said. 'Are those... udders?'

She nodded proudly. 'Actually, I have a little surprise for you.' She giggled excitedly and ran from the room shouting, 'You are gonna LOVE this.'

She returned with a parcel wrapped in Christmassy paper, and I could only guess at the horror beneath the pattern of pink Father Christmases adorning the paper.

'It's just one of your Chrissy prezzies,' she announced, handing me the parcel. 'I was saving them all for Christmas Day, but... here's something to keep you going until you find your case.'

I smiled and thanked her while carefully opening the squishy, Christmassy parcel. Inside, my hands alighted on bright pink and white fabric, and unfurling the 'gift' I realised the pattern was definitely cow. As the udders appeared I cried with dismay, which everyone misinterpreted as unbridled joy, and Jody clapped her hands together, delighted that she'd bought me just the right gift.

'I *knew* you'd just love it,' she said, her hands now clasped and her face smiley and pink with the pleasure of giving.

What could I say? Sitting there clutching at pink velvet udders, I was at a loss, then immediately thought of a solution. 'This feels like it would be lovely and warm. I'll be able to wear it as pyjamas... so...'

'Oh no, Jenny – you can't wear your best new onesie to bed.' Jody was looking around at the others incredulously. 'I'm only wearing this because it's my old one.'

'Oh... you have more than one... cow?'

'Of course. And anyway, you've got to save your cow because tomorrow's Onesie Day on the slopes, which is why I let you have it as an early Christmas prezzie.'

I must have looked bemused, sitting there clutching pink velvet udders and looking into the big brown eyes of the cow I would be tomorrow.

'Happy?' Jody asked, and I just smiled.

'Yeah... thanks for this, Jody,' I said. 'I need to embrace my inner cow.'

'Look – it's hard being over forty with your tragic love life.' She looked up to address the girls. 'But this is the way forward...' she started.

'Dressing up as a cow?'

'Not just that – but you have to get happy again – and forget the car crash that is your life.'

'Thanks for reminding me – I feel all warm and squidgy inside now,' I sighed, pulling away from her like a child. 'Perhaps you'd like to go further back and tell everyone about the guy I went out with at college who married my best friend. Or the one who took me on a day trip to London, offered to get the coffees on the train, asked what sandwich I'd like, headed for the buffet car and has never been seen since.'

'Oh God, I forgot about all that. Didn't you pull the emergency cord and get fined or something?'

'Yeah, dumped and fined... something like that...' I muttered, not wanting to relive that particular circus, involving British Rail police and fifty-two irate passengers on the 9.15 a.m. to Euston.

'Oh and I just remembered the comedian you went out with,' Jody said, smiling. 'You know... the one who made a whole stand-up act around your relationship...'

The others gasped and Kate giggled, adding, 'It was funny though.'

'You saw his show?' I asked, looking from Kate to Jody who both nodded. 'I can't believe it. He broke my heart and you went to watch him and laugh about it?'

'No, well, it wasn't quite like that – we didn't actually pay – he sent us free tickets,' Jody said, like that made all the difference.

'What about sisterly loyalty?' I asked.

'Well, that's why you're here now – your sister is going to get your 'happy' back. I know we haven't been like real sisters over the years and I want this to be special. I know you've always wanted to visit Switzerland and you love Christmas so I made it happen. I made your Christmas dreams come true – let's face it, this year it would have just been you and your cat.'

'Me and Mrs Christmas would have been very happy together,' I said, feeling a glimmer of homesickness.

'Sweetie, you saying you're happy with your cat is just confirmation that Jody was right to chopper you right out of there,' Lola piped up. 'This isn't a working holiday – it's an intervention, and just in time if you ask me.'

'I know it isn't ideal, and I know I'm not totally past it at forty,' I said, trying to convince myself as much as them. 'But I just thought by now I'd be having a different kind of Christmas – I thought I'd have babies, you know... sleepless nights, nappy changing... Look, all I'm saying is that I'm trying to readjust.'

'It's important to me that you have a great time here,' Jody was saying. 'And while we're here, it's your birthday too, so it's extra special, which is why I bought you this,' she said, touching the cow's ears. 'I want you to feel part of the group. We're a family, us four – and we're all we've got at Christmas, so let's enjoy it together.'

'So you're saying I have to wear a onesie to work tomorrow? What if my udders get caught up in the cappuccino steamer?'

'Then we'll all laugh our heads off.'

'Me too, I suppose,' I said and giggled, imagining this image.

Suddenly I felt exhausted; I had no idea how any of us were going to get up in the morning to do our jobs – we'd all need dark glasses. We started to get ready for bed but as my new thermal nightwear was now adorning an eight-year-old boy somewhere in the resort, and the onesie was out, I had nothing. Again, the girls were quick to offer their support, but it was a compromise given their eclectic and eccentric wardrobes, and for bed I wore Jody's pink fur all-in-one, with 'Come and get it – it's HOT!' emblazoned across the chest. After much conversation between the girls about 'losing heat from her head', Kate donated a purple bobble hat. I looked weird but was so tired I basically allowed them to put anything on me as Jody, who was now Googling 'death by cold', kept yelling words like 'layers' and 'hats', and the girls continued to add items of clothing to my ensemble, which was finished off with a bright blue diaphanous negligee, courtesy of Lola. 'This will trap warm air,' Kate said, as she helped me into it.

'It's trapped more than air in its time, that negligee,' Lola sighed.

I winced. Who knew what acts of indecency had been committed in this nasty blue fire hazard as I climbed into bed looking like Bette Davis in *Whatever Happened to Baby Jane?*

'You're being very dramatic, Jody,' I sighed, really tired now.

'Why does no one take me seriously?' she said. 'I also happen to be a nurse and know about these things.'

'And I'm a nursery nurse, so I know about first aid... mind you, only for kids, not for old people,' Kate added unnecessarily.

'Great, I'll get off to bed,' I said, finally heading for my sanctuary.

'OH. MY. GOD,' Jody announced loudly.

'What?' I sighed impatiently.

'I just realised people die if they fall asleep with hypothermia.'

'Oh my God,' Lola gasped. 'We're going to have to keep her awake all night.'

'No, no really, it's fine... it's only if you fall asleep while you're cold, or outside, isn't it?' I said – after all, my sister was apparently the medical expert in the room. 'As long as I stay warm I'll be okay – that's why I'm wearing these layers of clothing.'

'No, no, no. You're not playing the "I'll be fine game", with us,' Kate piped up. 'You have major issues, Jen... the nursery sent me on a counselling course last October – trust me, I know about these things.'

'Thank you, Sigmund Freud, but I don't have issues... all I want to do is sleep. I'm tired from the flight and stressed about losing my suitcase... and I'm absolutely exhausted after my ridiculous collapse tonight.'

'Ladies, I think we should take it in turns to keep Jen awake... let's all camp out in the living room tonight,' Kate kindly piped up.

'That's a great idea,' Jody said, clapping her hands together excitedly. 'We'll pretend we're back in the Brownies and toast marshmallows on the fire and sit round telling each other ghost stories.'

And so, until 5 a.m. (when they dropped off, leaving me to my fate after all) I was kept awake with stories of decapitated ghosts in forests, zombies under beds and chains that rattled on their own – and those are just the ones I can remember. I quite enjoyed myself, and after a while I forgot I had to be up early for work – I just laughed along and even told my own scary stories. I felt like a little kid again – in a good way (to quote Jody).

I finally dropped off about 5.30 a.m. which was why, when the door of our chalet was knocked at 8 a.m. and I opened it to

Jon, my gorgeous blue-eyed rescuer from the previous evening, I looked and felt like I was recovering from a fight. I was also still sporting a pink furry all-in-one and a bobble hat and a negligee, with my eyes ringed in black mascara and sleeplessness.

'Oh I... didn't expect to see you,' I started. 'I don't usually dress like this for bed – I just didn't want to die in the night.'

'Do you always dress like this so you don't die... in the night?' He was gesturing at the sequins across my chest and looked understandably confused.

'No... it's okay. I'm okay – I'm alive,' I said in a silly voice which made me wave my hands in the air, and I immediately felt very stupid.

'Good, I feel all the guilt about last night.'

I looked at him quizzically. Had I missed something that had occurred between us to cause this guilt? Surely I wasn't that drunk?

'You fainted because I kept you talking outside in the cold. It's all my fault. I couldn't sleep so I asked reception where you were staying and I came to see if you are okay.'

'That's very kind of you, but it's not your fault at all – in effect, you saved me. I was about to head off into the white unknown. It was only because you took me back into the club that I didn't die in the snow.' I always rambled when I was nervous, and given there was a slight 'lost in translation' element, I had to stop before I said something that might be misconstrued. He looked confused – it was either the language barrier or my insanity – so I tried to seem calm and normal and in the absence of words we both stood in the doorway in awkward silence, me on the inside, him on the outside in the snow.

'Would you like to come in?' I asked, not sure what was going on here.

He shook his head.

'I start work in the coffee shop today. You must pop over and I'll buy you a coffee to thank you for saving me,' I heard myself say. I still found him incredibly attractive, even when sober and in the cold light of morning. He nodded, but perhaps he was just being nice?

'And you ski today?' he asked.

I nodded my head vigorously. I'd never skied in my life, and I certainly hadn't planned to take to the slopes on my first full day in Switzerland, but I wanted to impress this beautiful man.

'Yes, I'll probably swing by the piste later,' I said, trying to sound casual. 'I love to ski,' I added unnecessarily.

'Ah yes.' He smiled and his eyes went a bit dreamy, which was nice to watch. 'It is the most beautiful feeling in the world... I love the rush – I think that's what you call it. The white mountains, the pure air, the absolute freedom, like all your worries flow away out of your body as you leave them behind, moving faster and faster away.'

I was slightly mesmerised by this description, and the way he moved his lips, and the way his eyes caught fire as he spoke of the mountains. When he stopped we were both standing in thick, snowy silence, and I was aware I was still gazing from his eyes to his mouth, which must have seemed a little odd.

I composed myself and focussed, only to see he was looking directly at my chest, which was a bit much even for a snowy Adonis. Everyone is so forward with the opposite sex these days, I thought, sounding about ninety-five years old, then realised he wasn't actually weighing up my breasts but trying to decipher the message across them inviting the onlooker to 'Come and get it – it's HOT!'

'It's not mine,' I said.

'You wear other people's clothes all the time?' he asked. 'Last night you were wearing your sister's shirt...'

'Yes, well no, well you see my case got lost and is probably somewhere in Europe by now and... anyway, what were we saying?' I said, covering my chest with my arms.

'Skiing... we were talking about the skiing...'

'Ah yes, I love to ski...' I lied.

Stupid, I know, but I didn't want him to know I'd never been skiing because it seemed like it was everything to him. I wanted to reach out to this lovely guy with the beautiful eyes who'd been so worried about me he'd found out where I was staying and taken the trouble to find out if I was okay.

'I hope you wear the warm clothes for skiing.' He smiled. 'You must wear the sensible clothing on the piste.'

'Yep, don't worry, I'm quite the ski bum...' I was trying to fill the silence with my noise and immediately regretted the comment.

'Bum?' He was now looking at me confused.

'No, no...' This was beginning to feel like a bad sitcom so I brought proceedings to a halt before I could confuse or offend him further.

'I'm just keen to get going on those slopes.' This was followed by an exaggerated mime of me skiing. Why?

'You are funny. You make me laugh,' he said, moving to leave.

'Oh... thanks.' I was a little nonplussed. I would rather have enthralled him with sex appeal and sophistication, but given my performance and my costume, I'd have to take 'funny' I suppose.

I thanked him again for checking on me and he nodded and headed off through the snow. He turned once to wave and I waved back, unable to stop smiling as I watched him disappear into infinite whiteness. Someone like him wouldn't look at me, but I couldn't help but wonder just what kind of woman would be able to capture his heart. I must have been miles away and was suddenly aware of someone standing behind me; a waft of French perfume and the rustle of silk told me it was Lola.

'He's cute,' she said.

'Oh he's way out of my league – he's gorgeous.'

'Stop that. You can have anyone you want, Jen. I could have said that about any of the A-listers I've bedded,' she sighed. 'But I didn't. I said "I'm fabulous, and if you don't think so then I'm not interested."'

She looked at me, waiting for me to say something.

'Jen, you're fabulous.'

'Okay, perhaps I'm just a little bit fabulous.' I smiled, sipping the coffee she handed me.

'That'll do for starters,' she said, and I gazed out of the window, holding my warm mug close, imagining Jon walking towards me in the snow, a twinkle in his eye and mistletoe in his hand.

Chapter 5

Cows on Skis and Coffee Shop Kardashians

'So, everyone, don't forget, our skiing lesson is booked for this afternoon when we've finished work – if we can all meet at the ski lodge we can take it from there,' Jody was saying as she emptied a box of cereal into a large bowl.

'Look, girls,' I started. I was about to make a million excuses why I couldn't ski, but then I thought about Jon and how he'd said it was the most beautiful feeling in the world and I thought, why not? It's something I'd always wanted to do and we were in Switzerland in a ski resort so it kind of made sense.

'The idea is that we'll all go skiing after work and just get acclimatised.'

'As long as you don't mind me tagging along... I can't ski and you're all friends and have done it before,' I said.

'And you are my sister,' Jody said, and it meant everything to me. I suddenly felt sad for all the years we had missed out on doing simple things like this. We would have had such fun if only I'd been more open to the idea of a sister. I wish I'd been able to see her in a different light, as an ally and a friend rather than an imposter trying to usurp my place.

'Sorry I gave you and your mum a bit of a hard time,' I said, putting my arm around her. 'I didn't mean it. I wished we'd spent more time together now.'

'Oh it was a long time ago, Jen. I was in awe of you – I never expected much so if you deigned to take me to the park or buy me some sweets, I was made up.'

'Did Dad ever say anything to you, when he died,' I said. 'Your mum called our house to say he'd gone... she said my name was on his lips but... I put the phone down on her. I was such an idiot at seventeen.'

'His death was tough. I remember his empty bed in the living room, all his pills lined up waiting to be taken. I remember asking Mum why they hadn't made him better. I was only eight, but I knew this was more than just being unwell. Jen... he wanted to see you, he always wanted to see you.'

'No, he didn't. Mum said he had his new family now – "bright and shiny", she always said. "We're old and rusty now, Jen," she'd say, and she'd cry and I'd plan to ask him to come home next time I saw him... but I rarely did. He let me down so often, Jody.'

She was shaking her head. 'He didn't, Jen. Dad came to see you so many times and was either turned away at the door or you and your mum weren't in.'

'Really?' I'd never realised and the thought almost destroyed me. So much going on behind the scenes – adults fighting and scoring, but no one thinking of the casualties, the children. What a terrible waste of time and lost moments we could have shared, and I could have been part of the family I always wanted.

'I do appreciate you suggesting I come here and including me in everything,' I said. 'I feel so lucky to have you, Jody. You're all

I've got now, and you could so easily have refused to have anything to do with me.'

'Jen, I told you – you're my sis... and that's all that matters. Everything else is water under the bridge.'

Jody was right – the past was the past and I had to move on, from my parents' break-up and my own failed relationship. Now I was ready to take on new challenges, taste different things and meet new people.

Part of this renaissance wasn't just emotional – it could be physical too, so why not try a new sport? Talking to Jon and pretending I could ski had made me think about the sensation of flying down a mountain, my hair behind me, the sun in my face, cold, fresh air in my lungs. I'd seen skiing on the TV. It was exhilarating to watch, and I could only imagine how exciting it would be to try.

'I'm looking forward to skiing.' I smiled. 'Count me in.'

Jody gave my arm a little squeeze. 'You'll love it – and I'm so happy that you're stepping out of your comfort zone, Jen.'

'Yeah, I know, and I can't wait to have a go on skis. I want to see the little gingerbread houses from above and take lots of photos so I can make them into Christmas cards.'

'That's good, but please don't try to take snaps while you're actually coming down the slopes, and Jen... it's not just about pretty pictures – enjoy the moment and be in it, won't you?'

I looked at her, puzzled. I'd just told her I wanted to ski, that I was looking forward to it – of course I would enjoy the moment.

'I mean, don't be fixating on how it should be – taking pictures, planning to use them as Christmas cards for next Christmas! Just be here now – when you're up there in all that wonderful white stuff you need to relax, let yourself go... don't be looking at little Swiss chalets and wondering how you can replicate them in gingerbread.'

I laughed, but what she'd said struck a chord. She was right – I was always trying to take photos, frame the moment, but now it was time to live in it.

'Sometimes you just don't get it – you don't have to go stalking Christmas; if you just stop a minute, sometimes it finds you. A bit like love.'

What she said made sense. 'Listen to you, being all knowing. I'm impressed by how profound and insightful my little sister is without the alcohol and the crazy clothes,' I said.

'Yeah, well, don't judge a book by its cover – as a librarian you should know that.' She giggled. 'Just because I have a good time and let my hair down, it doesn't mean I'm stupid and incapable of philosophy or analytical thought,' she said. 'Though Dad always said *you* were the clever one!'

'Did he?'

'Yeah. He was always saying "our Jenny's read that book" or "our Jenny got all As in her exams".'

I was quite touched by what she said, and even more moved to know my dad had spoken about me. I never knew he thought of me as 'the clever one', and I liked to think I had a place in his life, his heart.

'Yes, and for someone so clever, you don't half cock things up,' she said, laughing. 'All those Christmases when you've spent a fortune and so much time on getting things right – that's all about the moment too, love. So stop stalking Christmas!' She laughed again.

I'd thought Jody had been too obsessed with her own life to be aware of my catalogue of Christmas catastrophes over the years. I'd told her about them all but I'd never been sure she really took it in. But she had and not only that – she'd put them all together into one group with the heading 'Christmas Disappointments'. As a librarian I suppose I should have cross-referenced those Christmases and seen the writing on the wall. I liked things neat and perfect, labelled and in their place, yet all my Christmases since I'd met Tim had been a let-down. It's the time of year when all your hopes and dreams congeal into one and when they're unceremoniously spat on by the person you love, it can be tough to get back from that. Perhaps Jody was right? I should embrace the season, wear the onesie and go looking for Christmas.

'Get those udders on then... we should be mooooving or we'll be late for work!' Jody laughed.

'Are you sure about me wearing this in the coffee shop?' I asked.

'Yesss, it's Onesie Day – *everyone* on the resort will be wearing one, Jen.'

What choice did I have? Apart from a little boy's T-shirts, pyjamas and Rudolph jumpers, I had no other clothes. My new ski suit was somewhere on the outskirts of France now, according to reception, who had kindly called me with this non information earlier. And here was my half-sister, who I wanted to bond with, handing this to me as a gift – how could I refuse? Also I didn't want to be the odd one out at the resort if all the other staff were wearing onesies to work. So against all my instincts I donned the pink and white furry cow onesie with the bovine face and the velvet udders – which, to my utter horror, swayed as I walked!

❄ ❄ ❄

The coffee shop was lovely and looked like a gingerbread house standing there in the snow, twinkly lights round the window, a wreath on the door. It could have been a shop in a little, snowy village, but opening the door I saw the inside was very plastic and modern, which was disappointing really. A woman a little older than me stood behind the counter. She looked chic in a black shirt and smart trousers and was smiling as she told me they weren't quite open yet.

'Oh, I was told to be here for nine thirty,' I said. 'I'm Jennifer Barker – I'm here to work.'

She looked a little taken aback, which for a nanosecond surprised me, and then I realised she was looking at my udders.

'Oh, you came as a cow?' she said, straight-faced.

'Yes, I was told... it's International Onesie Day...'

'By whom?'

'My... sister?'

'Ah well, I bow to her superior knowledge – it's the first I've heard of this international day of onesie celebration. Quick, I must don my cat costume before I look silly.'

I was deeply embarrassed and wanted to kill Jody for her misinformation – I should have known.

'Oh... I'm sorry. It's just that my sister and her friends, they're all wearing them...'

She half-smiled. 'Sometimes the guests have onesie days and the staff join in, but we're the coffee shop, we have a uniform. I'm Maxine by the way.' She held out her manicured hand and my huge great cow hoof rose up and attempted a handshake.

I was actually relieved to hear there was a uniform, because this woman was not ready for my daywear taken from a suitcase full of boys' T-shirts and comedy pyjamas. I felt so foolish standing there like bloody Ermintrude, but Maxine, who turned out to be an ex-stewardess from Barnsley, suddenly laughed out loud. 'I'm sorry, you just look so... funny.'

I shrugged, which must have made me look even funnier.

'I don't have your uniform yet so just wear that today, but on the plus side, the kids will love being served by a cow.' She walked from behind the counter to join me. I could imagine her on a flight, elegantly serving drinks and flogging perfume – she looked all glamour, but the voice said salt of the earth. 'Now the most important thing you have to remember every morning is...' she started, hands on hips.

I took out my notebook (I'd stowed it in the cow's stomach region); I may have turned up to my first day at work dressed as a big, furry cow, but I was determined to do this properly and be the perfect coffee-shop employee. I couldn't mess this up.

'Yes, you really should make a detailed note of what I'm about to say, it's the most important aspect of your working day,' Maxine said, a slightly stern edge entering her voice. My heart sank slightly. I hoped she wasn't going to be a tyrannical boss – after the year I'd had, it was the last thing I needed.

'So... when you come in every – single – morning, turn on the hot water and put at least six croissants in the oven. This is imperative – have you written it down so far?'

I nodded, pen poised, waiting for more instructions.

'Then, take a cafetière, fill with this freshly ground coffee,' she said, holding up the jar of Italian blend like she was holding the life jacket when giving instructions on a plane. 'Pour hot water over the coffee and allow to percolate for about four minutes... got that?'

I nodded, writing down 'four minutes'. I kept glancing up from my notes, expecting her to start waving her arms around, pulling on lifebelt cords and explaining where the exits were in the unlikely event of an emergency.

'Then take two large cups and have them both filled with coffee, with the croissants warmed and ready, by exactly nine forty-five – so as soon as I get in we can sit down to breakfast!' She smiled at her own punchline while I sighed another big sigh of relief. And twenty minutes later, as we sat on the terrace in the chilly white morning sharing our life stories, and eating warm, buttery croissants and strong coffee before the day started, I thought, this will do.

❋ ❋ ❋

Later in the morning I could see why Maxine's coffee/croissant regime was so important – the coffee shop became so busy you didn't have five minutes for a break. Despite the cold outside the coffee shop was warm and my cow suit was disgustingly sweaty – but Maxine was right, the children loved it and I was in many photographs that morning. Those little kids were relentless, and as I ran the perimeter of the coffee bar with the kids and their phones in hot pursuit, I could almost imagine what it was like to be a Kardashian, chased by eager paparazzi.

Later, Maxine and I were enjoying a little post-lunch peace behind the counter when I looked up to see Jon standing in front of me. We said a slightly awkward hello because I wasn't sure whether he was there simply so he could claim the free coffee that I'd promised him – or if he had genuinely popped in to see me.

'Ah, so glad to see you took my advice on the "sensible clothing"?' He smiled as I placed his hot drink on the counter. I liked this gentle teasing – it reminded me of the previous evening when he'd tugged at my scarf, pretending to make me go on the dreaded luge.

'Yes, I decided to wear something more restrained – after all, I am at work and like to be professional at all times,' I said, matching his sarcasm and waggling the udders.

'You are making me laugh always.' He smiled as he wandered outside with his coffee, disappearing into the whiteness. I was disappointed – I'd hoped he might stay a while and sip his coffee and we could chat a little. Then again, I couldn't blame him. Not only was I a huge pink and white cow, I was also being followed round the area like the bloody Pied Piper as more and more children decided I was 'the chosen one'.

After work I met up with the girls at the ski shop where Lola was working. She was rocking her purple glittery shorts and tight top, and she'd met a 'gorgeous guy' again that day, so all was good in Lola's world.

Jody had promised me that the ski class was for beginners and that I would be fine. I was feeling positive about embracing this brave new world of winter sports, and I wandered with the others to the ski lodge where we were fitted with skis. Here everyone was wearing onesies, from Scooby-Doo to plum puddings, so my udders finally felt acceptable.

Once we'd been fitted with skis we were given a very basic talk involving instructions I didn't understand, which included words like 'A frame', 'camber' and 'linking turns'. I so wanted to do this, but a little voice on my shoulder was telling me I had to be careful because people died while skiing. I wasn't sure if this was my mother's insecurities coming through – she'd barely let me out after my dad had left and saw even a bicycle ridden on the path as a dangerous vehicle of death. Or maybe it was Tim's influence. He would often tell me I was 'too old', 'unfit' or even 'too dangerous' to take on any kind of physical challenge.

I felt slightly sick as we all trooped out into the snow on what felt to me like long planks of wood attached to my ankles. How the hell did anyone get anywhere on these, I thought as a giant pig whizzed past me down a very steep slope, followed quickly by a cartoon bear.

'I can't do this,' I hissed to my sister, who was dressed as a fat Father Christmas, as she wobbled onto a chair lift.

'Shut up, get in, sit down and hang on,' she said, holding out her hands to help me on. Kate pushed me under the bum, and I landed rather inelegantly in the chair, soon to be joined by a leopard and a gingerbread man. Once we were all aboard we were approached by a ski instructor called Hans, who had more on his mind than showing women how to ski. As he helped us to climb on the ski lift, he was all hands. Yes, they may have been gloved, but they still had intentions, and he came to be known as 'Hands-on Hans'.

'Now, girls, you must put on your seat belts. A seat belt in a ski lift is like a condom on a one-night stand,' was his opening line as he leered at Lola's ample leopard-spotted chest.

Sensing danger, we all lifted off our various creature heads and caught each other's eyes as he waxed lyrical about the amazing G-force of the slopes. I was petrified. Too high in the sky and clinging to Jody, I was feeling sicker and sicker as we rode higher and higher. Meanwhile Hans was going on and on about ramp angles and rise lines, which at the time I suspected were merely euphemisms for something unsavoury and was surprised to discover later were actually ski terms.

On arrival we all clambered quickly off the chair lift, the others to escape the lecherous Hans and me to simply kiss the ground and be grateful I'd survived the slopes so far. I was on all fours doing just this while trying not to scream and vomit when I heard a man's voice, 'You shouldn't be eating snow...'

'I'm not...' I said, looking up and seeing the familiar cobalt blue of lecherous Hans's ski suit.

I'd had enough of his cheap, lecherous comments and wasn't waiting for him to make an inappropriate remark about me being on all fours so I gave it to him with both barrels. 'Look, I don't want your sleazy jokes about one-night stands and no, before you ask, I don't want you to take me up the piste or put a condom on anything, so just bugger off and leave me to die here,' I hissed from my prone position.

'I am surprised to hear you say this,' came a different voice to the one from the chair lift. It was familiar, but it wasn't Hans. I felt my blood freeze as I looked up slowly, beyond the knees to the waist area and higher still, which slowly revealed the familiar gorgeous blue eyes of Jon.

'Oh God... I'm so sorry, I thought you were someone else... I hope you don't think I was saying anything about sex... or anything?'

I thought I detected vague amusement in his eyes, but it could have been the sun.

I tried to explain, but he just smiled and skied on past me with a quick wave.

I felt so stupid as I joined my friends Gingerbread, Panther and fat Father Christmas, who told me to put my head between my legs if I felt sick and to 'stop whingeing'. We must have looked quite a sight huddled together on the snow, waiting for our ski class to start, and I almost threw up there and then when Mr Blue Eyes whizzed back up, doing a rather dramatic turn on his skis and causing a flurry of snow in our faces.

'I'm Jon and I'm your ski instructor for today's beginners class,' he announced. I saw him look at me and attempted a coquettish stare, then realised I still had my cow head on so the effect would be minimal. I could see his eyes smiling at me though as he began giving out instructions on how to stand and how to gently propel ourselves forward. I have never been strong on coordination and my balance is dodgy, but the nausea had passed and this was the new Jen, the one who would tackle anything. I wasn't tied to my past – I was forging into the future, so I pushed myself through the snow with confidence, telling myself I could do this. But while everyone else was doing as instructed and 'propelling slowly forward', my legs were slowly parting involuntarily, and I didn't have the thigh strength to bring them together. And as my legs moved apart, I gathered speed, my udders now waving as I set off rapidly downhill.

As I whizzed past, I'd noticed that, unaware of my spreadeagled departure, Jon was busy helping some of the 'newer' skiers. Assuming I was a ski bum (serves me right for telling lies), he obviously didn't see the need to help me and prevent me taking the slope at a hundred miles an hour and becoming a serious danger to myself and others.

So, as he gently escorted a new skier down a very flat slope, I was hurtling towards my death on a very steep one. 'Turn, turn,' someone shouted. (I think it was Jody. She had no idea about skiing, but because she'd once been to the bloody snow dome, she thought she knew it all.)

'Jen, TURN,' she repeated, more anxious and louder this time.

'Turn what?' was all I could manage as speed overtook me, my legs now completely apart, udders swaying in the wind, my heart in my mouth. Unable to turn or break in any way, I headed for a mound of white that, when my skis hit, didn't slow me down but lifted me high up into the air. Mid-flight I recall seeing other skiers like ants scattering in all directions from my cannonball cow now eating up the slopes. I screamed in fear for myself and for those I was about to mow down, and after several heart attacks and several kilometres where I had no control of my body, I finally landed hard on my backside – so hard that I bounced into the air. My left ski detached with such velocity that it shot down to the end of the jump and landed in a group of Christmas puddings with legs, all hauling themselves back up the slope. The last thing I remember is shouting 'Sorry' before waking up in a hospital where my bum hurt and no one spoke English.

Jody was standing worriedly by my bed explaining that I had concussion and a possible broken coccyx. I then fell into a deep sleep to be awoken by an alarming bodily intrusion involving an overeager doctor and a tube of cold lubricant.

❄ ❄ ❄

I was eventually discharged from the hospital in the early evening and we were delivered back to the chalet in a resort snowmobile. I felt okay – a little bruised and humiliated – but the pain and the cold thawed when I was greeted by the most beautiful bouquet of white flowers. I gasped reading the little card that said: so sorry, my fault again! hope you feel better soon. jon xxx

'The poor guy will have a guilt complex,' Jody said, laughing as we drank hot chocolate round the fire.

'I know. He thinks he's the reason for my almost hypothermia and my damaged coccyx – but if it means he'll keep in touch, it's a small price to pay,' I said, and we all giggled.

'It's called emotional blackmail,' Jody warned with a smile.

'It's called desperate librarian,' I added.

The girls enjoyed my retelling of my encounter on all fours with Jon and laughed loudly about my later encounter with the doctor and the lubricant. 'He was humming Christmas carols as he "went in",' I squealed. 'It was horrific. I just lay back and thought of Christmas.'

The others screamed, but Jody took it in her stride, being a nurse. 'Oh, you'd be surprised what goes up there,' she sighed, almost admiringly. 'I've retrieved Coke bottles, deodorant canisters... once I even found a—'

'Stop,' I said. 'I'm recovering from an intimate examination of the worst kind, and you're making my buttocks clench... again.'

She screwed up her nose. '"Intimate examination" is the kind of phrase Tim would use. I can hear it now, all clenched teeth and sneering nostrils.'

I nodded – she was right. 'I think old Tim must be about due for a rectal examination,' she said. 'He's so damn anal, I don't know how you could have been with him for so long, Jen.'

'It was those clenched teeth and sneering nostrils – turned me on,' I monotoned, and everyone laughed. I was finally letting go of the last vestiges of hurt and pain – and anger too. Being in a different environment with new people was refreshing, I was beginning to laugh at my situation rather than becoming buried in it, and that was good for the soul. And the girls gave me a kind of respect that Tim never had, despite my spectacular fails at On the Piste, skiing, and Onesie Day – but the girls had all included me and had a kind of blind faith in me – now it was time for me to start believing in me too. I'd only been here a couple of days and yet already I was beginning to see my life objectively. The girls were so non-judgemental – they seemed to like me for who I was, and when I said something funny they laughed, and if I said something serious they listened – unlike Tim.

Just being able to say things I thought without worrying about offending anyone or being corrected was a breath of fresh air, and I liked it.

I looked around at the girls, laughing, sharing secrets, supporting each other and toasting the mallows Kate had found in a kitchen jar, and I suddenly realised what I'd never had. Here I was warm and safe among friends and I was saying stuff I would have filtered in front of Tim – I was a different person now he wasn't around – and that wasn't a bad thing. I began to relax. I hadn't felt truly relaxed in years.

I'd always kept things locked up inside. I suppose I was trying to please Tim. I was never scared of him, but I'd needed his approval, his validation of everything, from what I'd cooked to what I wore, to the person I was. Yet here I was regaling the girls with a story and I realised I had true freedom. I didn't have to edit or censor anything – including myself. I had no need to look across a dinner table and ask with my eyes, 'Is this okay for me to say? Do I look how you would like me to look?' I was free to be whoever I wanted to be, and I loved this rediscovery of something I hadn't even realised I'd lost. Sitting with the girls, chatting freely, finding myself again among the twinkly lights and the glitzy baubles, toasting marshmallows by the fire, I slowly began to see glimpses of my old self – the girl I had been in my twenties before I'd escaped my mother's sadness and run straight into the arms of Tim.

Chapter 6

Love, Lebkuchen and a New Year's Resolution

I hadn't seen Jon since my accident on the slopes, and as it was a couple of days since I'd received the flowers, I was keen to see him and thank him. I soon went back to the coffee shop, where Maxine treated me gently and allowed me to sit and stand in strange positions to alleviate my back pain while serving. But Jon was never far from my mind – I'd be working the cappuccino machine or the squirty cream and see a blue ski suit through the window, and my heart would start to race. I'd think I'd seen him in the distance, skiing or trudging through the snow, and my heart would leap, then it would drop to the ground as I realised it was Hans or one of the other ski instructors. After about three days of this hell I decided to try and save myself – why come out of a horrible relationship only to start stressing about someone else? Someone I didn't even know? The whole point of this trip was to be myself and to start to like myself, because it looked like I was going to be spending quite a lot of my life *by* myself. So I decided to embrace this freedom and the fact I had no shackles, no relationship and no one else to worry about, and do all the stuff I wanted to do in this lovely place.

'I'm going to spend today just taking things easy,' I said to the girls on my first day off. 'I've been looking online, and as it's almost Christmas, I really want to do something Christmassy...'

'Yes, that's why we're off to On the Piste tonight... you'll be back for that, won't you?'

'Yes, I think so. But today I'm going on a Christmas-shopping excursion. I want to see some of the Switzerland I've come for, the snowy valleys and Christmassy scenes, the stuff you told me about in the brochure, Jody.'

'You crazy bitch,' she sighed, crunching on cornflakes and absently flicking the channels on the TV.

'I know, I'm just bloody mad wanting to go out and look at stupid views from crappy mountains when I could be in a dark nightclub with you.'

'I know. Like I said – crazy bitch,' she said and laughed, acknowledging my sarcasm. 'You knock yourself out wandering round old ladies' tea shops and admiring piles of snow,' she said.

We were beginning to understand each other. Jody and I were very different people, wanting different things, but we shared the same values – we were both caring and wanted the best for each other.

Meanwhile, with my suitcase still missing in transit, I'd returned the little boy's suitcase to its rightful owner and was still making do with the girls' clothes. Even if my case did turn up, I wasn't sure I'd want to wear the clothes I'd brought with me – they seemed a bit frumpy now, and I wanted to buy something more fun to wear. I'd become used to the bright colours and fashionable styles, and although I'd thought I'd never be able to wear stuff like that, I'd discovered I could. I liked how it made me feel to wear younger clothes again.

'Are you sure you'll be okay on your own?' Jody said before I left.

'Not only will I be okay, I'll welcome it.' I smiled. 'I'm really looking forward to discovering this place and having some thinking time alone.' So after I'd promised faithfully to meet them at On the Piste for multiple Christmas Orgasms, they all headed off into the whiteness and the wandering hands of Hans and the chair lift.

I'd worn the coffee-shop uniform every day, and as I hadn't left the resort, I'd mostly worn the girls' stuff supplemented by a couple of tops from the ski shop. But this was a day out, so I decided to plunder the girls' 'winter collection' for my Christmas-shopping excursion.

I rifled through the drawers. Kate and Jody's wardrobes were all about tiny tops and skirts, not suitable for a day's sightseeing, so I looked in Lola's wardrobe of frills and faux leopard skin and there was, in my view, a fine line between 'fun and flirty' and 'escort service'. I held up a bright purple lace bra which definitely had something of the lady of the night about it, but I had no choice and it was kind of Lola to give me free rein with her clothes so I stuffed it with tissues to fill the parts I couldn't. It looked good. I think before this trip I'd have considered it a little racy for me, but I felt differently about myself now. I'd thought at the time I was reinventing myself, but as I dived back into the garish purples and sheer pinks of the girls' suitcase, I remembered how I used to wear things like this. Obviously some of the feather boas and the cropped tops weren't going to work on me, and I'd need to find something less pornographic than Jody's logoed tops and Lola's zipped leather trousers. (I won't mention where the zips were, but they wouldn't be appropriate for a touristy coach trip to a centuries-old Swiss village.) I was just about to give up when I came upon a red jersey. At first I thought it was too good to be true and, as it was in Lola's case, probably had nipple tassels. But on further inspection it appeared to be a simple jersey dress, and as I was now running a little late I quickly slipped the dress on and threw Jody's fake fur coat over it. Feeling exhilarated by the snow and the day ahead, I rushed off to The Ski Bunny, where the tour was meeting for the shopping excursion. I wasn't sure exactly what the trip involved, but along with buying a few Christmas gifts and some emergency clothes, I was keen to take in the sights. So far, working at the coffee shop had sucked up much of my time, and I'd only seen the ski resort – and that was from the top of a mountain on all fours in a cow costume.

There were a few people already waiting, and I waved to Maxine and we chatted for a little while before I joined my fellow travellers. There were some older ladies, a few couples and a family with two kids who were loud and kept fighting. In between their yells, the mother piped up with, 'JOSH, that will DO,' and when the father started with, 'THAT'S IT, we're going home if you keep doing that,' I wondered if I should have brought earplugs. Then all of a sudden, one of the children hugged their mum and said he wanted to whisper 'a secret' in her ear. It stopped me in my tracks for a few seconds, and an unspoken wave of emotion washed over me, reminding me I'd missed out on something very special along the way.

I batted the feelings out onto the snowy mountains and began a conversation with one of the older ladies about thermal underwear. She was just enlightening me about the joys of 'the liberty bodice' for 'us older girls' when I spotted him out of the corner of my eye. It was Jon. I tried to ignore the flutter in my chest, and suddenly felt incredibly nervous about approaching him, but at the same time had this urge to talk to him. I wanted to thank him for the flowers and to ask where he'd been for the past few days – I'd missed seeing him. I also wanted him to realise that I wore 'normal' clothes and there was nothing strange about me. Until now, the only times he'd seen me I'd been sporting a see-through shirt and miniskirt in deep snow, a costume with udders on a mountain or a top with an invitation to 'Come and get it – it's HOT!' in sequins across the chest – not to mention the bobble hat.

Being with the girls had given me confidence, and I was more sure of myself now. There was nothing wrong with going over to someone you knew and liked and just saying hi, was there?

So I made my excuses to my thermal-underwear friend and rushed over to him. Seeing him again, I knew I liked him and was keen to make a good impression and dispel any 'weirdo' or 'walking-human-disaster' vibe he may have picked up. So in my keenness to reassure him I wasn't half naked or wearing udders, I opened the fur coat and said, 'Hello, Jon, haven't seen you for a while – look, I'm normal!' Which probably wasn't necessary and implied the very opposite. I was holding open the fur coat like a flasher while insisting I was 'normal', and his face just opened up into a huge smile as my heart jammed into my chest.

'Ah yes, so you are,' he said teasingly.

'Thank you so much for the flowers,' I said. 'I was really touched.'

'I was feeling the guilt. You always fall or take on the illness around me.' He laughed. 'And now, here you are again, you are a glutton!'

My fellow tourists turned around at this to see 'the glutton' and I quickly added, for their benefit as much as Jon's, 'For punishment.'

'Ah, I think so. I worry you will have the accident on this trip... or we will lose you in an avalanche.'

We laughed and he gently touched my back as he escorted everyone out of the coffee shop and on to the waiting mountain bus. I'm not sure if he arranged it this way, but he suggested as I was the only single passenger I would need to sit at the front of the bus, and when he climbed on last, I was delighted to see him take the seat next to me.

I had hoped we could bond on the bus, but unfortunately he spent most of the hour-long journey dealing with various questions from the rest of the party. Once or twice he stood up at the front of the bus and pointed out a mountain or a glacier in his lovely Swiss-German accent. I was impressed by his knowledge, and he talked about local history, latitude, ski spots and climate. I liked listening to his voice and the way he described the snowy *picks* (peaks). I also warmed to the cute way he said 'wisitor centre'.

Our destination was a small village called Saas Fee, described by Jon as 'the pearl of the Alps', and stepping off the bus, I had to catch my breath. This was the beautiful little chocolate-box village I'd longed for when I'd first thought of coming to Switzerland. Nestled in a white, snowy valley surrounded by high mountains and glaciers, the village was the twinkliest, most Christmassy place I'd ever seen.

We had to walk into the village, and I walked alongside Jon, imagining what it would be like to be alone with him. Unfortunately 'liberty-bodice' woman had now latched on to me and was trying to engage me in more discussions on the joy of thermal underwear. By the time I'd managed to shake her off Jon was involved in some bloody drama regarding an older couple's flushing toilet in their chalet. Really? Couldn't they wait until they got back?

'Wow,' I sighed as I gazed out at the little streets dotted with wooden chalets, shops and cafés, all like fairy lights in the snow. It felt even more authentic and old-fashioned because there were no cars.

Jon gave us a talk about Saas Fee's fresh mountain air and how 'vonderful' it was to just enjoy the peace and quiet here. He told us it was home to the world's largest ice grotto, the highest funicular railway and a list of various measurements in metres about the surrounding peaks. I didn't care about the statistics – I just loved the fact that everything here seemed to be covered in Christmas glitter.

'It was also the setting for Wham!'s big hit "Last Christmas", in 1984,' he said, which caught my attention. No one but me seemed interested in this particular piece of pop history, but as an eight-year-old I'd loved the Wham! video that Christmas. I remember being obsessed with the video of George Michael's doomed love in the ski lodge among soft-focussed snowflakes and trendy young things at Christmas time. I suppose it was one of the last Christmases we'd shared happily as a family. Mum and Dad's marriage probably started to disintegrate the following year.

Jon explained that we were now free to wander until 5 p.m. when we had to meet the mountain bus back here. I was rather hoping he might suggest we spend some time together – I'd felt all the signals were there and I'd caught him looking at me a couple of times, and even when dealing with the various 'guest problems' he would sometimes catch my eye. I felt we definitely had some unfinished business, and I was excited – what a lovely setting to spend the afternoon with a good-looking, fun and knowledgeable man.

But just as we all split up and I was pretending to look for something in my bag in case he approached me, he announced that he wouldn't be walking through the village with us. 'I have to call the resort and tell them about someone's toilet problem,' he said, which caused a snigger from a couple of the kids. As much as I liked him, this was my day, doing my stuff, and standing on the snow-sugared street, a wave of something came over me, and – I know it sounds strange – but I felt like I was home. The Wham! video must have left such an impression on me that I think it's what I'd been looking for all my life without realising it. Each Christmas when real life let me down, I'd bake a big Christmas cake, some mince pies and I'd escape to this stunning winter wonderland nestled in my brain for over thirty years. And here I was – finally home for Christmas.

As it was winter there was little light in the village and all the shops and chalets were lit from the inside, often strung with fairy lights and mistletoe, with sprigs of holly and wreathes on the doors. Despite the village being busy with Christmas-seeking tourists, there was a tranquillity about it that appealed to me as I walked slowly past the shops and cafés, allowing the Christmas tingle to run through my veins, warming me in the sub-zero temperatures. Popping into a couple of boutiques I was a little horrified at the prices but managed to buy myself a few things to wear. I also bought three beautiful gingerbreads for the girls – I didn't have Christmas gifts for them yet, and Jody's was still in my suitcase – but at least I'd have something to give them on Christmas morning. There was a Christmas tree, a bauble covered in glittery icing and an angel with feathery iced white wings. They looked and smelled so delicious, I just hoped I'd be able to resist them myself before Christmas.

After a couple of hours wandering the beautiful streets, it was late afternoon and quite dark. This only added to the magic of the place as the lights twinkled and Christmas music played – I felt alive and happy for no reason, just pure happiness. All the walking had made me hungry so I wandered uphill towards a sign saying 'The Cake Café', which said it all for me. It was in the distance, snuggled under the towering white-topped mountains, and even though it meant walking a little further than I'd anticipated, I couldn't help myself – I was drawn there. When I arrived outside the café, I knew it had been worth the walk.

Looking just like a gingerbread house iced with snow, the café glowed in the winter dusk, welcoming me in with the smell of hot chocolate and freshly baked gingerbread. This was just like the café in my childhood book, *The Christmas Cake Café*, and I felt a little catch of excitement in my breath. The window was a huge display of the village created in gingerbread and icing, with the ice rink in the middle of the village green, children playing snowballs, a snowman – and even a sugar Father Christmas climbing down a chimney, his sack filled with real candy canes. There was the funicular railway, the snowy summits made from enormous peaked meringues, and strung through this little confectionery village were a million tiny fairy lights. The window was like something from an old fairy tale, a vision of Christmas as it used to be – as it should be – and I was transfixed. I don't know how long I stared into that window – there was so much detail, so many things to see – but when someone tapped me on the shoulder, it made me jump. When I turned around I saw Jon, smiling.

'Jon!' I said, fighting the urge to throw myself into his arms, and as we embraced politely, I was aware we held each other a little too long and a little too tight for acquaintances. Was it possible he liked me too?

'You okay?' he asked as we released each other. 'I've been looking for you, and then I give up and it's strange, but I come to my favourite place – and here you are!'

I nodded. 'Oh yes, this would be my favourite place too if I lived here – I'd spend all day every day just gazing into this delicious window. I'm mesmerised by this lovely gingerbread town,' I said, gesturing to the confectionery-iced buildings. 'It's so clever. It reminds me of a book I used to read as a child... it was mostly pictures, but they've stayed with me and this place is just like it. Uncanny really.'

'Do you bake?'

'No.' I smiled. 'I'm a librarian, but who knows? One day?'

'Ah yes, don't give up your dream to bake. I dream of baking the cakes all day.'

'Ah, I enjoy baking too, but I wouldn't know where to begin to create something like this.'

'Ah yes, this coffee shop she is very famous. Very sad though...'

'Oh why?'

'The lady who owns it is old and this might be her last winter here – she is moving away to live with family. I always loved looking at this window as a little child. Every December my parents bring me here and like you I gaze for hours at the gingerbread houses and the sugar snow.'

He was looking into the window, and I glanced up to see his face soften as his eyes took in the sweet winter wonderland before us. I could see from his face that underneath his rather detached exterior, there was something softer, capable of warmth and humour.

'I thought I might go inside and have something to eat,' I said, suddenly feeling rather cold and longing to enter the cosy café.

'Yes... I recommend the Sachertorte,' he said. 'It's Austrian, but they don't mind.' And then he laughed; it was presumably a Swiss joke, so I laughed along.

He was standing by the window as I walked towards the door and I felt rude just leaving him there, but what else could I do?

'I will take your advice and order the Sachertorte,' I said, smiling.

'Ah... erm, Jenny?' he said and I turned, my heart lifted, the door half open, one step in. 'Also the Brunsli... you must taste them... you call them the chocolate brownies, I think?'

'Oh yes... great. Thank you. I will.' I was now standing awkwardly half inside and half outside the café. I wanted to ask him to join me. He was clearly a Swiss cake connoisseur, which would be handy – especially if they didn't speak English. But I still lacked basic confidence with men and was rusty in the art of flirting, so I still wasn't sure if he was just being nice or if he really wanted to join me. There was also the issue of recent injuries I'd incurred in his company, for which he seemed to have taken on the blame. He'd sent the flowers and come to see me in the coffee shop and was being very friendly now, but perhaps he was just hoping I wouldn't sue him?

We both stood awkwardly in the doorway and one of us had to make a move. 'Okay... erm, I'll go and try those Brunsli...' I muttered, reluctantly walking away from him. I closed the door behind me, giving him a little wave but leaving him standing there. I entered the café and straightaway the warmth and the smell of Christmas engulfed me. Several people were sitting at rustic little wooden tables and benches, which had little heart shapes cut into the wood, drinking steaming chocolates and coffees. Two toddlers played with wooden toys, and their mothers chatted, watching them, loving them. I was stung again by the envy of motherhood, how I wanted to complain of sleepless nights, nappy changing and relentless nursery rhymes. My biological clock was a bitch.

I wandered over to a table, sat down and reminded myself there was more to life than being a mum, allowing the smell of vanilla and the shimmer of Christmas to soothe my heart. This place was so restorative; like Storm's comforting chamomile tea, it had almost magical qualities that calmed my head and my bones. I picked up the menu, and just as I was trying to decipher the German words, remembering some from school and wishing Jon had come in with me – if only to translate – the door opened, bringing in a blast of icy cold – and Jon.

'Jenny... I have to tell you...'

He seemed anxious and I was alarmed, worried he was talking about an avalanche or something.

I looked up, alarmed, dropping my menu onto the table and bracing myself for what he had to say.

'I have to tell you about the Schwabenbrötli.'

'Oh no? Is everyone okay?' I asked, assuming this was some kind of mountain disaster that had just happened since I'd walked in.

'Yes, everyone is fine. It's a cookie...' He looked at me like I was mad. 'And the Zimtsterne... oh and Lebkuchen, and you must try the Schokoladenkuchen.'

'Oh,' I smiled, relieved. 'I'm not sure I can remember, or even say, those things. Perhaps you'd like to join me and help me order my cake?' I said, hoping I'd got this right and he didn't think I was coming on to him. I was keen to talk cake... my favourite subject.

'Oh thank you, yes I would,' he said, making my knees go weak as he smiled and took the seat opposite me at the wooden table, which looked like something Heidi might have in her Alpine home.

He took charge and made a long and eloquent order of various cakes and cookies in Swiss German. He could have been ordering anything, but from his lips it sounded delicious. He was so animated, his hands waving around, his eyes smiling.

'You seem very happy here, very much at home...' I said as I watched him go forensically through the cake menu. I'd meant he was 'at home' in the metaphorical sense, choosing cakes, but he thought I meant it literally.

'Yes, I am at home here in Saas Fee – it's my home town. My family still live in the village and, to me, it is the most beautiful place on earth.'

'I agree,' I said as our steaming hot chocolates arrived with mountain peaks of fluffy cream dusted with cocoa powder and sprinkled with tiny mallows.

'Famous Swiss hot chocolate, like nothing else,' he sighed, breathing in the warm chocolate aroma from his mug.

I took a spoon and nibbled some mallow and cream before settling down into my chair. As it was so lovely and warm in the café and I felt so relaxed in his company, I decided to take Jody's big fur coat off.

I placed it on the back of the chair and continued to attend to the delicious hot chocolate. I was aware Jon was looking at me, perhaps admiringly, and I tried not to blush as I looked up and into his eyes.

'You very pretty, but you wear the strange clothes,' he said, which wasn't the comment I'd been expecting.

'Why do you say that?' I asked, smiling quizzically and leaning forward, which seemed to cause him some discomfort; he was looking around the café like he was embarrassed to be with me for some reason. I'm no body-language expert but I suspect this was textbook rejection and he clearly had problems, but I felt a little hurt. I wasn't trying to force myself upon him for God's sake – I just wanted to be friends.

'Is there something wrong?' I asked.

'I think perhaps your dress might be a little... cold? For... here?' He was looking at Lola's lovely red jersey dress with an uncomfortable expression on his face and I looked down and in an instant saw exactly what he meant. I'd been in such a hurry that morning I hadn't had a chance to check myself in the mirror, and the dress that had seemed like fine jersey on the coat hanger was completely transparent on the body! I yelped and grabbed at the fur coat from the back of my chair and quickly covered myself. I had, in effect, been sitting in a lovely rustic Swiss café with the handsome tour guide in just my bra and pants. Well, not even mine – because I was wearing Lola's purple bra stuffed with tissues under the red see-through dress, which I could now see left nothing to the imagination.

I should have known that Lola would never have worn a simple red dress. How stupid of me not to check the mirror, but I'd been in such a hurry.

'This is someone else's dress,' I said, like that made perfect sense. I tried to avoid mention of the enormous purple bra but explained about my suitcase and he seemed to find it all rather amusing.

'Damn those baggage handlers,' I said, after we'd talked through my catalogue of wardrobe malfunctions.

By now a large tray of cookies and cakes had been delivered to our table and, still giggling about my cow onesie with swaying velvet udders, he talked me through the different confections.

'Here is the Sachertorte,' he said, taking a forkful and putting it to my lips. I opened my mouth, trying not to dribble – that wouldn't be a good look – and as I took that deep, rich chocolate into my mouth I thought I had died and gone to heaven.

'Oh my God!' I said, groaning with pleasure as the chocolate danced with my taste buds and filled my mouth with something like stars. He was amused at my rapture and offered me another morsel. 'These are the Zimtsterne,' he said, holding a perfect, glittery cookie star, covered in icing and tasting of cinnamon.

'That's pure Christmas in a cookie,' I said, moaning and crunching and enjoying the combination of sweetness, spice and crunch. Next we tasted the Schokoladenkuchen – German chocolate cake covered in feathery icing, like a spider's glittery web. The taste was thick, rich chocolate – yet it melted in the mouth and is, to this day, the best chocolate cake I've ever tasted.

'Good yes?' he said, as we embarked on Chräbeli cookies, flavoured with anise that looked like tiny tree branches. Beautiful and aromatic, they were crisp and sweet with an echo of fennel and liquorice. Once or twice my moans of pleasure were perhaps a little too enthusiastic, and as one or two of the other customers glanced over, I became aware I might have been recreating the orgasm scene from *When Harry Met Sally*.

But I couldn't help it. These were new and exciting flavours for me, and I loved the deep, rich, sometimes surprising essences baked into the cakes and biscuits. 'These are cookies, but not as I know them,' I said, and smiling he offered me more.

I was reminded of a time when Tim and I had visited Belgium on holiday and the gorgeous little boutique chocolate shops selling every kind of chocolate.

'Food often tastes better abroad,' I said to Jon. 'In Belgium the chocolate was divine – flavoured with everything from fruit to mint to spice.' I'd wanted to try it all: the deep, dark seventy-per-cent cocoa was bitter and beautiful, the white was creamy and delicious and the milk was just chocolate heaven.

'Yes, I *love* Belgian chocolate. I always use Belgian chocolate chips when I make the cookies,' he said enthusiastically. 'My grandfather was a baker and taught me how to bake the lightest cookies, the deepest chocolate cake. My mother, she used to say, "Jon will eat chocolate and cookies and cake any time of the day – even breakfast."'

'That sounds like a delicious breakfast,' I said, smiling, remembering how Tim had scolded me for eating too much chocolate in that Belgian shop.

'I don't know why you're eating those – they'll make you fat,' he'd said as I paid for a beautiful box filled with a mixture of chocolates. I'd planned to share them with him but I never did – and when I got home they sat in a cupboard for two years until one day I opened them and they were white with age. I'd thrown them away.

'You are feeling sad?' Jon said, his head to one side, concerned.

'Not any more – but I'm afraid I've had a bad year and sometimes it just hits me,' I started.

He asked me why and I ended up telling him all about Tim (yes, everything – from the empty champagne glass on Christmas Eve to the fact there were now rumours of a new girlfriend). I explained how it was my dearest wish to be a mum, but that Tim had never wanted children and I'd foolishly believed we could work round that – and now it was probably too late for me.

'I can't believe I'm telling you all this,' I sighed. 'I feel like I have to keep apologising for my behaviour – first my dress and now the fact that I've just told you my life story without taking a breath. I'm not usually so self-obsessed, honestly.'

He smiled and I saw genuine kindness in his eyes – which made mine fill with tears.

I'd been thirsty for this, the Christmas nostalgia, facing up to my sadness and the strange, comforting feel of having someone who listened without offering me advice or telling me I had issues. I needed the girls' counsel and valued it – they were always telling me to pull myself together and offering all kinds of unsuitable men for me to date while at the resort. But I wasn't ready for any of that – I needed to find my feet, to pace myself and do it all in my own time.

'You will find another… you are lovely,' he said and smiled.

I blushed again. He made me feel all warm inside. It wasn't what he said, it was the way he said it. Yes, I was rusty and certainly no expert with men, but he seemed genuine.

'Oh, I don't know – men my age usually want younger women.'

'Not always. Some men are quite grown up enough to be with a real woman,' he said with a twinkle in his eye.

I looked back at him and returned the twinkle, wondering if there might be something here between us other than a table full of cake.

I'd just told him all about my love life, but he hadn't offered any information about his own situation.

'Men my age often have baggage,' I said, hoping this might prompt a response. 'You know, an ex-wife, kids...'

'I understand,' he said, wiping his mouth with a napkin. 'I hate the sadness luggage too – a broken relationship... much hurt.'

'Oh, I'm so sorry,' I said. 'I'm guessing we're a similar age. It's harder to meet people the older you get, isn't it?'

He nodded, but I doubt he really found it hard to meet people. He was a good-looking guy in a ski resort, and there were plenty of twenty- and thirty-somethings who I'm sure would have been delighted to go out with him.

'I suppose it's harder for women,' I added, acknowledging that he may not quite be in the same boat as me. 'For a start there's the issue of children...'

'Ah, the children...'

'Yes. I was an only child and I always wanted a sibling, then as I grew up, I wanted a baby. Now I feel it's too late for me to have children. Jody, my half-sister, says it would have to be quick – a whirlwind romance. I'd have to meet someone who's also single and wants what I want – and then we get down to it... Oh I didn't mean... that.' What was I saying? I really liked this guy, but I was turning this into a speed-dating experience, desperately trying to find out if he was single and if he wanted kids – with me. Now I really had to calm down.

'Yes, it can be difficult to find someone who wants the same as you.'

'Yes, I just don't have time and I don't need someone else's baggage.' He nodded slowly. I think he understood, but then for him things were different; even though he was probably my age, he had plenty of time to have children.

Then, out of nowhere, big, wet tears dropped onto my cheeks. At first the tears were for lost chances, but then, as these things do, my tears reached further. I cried because all my clothes were still sitting somewhere in Zürich, and I cried because I couldn't ski like everyone else and even though I made out it was hilarious, I also wanted to feel that wind through my hair as I swooped through the snow. Then the tears became very dark and distant and I cried for my mother, abandoned by my dad as she dressed the tree, and my own loss the previous year when Tim had abandoned me too. Throughout this whole process I said things through my tears like, 'Zürich... Mum... Christmas... and Tim, the bastard,' which didn't make any sense to anyone – especially a Swiss German I'd only just met.

'Hey... hey...' Jon got up from his seat and sat in the chair next to me. Putting his arm on my shoulder, he gently rubbed it. 'Please don't cry...'

'I am so stupid,' I said, hating myself. 'I'm upset – but honestly I'm happy too. I never thought a place like this existed... the village, the mountains and this perfect little café.'

'There's no need to cry then... It's all good, yes?'

'Yes.' I nodded through tears and he handed me a napkin from the nearby table, and I made it very, very wet.

Eventually the tears subsided and I felt calm. Here was a very handsome, probably very kind man who would have perhaps made someone a perfect boyfriend – but not me because even if he'd had a glimmer of 'liking' me, I had now just ruined any hope of that. I'd sobbed all over the cakes and cookies and probably scared him more than when I'd opened my coat that morning like a bloody flasher to reveal a see-through dress while shouting, 'Look, I'm normal!'

'I've just ruined a perfectly good Schokoladenkuchen,' I said, knowing I would always remember the lovely chocolate cake with the same bittersweetness I remembered the Belgian chocolates with Tim. Thinking about that made me cry all over again.

'You haven't ruined anything,' Jon said, looking at his watch. He'd obviously had enough of my whingeing and sobbing and was looking to find an excuse to escape.

'I have to tell you something, but I think it will make you do more of the crying,' he said.

I looked up. What could he possibly add to my list of misery?

'Please don't start the crying, but it's after 5 p.m., and you've missed the mountain bus back to your resort.'

'Oh God!' I hadn't even considered the time, and even if I had I would have assumed we were okay because I was with the tour guide.

I leapt up from my seat and gathered my bags. 'If we run we might make it? But if not – what will we do?' I said, now panicking. 'Is the bus allowed to leave without you?'

'Ah no, *I'm* not coming back to the resort. The driver will look after the passengers on the return. I'm staying here tonight... I live here.'

'What? Oh of course...' I plonked myself back down on my seat. What the hell was I going to do now?

'I'm so sorry, it's my fault,' he said, once more taking the blame for my predicament.

'No, no, of course it isn't,' I said, shaking my head vigorously. 'I'm a grown woman, I should have thought – but I was having such a lovely time... crying and complaining and being generally miserable that I lost track of the time.'

He laughed; he seemed to understand my sarcasm. I hoped he also understood this was an acknowledgement of what terrible company I must have been.

I wiped my eyes and tried to sound perkier and less suicidal. 'Is there another bus I can get?'

'No... er, I feel bad – I kept you talking.'

'Hardly. I've just given you my life story and wept salty tears all over your cake – please don't blame yourself.'

'It is not a problem. Don't worry, I will drive you back to your resort.'

'No, really, I'll be fine,' I said, unconvinced. This was all I needed – to be stranded in a snow-bound village in a see-through dress. The girls were going to think this was hilarious. I didn't know what to do and just stood there, clutching at all my shopping, my eyes back to their natural panda state and most probably with chocolate icing round my mouth.

Oh God, I'd sat here sobbing and going on about myself and all the time he was probably wondering when I was going to realise and go to the bus. I really needed to train myself in the art of men again. It had been such a long time since I'd been alone with a handsome stranger, I just didn't know how to behave any more, and I hadn't picked up any signals.

'If the worst comes to the worst I can get a taxi. You probably have plans. You don't want to take up your evening driving me back, it's miles.'

'Please, sit down. The taxi will cost too much, but I could drive you back and I will stay at the resort. I can stay with my friend.'

I bit my lip. This was looking like the only option if I wanted to get back tonight.

'You must hate me,' I sighed.

'Hate? Why would I be hating?'

'Because I just seem to have lots of drama around me at the moment – and now this. I'm stranded in a village I was only supposed to visit for the afternoon.'

'It doesn't have to be the tragedy,' he said. 'I can show you Saas Fee and we can have dinner here – then I'll drive you back to the resort... my village, she is very beautiful by night.'

'Oh, I don't know. The girls will be expecting me,' I said, rather ungraciously.

'Then I will drive you home now.'

I thanked him and asked if he'd mind waiting while I changed in the toilets into my newly purchased cold-weather clothing. Along with one or two other items, I'd scoured the sale rails to find a jacket in bright pink, some matching waterproof trousers and a glitzy red dress that screamed 'It's CHRISTMAAAS' louder than Slade. I went for 'cute', 'colourful', 'figure-hugging' – words I would never have associated with clothes buying before now. But in the light of recent wardrobe malfunctions I checked forensically for inappropriate logos and unexpected transparency in each item before I left the toilets. I felt good in the French navy jumper and tight jeans, topped with the pink padded jacket, and the smile on Jon's face was definitely one of relief when I walked back into the café.

I liked how I felt as he watched me walk over to the table and lifted all my shopping bags. In my rush I'd forgotten about paying and suddenly realised as he took out his wallet. 'No, no, no... I insist on paying for the cakes,' I said, virtually rugby tackling him to the ground. 'I've caused you enough inconvenience without you having to pay for me.'

But despite me almost literally having his arm up his back and hurling him across a table, he insisted on paying for the cakes before we left the sugary warmth of the café and braced ourselves for the icy sting outside.

As we walked out into the snowy street we began walking towards his car, which was apparently several streets away.

'I'd love the recipe for that Lebkuchen,' I said.

'I have it at home. My grandfather, he wrote all his recipes in books – I have them all. He left them to me when he died and sometimes, especially at Christmas, I use them... I will print them for you.'

'Oh thank you, I'd love that,' I said, genuinely pleased at the offer but also noting that he planned to stay in touch, if only to deliver recipes. 'If I lived here it would feel like Christmas every day,' I sighed. 'I would make a daily batch of Lebkuchen and chocolate brownies and...'

'And Christmas cookies...'

'And cupcakes. Everyone loves a cupcake. Your Glühwein cupcakes would sell like... hot cakes.'

'No, not hot,' he said, misunderstanding – but it didn't matter.

'No, okay.' I smiled. 'But with a stick of cinnamon in the top...'

'Or a candy cane?'

I'd often had ideas for recipes when I was with Tim, but I wouldn't have shared them with him – he wasn't interested. I remember enthusing about a delicious almond cake we'd eaten once in a tea room and he'd said, 'It's cake, Jennifer, get over it.'

We wandered through the snow chatting about recipes, ingredients, ideas – both animated, both adding to the other's inspiration, never taking from it. On the walk to his car we shared theories and wondered aloud about interesting flavour combinations and the best kinds of syrups and toppings.

'Perhaps you're in the wrong job as a ski instructor and tour guide?' I suggested.

'Perhaps so are you in the library,' he said, laughing.

I loved my job at the library. The customers could be irritating at times but mostly they were nice, bookish people who shared my love of books. But did I want to be there for ever? I loved sorting the books, classifying them, discovering new authors, discovering old ones – but perhaps it was time to take inspiration from those books and live a life instead of reading about one?

'I think you've just given me a great idea.' I stopped walking and looked at him. 'I might take cake-decorating classes when I get home. No, I *will*. It will be my New Year resolution. I can bake, but I've always wanted to really bake and to ice cakes to a professional standard – you know, wedding cakes and proper themed birthday cakes, mountains of cupcakes all exactly the same.' I liked the uniformity: like books all in a row on a shelf, I could create beautiful stories of my own – in cake. I was reminded again of *The Christmas Cake Café* book my mother had given me as a child, and how I'd carried this seed of something in my heart all my life – without even realising it.

'That sounds like a wonderful idea,' he said. 'And I too will make a New Year resolution, to go through my grandfather's recipe books and make everything... from his special *bündnernusstorte* to Zopf to Gugelhupf.'

'Absolutely,' I said as we continued to walk quickly through the snow. I hadn't a clue what he'd just said, but I nodded vigorously, lost in his enthusiasm and those flashing blue eyes.

Perhaps I should stay here with him for dinner and offer to pay? That way at least it might make up for the trouble and the petrol he'd use driving me the hour's journey back later. And what was it Jody had said about not being so closed to new ideas? That I needed to let go and allow Christmas to come to me?

'Jon, I'm just thinking... it would be lovely to stay here for dinner, it's such a beautiful place,' I said.

'Ah, I'm so glad you are going with the flowing.' He smiled. 'I know the perfect restaurant, majestic views across the mountains and the glacial lake. I would love to show you round my village – I'm very proud of where I live. I think you like it almost as much as I do. I know you will love it if you see even more.'

'That sounds wonderful – but I'll only join you on one condition.'

'What is the condition?'

'That you let me pay for dinner.'

He agreed, and while he called the tour company to let them know I'd missed the bus but was safe, I called Jody and told her I wouldn't be joining them for après ski because there was an 'evening option' on the trip and I would be staying until late.

'There's a lovely restaurant with majestic views over the glacial lake,' I said, repeating everything that Jon had told me about but missing out the key factor – that I was with him. Alone. I knew if I told Jody she'd be supportive and lovely, but she'd also be texting and advising me throughout the evening. I turned off my phone. I wanted some peace and some time to enjoy the company of this lovely man without being interrupted by the girls with advice on contraception, sexual positions or demands for a blow-by-blow account of the evening.

'Oh, majestic views over your chicken dinner... that sounds great,' she said sarcastically. 'I mean you and a load of OAPs in a bloody restaurant eating soup looking out over a lake – don't get too wild. I told you to relax and let Christmas come to you, but I doubt it'll find you in a Swiss nursing home, love.'

'Oh don't worry.' I smiled. 'It might not be your idea of a good time, but I think it might be mine.'

Chapter 7

Gruyère and Wham! with a Gorgeous Man

Jon's car was parked on a snowy side street and when we arrived he opened the door for me to sit inside while he spent a few minutes clearing the snow from the windscreen. I watched him through the powdery white windows and wondered at how life can take you places if you let go and open up a little. This was a fine line, and along with the new, more carefree me, there was still a little voice in my head asking me if I'd taken leave of my senses. *You don't know this man*, it was saying. *You could be in grave danger – he might be a serial killer.* So to be on the safe side I risked a tsunami of sexual advice and turned my phone back on and texted Jody and told her I was with Jon and under no circumstances must she text me with ridiculous comments or pass this information on to the girls. However, if I wasn't back by midnight she was to call the National Guard, the mountain police or whatever they have in Switzerland to find murder victims in snow. She responded with several emojis I didn't understand and an *OMG!!* She also texted back that even if he was dangerous, I'd have a better time fighting off a good-looking killer than sightseeing with a group of wrinklies. 'Enjoy your last hours,' was her final comment, and I smiled as I put my phone away.

'It's turning into a blizzard,' Jon said as he climbed back into the car.

'Will we be okay?'

'We will be fine,' he said, his eyes locking with mine, his hand on my knee in a comforting gesture.

A year ago I'd have seen this as sitting in a stranger's car in a foreign country – but Jon wasn't a stranger; he was someone I'd yet to know. I was in a beautiful country, and I was finally strong enough to embrace the unknown, take a few little risks and even trust again.

We drove to the restaurant, which was just how I'd imagined. It was in the wood-cabin style, with roaring log fires, tinkling glasses and a warm, glowing respite from the freezing cold darkness outside. Here we ate tangy cheese fondue, hot and comforting, dipped with crusty chunks of bread – it was manna from heaven.

'I've had fondue before, but it never tasted like this,' I said, eating hungrily while skewering sturdy chunks of bread to immerse into bubbling rich cheese.

'Only here in Switzerland,' he said and smiled, watching me eat. 'We use the Emmental cheese – the perfect marriage with strong Gruyère, and the splashes of kirsch and white wine.'

I lifted a steaming chunk of heaven-soaked bread to my mouth as our eyes met and my insides felt just like the hot, melting cheese.

After the 'fondue heaven', we drank strong coffee and gazed out over the stunning views, a glittering pale blue landscape framed by mountains, lit by moonlight.

'I've had a lovely time,' I said.

'I like spending this time with you too,' he said, finishing his coffee and sitting back, looking at me. 'I have been away from the resort, but was looking for you... I like you, Jenny. I liked you when I saw you...'

'Standing outside a nightclub in a see-through top? Or was it the cow costume that did it for you?'

'Ah the cow, she was so cute.' He laughed. 'Especially in skis.'

'Don't remind me.' I put my head in my hands.

'I teach you to ski, Jenny.'

He reached out his hand across the table and touched mine, and the way he looked at me made me feel that I was just a little bit fabulous.

This was what I'd longed for, and I didn't even know it – my life had been missing this for so many years. A man who looked at me like I was special, who spoke to me gently, smiled when I spoke and listened instead of waiting for a chance to leap in and put me down. It was also lovely to have a break from the girls, who I have to admit I was growing to love – but their drinking and carousing sometimes went on until dawn. Yes, this was perfect, a handsome, appreciative man, and delicious food in a perfect Christmas setting. And I wanted to remember every moment so I could take it home with me when Christmas was over and the snow had all melted.

'I can only imagine what you must have thought of me that first night.' I pulled an 'awkward' face. 'I was out there drunk and half dressed.'

He laughed. 'I thought, she is an English tourist and she has no idea. Then I see you dressing in the cow and I think, she is an

English tourist and she has no idea. Then this morning you open your coat and I see your underclothes in a dress that shouldn't be worn in the cold and I think, oh dear this English tourist, she is...'

'Yes, I get the gist. I can see exactly what you must think of me.'

'Ah but... then later, in the café, I think to myself this English girl, she is good... nice. She is loving the tastes and exciting to talk to... and we both love the baking... and she isn't afraid to cry and show her feelings.'

'Yes, sorry about that nonsense,' I said, shifting in my seat. 'I'm afraid I sometimes go on a bit. I just found you very calming, easy to talk to and I'm afraid it all came spilling out.'

'Today I see the sadness in your eyes,' he said, looking down – a little embarrassed at his own feelings perhaps?

I was touched. 'Yes, it hurts that I gave my best years to someone who never had any intention of spending the rest of his life with me. But it isn't about him any more – it's about having a family. My own family was fractured and broken, and I suppose I've always dreamed of creating one of my own.'

'I'm sorry you are sad. Children, family... they are a blessing...'

'Yes, they are.' I had to quickly change the subject – I didn't want to end up in tears again. I'd managed to contain myself for at least two hours and he seemed to like me – I didn't want to ruin everything with an encore.

'I know you thought I was just...'

'An English tourist, she has no idea?'

'Erm... yes.' I laughed.

He asked me about my job and my home, and I shared photos of Mrs Christmas on my phone, and Jon told me he lived alone in the village, his parents were both dead and he was an only child – and it seems we shared a lot of similar experiences. He also had a difficult break-up a few years back but didn't seem to want to talk about it; I saw his eyes moisten and I didn't think it fair to probe too much.

'I come with the big, heavy suitcases,' he said, and I assumed by this he meant emotional baggage.

We finished our coffee, and I wondered what he was thinking as he gazed into his empty cup. It occurred to me that he might be troubled but couldn't tell me, or didn't want to.

I caught sight of the beautiful Christmas tree in the corner, decorated in the traditional way, with scarlet baubles and striped candy canes. Huge red bows were tied on the branches, and the tree was topped by a big, gold star. It was the perfect tree and, turning to look out through the windows at the huge landscape, I saw the snowy Christmas scene was perfect too. I felt lucky to be here in such a wonderful place this time of year, and I recalled how, as a kid, I'd watched that Wham! video and sang along and dreamed of a moment like this. And I remembered something my mum used to say: 'Stop worrying about tomorrow', which was pretty much what Jody had advised too.

I'd spent most of my life worrying about what would happen next – from the moment my dad left I'd started worrying about the future, how we'd manage without him, where Mum and I would end up.

'We'll be fine – what doesn't kill us will make us stronger,' she'd said. But Dad leaving was my mum's final chapter, the beginning of a slow decline – and subsequently the fear of being left had followed me into adulthood.

And after all the hurt and the heartache, I'd survived, it hadn't killed me. Mum had been right – I was in fact stronger. Being abandoned by Tim had made me dig deep into myself and now I knew I could survive – anything. Alone if I had to.

As a result of my strength and my recent willingness to say yes to what life had to offer, I was also finding little shards of happiness everywhere. And that night was a perfect example. I was now in a beautiful restaurant with a beautiful stranger a few days before Christmas – and all because I'd said yes.

So I drank in the view and relaxed into the conversation. I didn't know where it would take me, and it didn't matter. And if Jon didn't ask to see me again it didn't really matter. I'd be disappointed, but no one could take away this wonderful Christmassy memory of me finally being in the winter wonderland I used to dream of. I'd finally arrived, walked the same streets that George Michael once walked – and what's more I was with a lovely man who, for tonight at least, was mine.

After dinner we braced ourselves for the toothpaste-fresh air and walked back through the village arm in arm. I longed to hold his hand, put my arms all the way around him and feel him close against me – but for now I would be happy with this.

'I grew up surrounded by these mountains; they are like old friends,' he sighed. 'I miss them when I'm away.'

'How lovely to be born somewhere like this – for it to be your home, to feel part of the geography, the landscape. It must feel like Christmas every day,' I said, laughing.

'Ah but the summer... She is beautiful in the summer too. You should visit in June when the sun is high and the sky is deep, deep blue.' I imagined that sky and looked into his eyes as he talked, his lips moving. I ached to kiss him. We eventually stopped walking to gaze at the Christmas tree in the village square. It was huge and twinkling, decorated by nature with real snow and glistening icicles, their sparkles caught in the lights twisting through the branches.

'This is how a Christmas tree should look,' I sighed, remembering all the Christmases I'd tried to get it right with my Marks and Spencer baubles and Homebase fairy lights. Perhaps it wasn't about the kind of baubles after all?

Then, from nowhere, came a sound – children's voices wafting along the iced air, a familiar yet different sound as it shimmered through the village.

'The children's choir singing "Stille Nacht",' he said.

They were singing 'Silent Night' in German. It was the most beautiful, ethereal sound I'd ever heard, and I was transported through the silence of the mountains. My head and my heart were high above, looking down on this beautiful place.

'It's my favourite carol,' I said, 'but it's so much more beautiful in German.'

'It was written in German. One snowy Christmas Eve the minister walked through thick crunchy snow, uphill to his church. He was going to practise on the organ so he could make the most beautiful sound for his parishioners the next day, Jesus's birthday...' Jon started.

I listened intently, vaguely aware that I must have looked like a little girl being told a bedtime story as we stood by the tree, the music all around us.

'But when he sat down to play, not a sound came from the instrument. So he looked at the pipes and discovered they had been chewed by mice. He was so sad – he had nothing to play and went back home, where he began to think about how quiet it was in the church without his music. The thick silence of the night before Christmas was all around – and on that special night he wrote "Stille Nacht" on his guitar and sang it to his village...'

He told this with all the inflections and facial expressions that would delight a child. And I tried not to think about what a good dad he would make.

'My father used to tell me the story of "Stille Nacht" and he always said "Jon, what a magical night that must have been. When you say your prayers tonight, thank the little mice for that beautiful carol."'

I was so touched by this I felt my eyes filling with tears. Again!

'Oh, Jenny, I made you cry?' he said tenderly.

I nodded. 'I'm an idiot, really – take no notice. I just love Christmas and your story was so lovely...'

He reached up to my face and wiped a single tear from my cheek with his gloved hand.

'Your tears are happy tears?'

'Yes... yes. I'm not sad, Jon, just moved, by the magic. Someone once told me I was the most important girl in the world, and tonight, for the first time since then, I've felt... important. You've made me sparkle.'

'No, Jenny, the sparkles are yours... I just brought the starlight.' He looked up and I followed his eyes to the huge, black sky twinkling with stars.

'Thank you for bringing the stars,' I said. 'And for reminding me they're there – I haven't looked up at the stars for a long time.'

I was mesmerised by him and as we stood together under the dark sky, the white ground lifting everything to new, sparkly heights, I looked into his eyes. He was smiling and gazing down at me with a look on his face that I hadn't seen for a long, long time from any man. He liked me, and I knew he was going to kiss me, and when he did I kissed him back. It was a little clumsy, a little awkward, our lips and timing weren't quite in tune with each other, but in spite of this it felt so good to be kissing him under the tree in the middle of the village square as the snow fell, the stars twinkled, and I – apparently – sparkled. Now we had a secret; that kind of feeling when you first realise you like someone and your feelings are returned, like no one else in the world has ever had those feelings before – just the two of you. It was wonderful clinging to him in the cold night, locked in a passionate embrace. All the emotion I'd wanted, longed for, was here tonight and as we pulled away, we both smiled.

'I've wanted to do that since the first time I saw you,' he said as we walked on, my head now nestling easily in his neck.

'Me too,' I sighed. 'But I never thought for a moment you'd feel the same.'

'You think I wouldn't like you?' He slowed down and turned to face me. 'Here, let me show you another time again.' I giggled at his English and the way he was gently tugging my scarf towards him, as he had on that first night. He pulled me into him and we kissed again, this time both more in tune, more sure of each other, both wanting this so much. As our lips met my heart flew high over the snowy peaks – I was in a cable car over the Alps, hotels and chalets below like fairy lights sprinkled through the snow. I thought about how lonely I'd been and how cruel life could be, and at the same time, how wonderful and surprising it was too.

Eventually we wandered back to the car, Jon pointing out various buildings and shops belonging to friends or family while drawing me back to the beauty of the mountains with his gorgeous accent. His voice belonged here in the rugged terrain and the unforgiving chill of the wind, and just hearing him made me shiver – and not with the cold. And inside I was tingling, because suddenly, out of nowhere, here in this little Swiss village, I saw a glimmer of something on my horizon: a change of luck, a new start... And, dare I say, a future?

Chapter 8

Sparkly Baubles and Crispy Onion Rings

After a final goodnight kiss with Jon in the doorway at midnight, I tore myself away from his arms, left my glass slipper on the stairs and tiptoed into the chalet. However, I needn't have worried about waking the girls because the racket coming from the balcony told me they were all wide awake – and probably keeping the rest of the resort in that state too. I opened the balcony door to see them all in their underwear or worse, in the steamy hot tub. There were a couple of faces I didn't recognise, both male, and I wasn't quite sure where they fit in, but who was I to judge? I'd just been on an evening out with someone I hardly knew – I was definitely becoming one of the girls.

I stood in the balcony doorway, an observer. I wanted to chat, to tell them all about my day, how I'd just been kissed. I was ready to talk about things like this in a way I never had before. The girls had brought me out of my shell, and I'd marvelled at the way Jody and Kate discussed their sex lives with each other. I'd listened to them all and imagined it took the sting out of life when you could share these things.

The hot tub was a new acquisition. Lola was seeing the resort plumber and he had access to all kinds of amenities four resort workers could only dream of.

'Aren't you cold?' I asked Jody, unsure how to join in on this hot-tub action.

'*No*, that's the... point. It's a *hot* tub, get in,' she slurred, waving her arms around, almost hitting Lola, who didn't seem to notice – she was too busy having an intimate conversation with one of the male guests.

'And before you ashk... yes, I've been on the orgasms again.' Jody and Kate were now laughing so hard they inadvertently went underwater.

'Jody says you hooked up with that guy again,' Kate spluttered, coming up for air. I could see through the steam she was holding a flute of champagne high, and I was reminded of being in the Maldives with Tim. It had been such a romantic place I'd suggested we drink champagne in the pool, but he wouldn't. 'That would be dangerous, Jennifer. Deep water and alcohol don't mix,' he'd said.

'Have you had a good time with that hunky ski instructor... you coooogar?' Jody was calling loudly from the bubbles.

I smiled and they all made a loud whooping noise, and one of the guys in the hot tub said, 'Go, Jenny!' I just felt embarrassed and all I could think was 'deep alcohol and water don't mix'. Perhaps Jody was right and Tim had brainwashed me?

They all carried on laughing and drinking and splashing, and I went back inside and found the bag with my new underwear in. I took out the purple bra, put it on with the matching pants, wrapped myself in a towel and walked out onto the balcony.

'Okay, okay, we know. You're trying to sleep, Jen, and we're making too much noise – don't worry, we'll keep it down for the pensioner,' Jody sighed. I had sometimes asked that they keep the noise down if I had an early start, and I had an early start the next day, but when was I going to get the chance to drink cold champagne in a hot tub with my friends?

'I'm not a bloody pensioner. Budge up, Jody,' I said, dropping the towel and climbing in. The air was icy and the shock of the hot water made me yelp slightly as I slowly lowered myself down into the heaven that was the hot tub. Jody was pleasantly surprised that I was joining in, and Kate was clearly delighted.

'Bloody hell, Jen, get in and get some of this champers down you,' she said, offering me a high five with one hand and a glass with the other. I struggled a bit with this. I've never been dextrous, and I high fived the champagne and grabbed her hand, but once we'd sorted that out I sipped my drink and told everyone about my day in Saas Fee. They loved hearing all about it and sitting in the hot, bubbly water I began to feel part of things. 'So what does a girl have to do to get another glass of fizz around here?' I asked, finishing off my drink within seconds and waving my glass in the air. They all laughed and Lola poured more icy fizz into my flute – as I shared everything.

'So you can imagine why he was a little odd with me when I whipped open Jody's fur coat saying, "Look, I'm normal," and all he saw was pretty much my underwear!' I said, telling them all about Jon's reaction to Lola's transparent dress.

'I've had better reactions in that dress, I have to tell ya,' Lola said, laughing.

I described the village, Jon's blue eyes, his strong hands and his lovely smile. I talked them through his accent, everything he said and how all this had happened in the Christmas location of my eight-year-old dreams.

'Oh God! Yes I remember the "Last Christmas" video,' Kate said. She found it on her phone and as she passed it round for us to see the snowy landscape, I heard the opening chords and felt that frisson of Christmas. George Michael, Andrew Ridgeley, Pepsi and Shirley and all their friends at the ski lift, and then all round a Christmas table in a great big house in Saas Fee, warm and bright inside, snow falling outside. And I stopped a moment. I felt like I was currently living in a video just like that. I'd always dreamed of living a life filled with snow, fizz, food and friends at Christmas, and at almost forty-one years old, I was starring in it.

'And before you ask, no he hasn't asked to see me again,' I said.

'Who does that any more?' Lola said.

I smiled as Lola winked and poured me another drink before leaning in. 'Did you sleep with him?'

'When, tonight? No, we just went for dinner... Lola, I hardly know him.'

'That doesn't mean anything. I hardly knew my first husband, but we had sex one afternoon and I married him the next.'

'Well, sex wasn't on the menu, I'm afraid. We spent most of the evening in a restaurant surrounded by other people.'

'Since when has a full restaurant stopped anyone having sex?' Lola said incredulously. 'You are hilarious, Jen... all I'll say is *The Hungry Horse, September 2009* – I got a large portion of crispy onion rings afterwards.'

I didn't ask; I didn't need any more details.

'Well, I'd like a relationship, but I don't want sex... or crispy onion rings,' I said with a giggle. 'Anything that happens here is like a holiday romance – I'm only here for the season, we live in different countries... it just can't happen.'

'Can't happen? I give you Magaluf 1999, New Year's Eve – me, a water cannon and a buff dancer called JJ...' Lola was off on another trip down her sexual memory lane.

'No, I'm not going to get involved. It's too bloody painful when it ends – and with this kind of geography involved – trust me, it would end,' I sighed.

'Suit yourself. Distance relationships can be testing but worth the effort, as can male dancers with taut thighs and hard upper bodies... but I digress.'

'Well, I'm not going to think too much about men with taut thighs,' I joked. 'I'm just going to enjoy being in a lovely snowy place over the Christmas season and if fate wants to intervene then that's good enough for me. And I really don't mind that he didn't ask to see me again.' I realised by now I was lying to myself. I liked him, I was here working for a little while longer and it would be wonderful to spend time together, but perhaps he didn't feel the same.

'He didn't ask to see you? Well, didn't you ask to see him?' Jody asked, apparently amazed at my lack of chutzpah.

'No, I didn't. The man has to ask.' But before I'd finished speaking there was a roar of disapproval from the tub.

'Ooh, and I suppose the man decides when you'll have sex and when you'll eat your dinner too?' Jody said.

'Look, it's just me – I couldn't bring myself to ask a guy. I've always waited for them to ask... it's just the way things are.'

'Is that what Tim told you – that the lady has to wait for the man?' Jody asked, shaking her head.

'Tim? Who's Tim?' I said. At this, Jody gave me a high five, which I managed this time.

'Yeah exactly,' Lola said. 'You're a strong woman, Jen. I never met Tim, but I can't understand how someone like you would put up with someone like him. I mean, we've all been there and being with a domineering man doesn't have to mean whips and chains and pain. Unless of course we want it to...'

I laughed, but what Lola said did make me think about why I'd put up with Tim. I think we all have times in our lives when we make choices. Sometimes those choices are wrong for us, but we don't always realise until it's too late.

'Now is your time, Jen,' Jody was saying.

'I agree, and I really do want to grab it, Jody. I like Jon, but I'm not going to chase him – if it's meant to be, it's meant to be.'

'Ahhhh,' Kate and Jody chorused.

'Sod that,' Jody suddenly said. 'You can't live your life waiting for fate – trust me, she has a way of letting you down.'

We went to bed that night and I lay in the dark, knowing they all meant well, but thankful for the peace their sleep brought. I was awake for hours just thinking about Jon and his lovely smile and the way he said 'vonderful'... and just hoping against hope I did bump into him. I know it sounds silly, but I really did believe in fate and had this strong feeling I'd see him again.

Chapter 9

Seven Christmas Orgasms and Sex in the Snow

The next day we were busy at The Ski Bunny and it was late afternoon when I finally managed to get a break.

I took a drink out onto the terrace and marvelled at where I was. I could be sitting in the library now in a big cardi playing a game of 'librarian charades' with one of our older readers who would ask things like, 'Do you have that book with the blue cover by that famous author?' Instead, I was drinking hot chocolate on a terrace in Switzerland, people watching on a morning lit by snow.

The hot chocolate was very strong and topped with the fluffiest cream and baby pink mallows, and I felt happy and relaxed. I thought of Jon for the millionth time that day, going over everything he'd said in my head. I could still feel his kiss on my lips, and my heart leapt every time I caught sight of a cobalt ski suit. Today there seemed to be hundreds of ski instructors wearing the resort's blue suit, but sadly none of them were him.

The rest of the day dragged a little and after work we were tired, but instead of going back to the chalet I joined the girls in the bar, drinking lurid cocktails and flirting with unsuitable men – we called it 'après ski'. Lola's 'après' lasted longer than the others – she disappeared with a guy around 6 p.m. and didn't return until midnight.

'So, Lola – you didn't exactly play hard to get this afternoon,' Jody said later as the four of us sat in the hot tub.

'Neither did he,' she answered. 'We had a good time, no strings, no messy love stuff, just a few toys, good old-fashioned fun and a big cigar afterwards.'

'Ew, he smoked?'

'No, I had the cigar,' she said.

I had to admire Lola. She took what she wanted from life and threw away the wrapper. There was no aftermath, and no self-doubt.

'Lola, you really have got it sussed,' I said. 'There's me fretting about what I should have said, what I should have done and I only kissed Jon. I'm worried I was being too pushy – I keep asking myself if I should have held back.'

'Why the hell should *anyone* hold back?' she said, almost dropping her champagne glass in shock. 'I don't know why you feel like they are doing you such a big favour. Men don't hold all the power – we do – and the sooner we all realise that the better. You've been with some guy for ten years who told you a story that just wasn't true – now it's time to write your own story.'

'That's why you should take things easy with Jon,' Jody started. 'I've told you before, and I know I'm younger than you and you're cleverer than me, but sometimes I'm amazed at your naïvety.'

'Ha... you're kidding, aren't you?' I said, a little put out at this.

'No. I can be immature, but I'm not naïve when it comes to men, but you love being in love. Trouble is, you want to be loved so much that you create this whole world where he's perfect, when often he isn't. Life isn't picture perfect, Jen, and you can't paint it to be how you want it to be. It's like you're scared of being on your own so much you'll put up with anything... anyone and tell yourself and everyone else it's great,' she said, reaching out and putting her hot, wet arm around me.

'I can see that now, and yes you're right, I probably am naïve. When Tim dumped me last year my darkest thoughts were about being alone – not being without Tim.'

'Exactly, so don't just jump at the first guy who comes along and is nice to you.'

'Jody, that isn't the case – honestly, I'm not building up this thing with Jon, so don't nag me.' I smiled and reached for the bottle of fizz behind me and we toasted strong women.

It was okay for Jody. She was only in her twenties – she didn't know how it felt to lie awake at night and feel life creeping up on you then fading just as quickly in your forties like a dying flame. It made you want to settle for what you had in case there wasn't anything else out there – but spending a short time with Jon had shown me that there was still so much out there for me. I'd spent a year on my own and coming away to a new life was teaching me that the world was a big place and this 'bigger' life I was leading made my life with Tim feel very small. Being with the girls, meeting new people and doing different things had opened up my horizons. I liked Jon, and if we spent more time together it would be wonderful, but I didn't *need* a man to make me happy or complete – I was beginning to believe in me again.

Jody was right. I hadn't seen it so clearly before, but I had been vulnerable when I met Tim and instead of giving me confidence, allowing me to develop and fulfil myself within the relationship, he'd pushed me down, kept me vulnerable, filled me with self-doubt and made me scared to live my life. He hadn't helped me in any way to recover from my childhood, merely exacerbated my vulnerability and low self-esteem.

'I remember one Christmas Dad asked me if I'd like to go and see Father Christmas in Lewis's department store,' I started. I couldn't look at Jody; I just continued to talk. 'I was twelve by then. I knew Father Christmas didn't exist, he was just an old man in a fake beard sitting in Lewis's grotto, and I said, "No way." But I wanted to see Dad... I longed to see him, but out of loyalty to Mum I said I didn't want to go with him.' I looked at Jody. 'That Christmas he sent me a voucher through the post – I thought he couldn't even be bothered to try and see me. You were born the following April. Looking back now I suppose he'd wanted to tell me about the new baby – about you.'

I'd misunderstood my dad all these years, and it had caused me to doubt his love and doubt myself. Someone like Tim had compounded these feelings of being unworthy, and it was only now I was beginning to see the light and become the stronger, more confident me who'd always been there, waiting in the wings for her time.

Jody raised her eyebrows. 'That makes me feel bad – that me being born was the end for you and Dad.'

'No, don't. I overreacted, but I was just a kid. I blame the grown-ups – they handled it badly. No one prepared me for you. But in the last few months, Jody, I've realised how lucky I am to have you in my life.'

She smiled.

'I just feel sad that we didn't get to spend much time together when we were younger,' I sighed. 'Dad would invite me over, suggest I spend holidays with you – but I felt like I was betraying my mum... I was very torn.' Mum wasn't openly hostile to the idea of me going off on holiday with Dad's 'new family', as she referred to Jody and her mum, but it was clear how she felt. I understood her feelings. We were close and even at my young age I related to her feelings of betrayal. I suppose if I'm honest I think we both harboured a secret wish that one day he'd just come home and we could carry on as a family – the fact that she called them 'Dad's new family' suggested a temporary status, like he'd plucked them from a clothes rail and could just as easily put them back when he was finished.

'Anyway, I'm glad we're doing this... spending time... and especially Christmas together,' I said. 'I feel stronger now. I can still drink and dance until dawn, if I want to, but the key here is "want". If I don't want to, I don't. No one tells me what to do or makes me feel guilty for not doing it. I love being with you and the girls, and yet at the same time I enjoy doing what I want to do. I'm not a people pleaser these days – I'm more of a Jenny pleaser.'

'Good for you – but I still think you need to let go a little. You still haven't been down the luge.' She raised her eyebrows and looked at me. 'You're old, but you're not an OAP, Jen.' And she laughed.

'I'm older,' I said in my big-sister voice. I hadn't had much opportunity to use it over the years, and I liked how it sounded. 'You can thrash around nightclubs and date different guys, but I have mature tastes. I need something more sophisticated, more cerebral. These days, a night out for me doesn't necessarily involve drinking and dancing on tables until I fall off, Jody.'

Fast forward to the following evening when, after seven Christmas Orgasms and a Sex in the Snow, I'm screaming, 'Do they know it's Christmas...?' at the top of my voice while balancing on a precarious table in the middle of the On the Piste nightclub and bar. I'd also been down the luge six times and gone round the club twice on somebody's back – so perhaps I'd spoken too soon about being mature. Perhaps there was still some fun to be had... even for an 'OAP' like me?

Chapter 10

Lola's Dangerous Pants

Staggering back to the chalet at three in the morning, the four of us clung on to each other in the snow. Fortunately it was packed down with no fresh snowfall for us to sink into – which was just as well because we were all in Christmas jumpers, all singing Christmas songs – and all very, very drunk.

'It's been like old times,' Jody said, laughing as we arrived back and fell onto our beds.

Later, as I lay in bed, I let the madness of the evening wash over me. It had been a wonderful night, but something had been missing – Jon? I longed to call him, but I didn't have his number, and it was probably just as well – I'd had too much to drink and was likely to profess undying love, or lust, and that wouldn't be good. But I felt excited: so much had happened – not just the place, the people, the fancy dress and Jon – but I felt different inside.

This was a different Jen to the one who'd sat waiting expectantly for Tim to propose, for Tim to take a decision on my life – and a different Jen to the one who'd boarded the plane for Switzerland just two months before.

I'd learned a lot about myself – that I could be grown up, mature, sensible and in control of my own life – but that didn't mean I couldn't sing out loud or dance on tables. The two things weren't mutually exclusive.

The following morning I woke with one hell of a hangover and headed straight for the kitchen and a large cup of caffeine. But feeling rough and not being as supple as perhaps I once was, I entered the kitchen and slipped on a pair of Lola's silk pants. I was halfway across the kitchen, clinging to the counter and calling for help for several minutes before Jody finally arrived.

'Oh my God, Jen, what are you doing?' she was saying – like I'd been partaking in some kind of kitchen sport.

'Lola's pants... dangerous,' was all I could say.

'Lola's pants? Have you lost it? Can you hear me, Jen?' Jody was now shouting in my face while checking my pulse, before making a panicked phone call to resort reception shouting down the phone for medical help. Meanwhile Kate was sobbing saying, 'She'll never walk again,' and Lola was asking if I could feel her sharp pinchings all over my legs (which I could!). Jody was in nurse mode now, ordering first-aid equipment. Reception said they'd send equipment as soon as someone was free, but if my life was in danger they'd call the emergency services for us.

'Is her life in danger?' Kate asked.

'I've twisted my ankle... ooh and cricked my neck,' I said, trying to diffuse the drama, as they lifted me onto the sofa.

Within minutes there was a sharp knocking on the chalet door and Jody rushed to answer it. She came back in with a smile on her face, followed by Jon, who I was delighted to see looked rather concerned.

'Hi, Jenny, I was in reception when the call came through. I have brought the first aid... again. What happened?'

'I hurt my neck,' I said, trying to position myself elegantly on the sofa where the girls had dumped me like a bag of washing.

'They're not mine... these bed shorts,' I said, like it even mattered to him. It mattered to me, though, because they were Jody's and they had 'KISS IT' emblazoned across the bum region in sequins.

'Why do you tell me all the time you are wearing clothes belonging to other women?' He laughed and sat down next to me. He was easy, open, smiling, and the girls watched open-mouthed as he hugged me hello. 'I think you like the crazy clothes...'

We both laughed and the girls seemed to disappear into their rooms.

'Anyway, where are you hurt?' he said, looking into my eyes and making my heart skid across the shiny floor.

'Let me see,' he said, looking closely now at my ankle then my neck and causing my knees to feel weak. I leaned towards him slightly as he moved closer, and as his strong, gentle fingers caressed my neck, I caught his eye and for a few moments the world stood still.

Then he took off his jacket and opened up his first-aid kit.

'I enjoyed the other day,' I said. 'It was fun... the cake was fantastic.' I thought of how Lola said I should be bolder, and I rested my hand on his knee. I was clever – I did this in such a way that I could pretend it was more of a balance thing than a sign of anything more. At the same time I was hoping he'd get the message.

'Yes. What were you doing?'

'Nothing, I wasn't doing anything,' I said, guiltily snatching my hand off his knee.

'No... I didn't mean that,' he said, taking my hand and putting it back on his knee without taking his eyes from my neck. 'I mean, what were you doing to cause the injury?' He was still stroking my neck.

'I slipped on Lola's pants.'

'Were you wearing the shorts at the time?'

I nodded. And he smiled again, like he wanted to laugh but was trying to be businesslike. I kept my hand on his knee as he continued caressing my neck. I could feel his breath at the side of my face and, turning slightly, my lips met his. It was so much better than even the wonderful kiss at Saas Fee – this was deeper and more passionate. His hands moved around my back, round my waist, and he opened my mouth with his tongue, pushing me gently into the sofa. Then in the middle of this pure bliss, this tidal wave of ecstasy, I heard a giggle coming from Jody and Kate's bedroom and remembered we weren't alone.

I pulled away.

'I'm sorry, I shouldn't have. I am not in the position to be kissing you.'

'No, it's fine, your *position* is... fine. It's just that my friends are here and I would hate for them to walk in and...'

'Ahhh, I see. Yes, then I will go. You can stand on your ankle and your neck is good, yes?'

'Yes,' I said, working out how to stop him leaving, just disappearing into the snow forever. The girls were right. You couldn't just rely on fate – you had to go for it.

'I was wondering if I could perhaps buy you a coffee? To thank you for the lovely time we had in Saas Fee?' I heard myself say.

'That would be... nice,' he said. It wasn't quite the overwhelming response I was hoping for, but perhaps the staff weren't allowed to fraternise with each other?

'Later today?' I suggested.

'I can't today, I am, er... busy today...'

I wanted to die. All the signals had been there, hadn't they? Or was I just naïve like Jody said I was and because I wanted a big love affair, I was creating one in my head? And why did he hesitate before saying he was busy? There was definitely something he wasn't sharing. Did he have a girlfriend? I'd assumed he was single; he said he'd been in a relationship and it was over. All this was going through my head like a freight train, and as he got up to go, he brushed my hand with his fingers.

'Tomorrow? Coffee... we can meet tomorrow? We can have drinks and talk and... I like to spend time with you, Jenny.'

I agreed, delighted at this 'almost date' but still a niggle in the back of my mind worried that he wasn't quite what he seemed, or what I'd painted him to be. Perhaps over a coffee in the light of day without neck pain or a hangover I could work out what was actually going on here – in reality as opposed to in my head.

The following day my neck was a little stiff, but fortunately my ankle was fine and my only concern was what little I had to wear, lamenting the fact that somewhere in Europe my perfect pastel-blue cashmere jumper was lying unworn in an airport. 'That would have been perfect for a casual coffee,' I said. 'Not too much, not too suggestive or "I'm on a date-ish", just a subtle, "It's only coffee with a friend, but I'm open to more" feel to it.'

I had bought some practical outerwear in Saas Fee but nothing in my current wardrobe said 'casual coffee with a promise'.

'What about my new pink padded jacket?'

'Miss Piggy,' Kate said absently. 'No... not Miss Piggy... someone from *The Biggest Loser*, before they lose all the weight.' She giggled to herself and I wished she wasn't quite so honest at times.

'There's the dinosaur pyjama top?' Jody joked.

'Sadly that's gone back to its owner, but you can laugh,' I said. 'He's seen me in worse.'

'There's my special jumper. I was saving it for a special occasion,' Kate said, pulling out a lovely coffee-coloured merino-wool jumper from her drawer.

'That's so lovely,' I said. 'Thank you, Kate, but it's your special jumper and probably cost a fortune. It's beautiful, but I would only worry about spilling coffee down it, so thank you but I won't.'

I was touched she'd offered to lend it to me – that's what friends did for friends. I hadn't realised, but I'd missed female friendship in recent years. They were good for the soul.

I arrived at the coffee shop and as Jon hadn't arrived yet I ordered one for myself and sat outside to watch the snow and the skiing. It was so Christmassy. I could hear 'Jingle Bells' coming from inside as I sipped on the hot, strong coffee, which warmed me and soothed my nerves, and I thought how perfect everything seemed at this moment. I had to smile to myself. Jody had been spot on when she said I always wanted the perfect picture – but I knew now that it was what was underneath that mattered.

I was thinking about this when Jon appeared at the table. He seemed so big and handsome and gentle, and he hugged me with both arms and kissed my cheek – it was more continental than sexual, but I enjoyed it nonetheless. I offered to buy him a coffee, but he said he'd ordered and once he'd sat down, the waitress arrived with a tray carrying two large glasses of Glühwein.

'I know it's a little early for the après ski, but it's almost Christmas,' he said and smiled as the waitress put one of the glasses down in front of me.

'It's my favourite,' I said, holding the warm glass with both hands and breathing in the cinnamon-laced alcohol of Christmas. Sipping it as we chatted, I was filled with a warmth inside and out. I liked his smile, I loved his accent and I enjoyed being with him. He talked animatedly about the skiing as we watched people swooping down the slopes in a rainbow of colours, laughter, shouting, and excited children having snowball fights nearby. The landscape was spectacular, snow falling gently – huge fragile snowdrops floating to the ground and forming a lace curtain in the air that framed the spectacular mountains looming in the distance.

'I can't believe I'm here,' I sighed. 'This is just pure Christmas. How could anyone be anywhere else this time of year... well, any time of year really.'

'Yes, she is a beautiful country. Everything is here.' He smiled. 'Tell me about your home. I went to London once, with my school... Big Ben... a big clock and a big river – the Thames?' he asked, making a 'th' sound as he said it. 'You will come with me and see Saas Fee again one day?'

I said I'd love to and he talked about the chair lift that we could take at night, flying over the village and up the slopes. 'The village, she is like a million stars on the ground,' he said. And like those fragile snowflakes falling all around me, I just melted.

He asked me about my work and I told him all about the library. 'It wasn't my dream job,' I explained. 'But once I started I quite enjoyed the idea of neat books all on a shelf and the job involves cataloguing and cross-referencing so it's okay – but I long to do something else, live another life.'

'Ah yes. But...' He looked puzzled. 'You don't look like a book lady to me...'

'Yes, well I think people have a rather limited view of librarians.' I laughed. 'Librarians are often considered to be boring and a bit dry... always telling people to shush. I can understand that. I mean we're stuck inside buildings full of old books all day – what are people expected to think? But it isn't true. I spent the first few years of my career trying to prove to everyone how interesting I was.' I smiled. 'And I may work in a dusty old library, but I have my dreams and dance on tables.'

'Like the other night? In On the Piste?'

'Oh no, you were there?'

He nodded and smiled. 'I was on duty – I am the first aider, and I had to be holding my breath as you danced on the table.'

At first I thought this was because I was dancing so seductively, but he explained he was worried about me having another accident.

'You should have said hello,' I said, aware of my face flushing; if I'd known he was there I would have restrained myself – but then again...

'You were too busy having the fun with your friends. And I worried if I waved you would be waving back and uh oh... on the floor.'

'Ah, good point. I don't think I have good coordination.'

'Your coordination she is beautiful.'

'Thank you,' I smiled. No one had said that to me before, not surprisingly. I tried to bat away the horrific images of me singing and staggering and laughing loudly. 'So, now you've seen me at my worst...'

'Your best.'

He looked at me intently when he said this and made me feel all warm and soft inside. I was still having the odd struggle with enjoying the moment, and it suddenly occurred to me that I might be one of many women he'd kissed at the resort. Perhaps I wasn't special at all, just another one on his list?

'Do you often go out for coffee with single ladies?'

'I'm not what you call the escort – I don't get paid to be with the single ladies.' He was shaking his head and laughing.

'No. I wasn't suggesting you were some kind of male prostitute,' I said, thinking, why did I have to say that? When is it ever okay to use the phrase 'male prostitute' when you're on a potential first date?

'I like you, Jenny. You make me smile with your wacky clothes and your weird dancing.'

I didn't hear what he said; I just melted again at the way he swapped W for V.

We finished our drinks and he ordered two more and not once did he say, 'You're a bit tipsy,' or, 'We shouldn't really be drinking in the daytime,' the way Tim used to. I was discovering this lovely new-found freedom where I made my own decisions, drank too much, ate cake for breakfast and wore pyjamas on my day off – and after all this time it made me giddy.

'So, Jenny, do you have a... boyfriend in England?'

'No. If I did, I wouldn't be having coffee with you. Not that I see you in that way, I just mean – if I had a boyfriend I'd be here with him now, sitting by a log fire, toasting marshmallows with the man of my dreams.'

He smiled and looked into my eyes and I could almost smell those toasting mallows and see firelight glinting – or perhaps it was just the Glühwein running through my veins.

'You have the sadness,' he suddenly said, still looking into my eyes like he was searching for something. 'I understand... I have it too...'

'Oh no, I'm great. I'm not sad really. I was a little, but being here seems to have lifted the sadness I was feeling.'

He shook his head while continuing to smile and reaching out his hand to touch mine. 'You have a sad time, Jenny. I want to make you smile again.'

As the Glühwein flowed so did my conversation and by mid-afternoon I'd told him even more of my life story. He had it all, from my father leaving, to a repeat of the final, festive romantic denouement with Tim and even the aftermath of confined dough-nut consumption and self-loathing that followed.

You are lovely, you don't deserve the sadness,' he said, looking into my eyes.

'Don't be nice to me – I'm just being silly,' I said. 'There are lots of women who have had break-ups or who can't have children, or leave it too late like me… it's not the end of the world.' I hated the way he must see me: self-pitying and self-obsessed.

'Perhaps you still have time… to have a child?' he said.

For the past twelve months (ironically since Tim and I had broken up) my periods had been coming irregularly, or sometimes not at all. I'd been to the doctor, who said it was probably early menopause and offered me hormones, but Jody said I should try getting through it without medication, so I threw them away.

'No. I think I have to give up on that dream. Children aren't going to be part of my life, and I need to accept that,' I said unconvincingly as I wiped away a tear. 'I'm so sorry. You must think I'm an awful, self-obsessed person. I keep bursting into tears and going on about myself. You hardly know me and here I am rambling about lost dreams and never-to-be babies.'

'No, I feel for you. But don't worry, another dream will come along,' he said.

I liked his optimism; it filled me with hope and made me think that one day I might just be able to be in a relationship again, with someone like him.

'Yes, I'll have to think of another dream.' I smiled.

'No – you can't "think" of a dream,' he said gently. 'You must let go and it will find you. We call it *Schicksal*. I think in English it's called fate.'

'Yes, I'm a great believer in fat.' I smiled, thinking of how we'd met again because he'd been sent to perform first aid on my neck.

He ordered more drinks and I asked him in more detail about his own life and was surprised to learn that he'd been married.

'It was short – we didn't last very long.' He sighed. 'She lives in Germany now...' He was about to say something else then seemed to think better of it.

'What?' I asked, hoping he'd share it with me. After all, I'd shared everything with him, my whole life until that moment in fact – whether he'd wanted to hear it or not.

'Nothing, I just... I feel like I failed... I understand you when you say you're frightened to go into a relationship.'

I nodded. 'Are you? Frightened?'

'I think so, yes. I haven't had a girlfriend since my marriage ended. I have resigned myself to being single, like you.'

'Yes, it seems so much easier,' I said.

'That is until someone comes along...'

He looked at me across the table and reached his hand towards mine again, brushing my fingers with his.

'Jenny, I liked you in Saas Fee... a lot.'

'Oh, do you like me here too?' I smiled.

'Very much.'

He leaned forward and so did I, and instinctively our lips met and we kissed, and all I could think was that I never wanted this moment to stop.

I thought about all the books I'd read where the romantic hero is impossibly perfect, which was why I'd given up on finding one – but here he was, straight out of a novel. He had Mr Darcy's cool, Rhett Butler's kisses and Heathcliff's wild, unruly hair – I could only imagine what he was like in bed. I tried not to think too much about this as I was becoming dangerously drunk on Glühwein and any moment now I might clear the table, climb on top and begin a loud rendition of 'Last Christmas'. I had to be stopped.

I can blame the Glühwein, the music, the setting, the fact that it was close to Christmas and I knew the girls would be après skiing until late. On the other hand I could take full responsibility for what happened next.

Chapter 11

Frosty Skies and Gingerbread Kisses

We wandered back through the snow, passing children's snowball fights and smiling people in padded suits. 'Last Christmas' was playing in one of the chalets, and I was reminded with a frisson that Christmas wasn't far away. There was snow on the ground, music dancing through the frosty skies and I was going back to a Swiss chalet with a handsome guy who'd just told me he liked me 'very much'. Did life get any better than this?

I was finally the heroine in my own Christmas story – and everything was perfect, like a well-crafted scene from one of my favourite books.

Back in the chalet we lit the fire and opened a bottle of red, letting it breathe while we lay on the rug just looking at each other. The firelight twinkled in his eyes and I kissed him, pushing my hands under his thick jumper, feeling the warm, hard flesh underneath and the softness of his mouth on mine. We tore at each other's clothes until we were both naked, rolling around in front of the crackly fire, the dancing flames the only light in the room. He was light and gentle at first, placing soft, tender kisses everywhere and then he was inside me, panting, my cries of ecstasy filling the air and taking me somewhere I'd never been before. And when it was over we just lay there naked and entwined, letting the firelight dance over our bodies.

We lay in comfortable silence for a long time. I was happy we'd had this time together, but it was tinged with sadness, because I knew if anything this could only ever be a holiday romance. We were just two wounded people finding each other in the snow, so I didn't dwell on the future, or compare it to the past. I lived in the now, pouring two large glasses of wine and smiling as we chinked them together.

He got up and began to look through his jacket pockets, retrieving a paper bag filled with gingerbread and handing it to me.

'My favourite,' I said, opening up the bag and just breathing in the delicious spicy scent.

'I wish you could taste my gingerbread. My father used to bake it, and I have the recipe... one day perhaps?'

I nodded. It was sad to be with someone whose life was lived so far away from mine. If Jon's home was down the road and we were on a date it would be so different – it would feel like so much more. But we were both from different worlds, and we just had to make the best of what we had, here and now. I hoped he felt the same and wanted to spend time with me while I was here. We both knew that this could only last a short time, maybe even only a matter of days, but it didn't matter. I had to start living for now and not worry about tomorrow – that's what Jody and the girls kept telling me. And then we kissed again in front of the crackling log fire, carols playing and the snow falling outside. This was the

Christmas I'd always dreamed of. It wasn't planned, it hadn't been shopped for and I hadn't had time to consider what the musical accompaniment of choice would be. Yet here it was, the perfect picture, the perfect man in the most perfect setting – and I hadn't done a thing; I'd just let it happen.

We snuggled together, just talking and kissing, but it was and always will be one of the most romantic, most wonderful evenings of my life – it was pure bliss.

'A match made in heaven,' I said, sipping the wine then chewing on the delicious biscuit.

'I am thinking if there's a recipe for red wine and gingerbread?' he said.

'I suppose it's called Glühwein.' I smiled.

'Ah yes, I will try to make Glühwein biscuits one day... I will let you know what they taste like.'

'Yes do,' I said, knowing that he probably wouldn't, because by the time 'one day' came and he made the biscuits he'd have forgotten all about me. He'd be with someone else, and I'd be alone again, and for me his Glühwein biscuits would simply be a reminder of what might have been and a like on Facebook.

Later we said goodbye, and though I tried not to let myself get carried away, I hoped he might ask to see me again as we kissed in the doorway. And when he didn't I decided to take fate into my own hands.

'Would you like to meet for dinner tomorrow? Or the day after?' I asked.

We were mid-embrace and I felt him pull away slightly. 'I can't, Jenny – I'm really sorry, I'm busy all weekend.'

Despite trying desperately to convince myself this was only a holiday romance, I knew differently. I couldn't help it – my heart had been thawed and I was falling hard for this man, and it hurt me so much when he pulled away. I wanted more – I wanted to ask what he was keeping from me, why he could go from being warm and open to cold and detached, not wanting to reveal himself. I couldn't push. I daren't ask what he was concealing from me because I was still protecting myself from being hurt again and perhaps I didn't want to know?

He left soon after, and when he'd gone I felt cold, like the roaring log fire had gone out and all the fairy lights had fused and my heart was the last one flickering in the darkness. What the hell was going on with him?

Chapter 12

Bail Early, with Diamonds

I'd had a wonderful evening with Jon, but his rather abrupt departure and the vague way he referred to being busy all weekend had left me feeling very uneasy.

I tried to rationalise it to myself, putting the whole thing into perspective – but somehow things weren't adding up. I didn't expect him to give me forensic details of his every move – but surely a quick 'I'm working' or 'I'm out with friends' would have been softer than the pulling away and the vague but determined 'busy' he'd offered me? I understood that he had a life of his own, and I certainly didn't want to fall into the 'needy' trap I'd fallen into before – so I hadn't pushed for anything more and after a final kiss he'd disappeared into the white night.

It was late when the girls returned from their après ski and I appreciated that they'd stayed out late for me, but I suddenly didn't want to be alone with my swirling thoughts. I wanted to talk and they were keen to know all that had happened. I felt like I had as a teenager when a boy at school had asked me out and all my friends had phoned me for details. Being in the company of these girls had changed me, and instead of resenting their drunken laughter and noisy, nosy enquiries about Jon, I welcomed them.

'Thank you, yes, I had a great time... he's lovely,' I said, opening another bottle of wine. I would need to start drinking if I wanted to catch up with them – they were singing Christmas songs and Lola had mistletoe firmly fastened to her cleavage. I didn't ask.

'So are you seeing him again? Or are you just a one-night stand?' Kate asked with her usual candour.

'Who knows? And who cares? All I know is I had a wonderful time.' I looked at Jody. 'I'm living for today, just as you said,' I said, smiling.

'Yay! You go, girl. Love 'em and leave 'em, that's what I say.'

'Yes, but be careful and carry condoms,' I said in my big-sister voice.

'Gee thanks, Jen. Shame you weren't around when I was young enough to need that advice.' She laughed. 'I've seen a cute guy myself, got talking to him tonight and he's funny, easy on the eye – I think he's Canadian, but I'm not rushing into anything.'

'Good. I'm glad... I don't want you to go down the same stupid road that I did.'

'Jen, you must be kidding. I've learned from your mistakes, like little sisters do – I swear the next time I go out with anyone I'll have a ball and bail early... with diamonds.'

I had to smile. I liked the idea that Jody was my 'little' sister and had learned from my mistakes – but it was like she came from a different world. Despite my disappointment in love I was the optimist, always hoping this time would be different – a fairy tale where it all ended happily ever after, which was ridiculous at my age. But here was Jody who never talked happy endings but saw engagement rings like they were an insurance policy. Who was I to criticise? At least she'd get to keep the ring and a bit of herself – while I'd spent almost a year getting over being dumped with not even the sniff of a ring.

'I can be romantic, but my head isn't filled with confetti,' she said, sitting on the sofa, curling her legs under her. 'I just know that nothing is perfect – and once you know that, then you can relax, because there are no surprises further down the line.'

'I suppose you're right,' I sighed, walking through from the kitchen area with two glasses of wine. Inside, a little part of me was disagreeing with her. I so wanted to believe that there was such a thing as the perfect relationship, the perfect ending, the perfect Christmas.

'You're so much wiser than me, Jody, but try and join me on the other side of the rose-tinted glass now and then?' I smiled, handing her a glass of wine and sitting next to her.

'No, thank you. That rose-coloured monocle you carry around makes you very vulnerable to disappointment,' she said, taking a sip. 'I bet you're already thinking about what kind of ring this Jon will buy you, and I bet you've designed the bloody dress in your head.' She laughed affectionately.

'No, I haven't. How dare you,' I said in mock anger.

'I love you, Jen. I don't want some tosser taking you for a ride again.'

'Don't worry – I learned my lesson. And as for Jon, it's not even a holiday romance at the moment. I'm not even sure if I'll see him again – he just wandered off into the snow. I don't know anything about him, so don't worry about me getting carried away... but you would look lovely in pistachio green as my maid of honour.'

She threw a cushion at me.

'I was joking.'

'Not funny.' She smiled indulgently at me and I thought how lucky I was to have someone who cared so much about me.

'But as you say, you don't know anything about him, so please tread carefully, babes.'

My heart jolted a little. She was right. He could be telling me exactly what I wanted to hear. On paper it was good, perfect even – so why had I had that funny feeling as he'd left? Yet despite my mental turmoil, trying to work out what could possibly make him be this way, I was convinced he cared about me. He had such tenderness in his eyes, and the way he kissed me made me feel wonderful, like I'd never felt before. Surely if we had the connection I thought we had, we could talk and he could share this with me?

❊ ❊ ❊

We chatted more and drank a little more and then Lola appeared in her towel demanding we all have 'a girls' hot tub'. I was about to say no; I was tired and they were all tipsier than me. It would be loud and messy, like a big, hot, alcoholic girl soup.

But it would also be fun and just the thing to lift my gloom over Jon. I stripped to my underwear and threw myself into the tub on the balcony... which hadn't been heated and was freezing. And I screamed. A lot. And as I screamed I saw Jon waving from down below. 'You okay, Jen?' He was alarmed, and who could blame him?

'I'm fine... just fine...' I called, emerging from the sub-zero water in my underwear, the light on the balcony revealing everything.

He was now standing under the balcony, and I couldn't help but think of Romeo and Juliet – and how it couldn't be further from the teenage love tryst as I leaned over, all big pants and goosebumps.

'Why are you here?' I called through the thick, cold air.

'I want to... I was just going to see Hans, my friend. He has my keys,' he said.

'Oh... okay.' I couldn't help but feel he'd hesitated when he answered me. Was he telling the truth and, if not, what was he really doing walking through the snow past our chalet after midnight? 'Night,' I said, a shadow now hovering over me that I tried to shake off.

'Hi there,' Lola called as she arrived on the balcony in full metal jacket – leopard-skin swimming costume and matching hair accessories. I noted her cleavage was still decorated with mistletoe. This girl never clocked off.

She was now leaning over the balcony rail next to me to see who I was talking to.

'I didn't realise you were under us,' she roared, laughing at this, which was lost in translation for Jon, thank goodness.

'I have mistletoe and would offer you a Christmas kiss, but it's not quite Christmas and I think Jen's got that covered,' she said, smiling.

I looked out at Jon standing in the snow. I couldn't see his face. He'd moved away as Lola and Kate had appeared, said 'Goodnight ladies,' and set off through the snow.

'Well, that's the last I'll see of him,' I said. 'Thanks, Lola... and it was all going so well.'

In spite of everything I'd told myself about not appearing clingy or needy, I couldn't leave it like this, so I rushed downstairs and threw open the front door.

'JON,' I called loudly into the white night.

After a few seconds he reappeared, walking slowly back and greeting me at the front door with a warm hug.

'You okay?' I asked.

He nodded.

'I just wondered if everything is good between us... you and me?'

'Yes, yes of course – it's better than good for me.'

'Oh, me too and if you want to talk... any time, I'm here to listen,' I said, hoping to prompt him into telling me what kept him away some weekends. 'You seem reluctant to tell me about... some aspects of your life,' I said, walking the tightrope between finding out and being too pushy and scaring him away.

'I really like you, Jenny... I just need some time.'

My heart did a little jolt. Did he want space too? What was he saying exactly?

'Do you want to finish... this? Me and you?' I asked, holding my breath, my heart stuck somewhere in my gullet.

'No, I just need to have the time before we talk.' He smiled and kissed me on the lips. 'I will call you tomorrow, Jenny, yes?'

I nodded, unable to speak, tears filling up my eyes and confusion twisting around my head and heart.

Chapter 13

Uncle Albert and the Flirty Goddess

I had the weekend off so I pottered around the chalet for a while, and the girls set off to the slopes in their sunglasses looking like the cast of *Reservoir Dogs*. I couldn't stop thinking about Jon, and I needed to be distracted from the maelstrom in my head, so I settled down with my drink and called Storm. She'd posted a picture of Mrs Christmas on Facebook the previous night and it had made me a little homesick. I just wanted to know everything was okay at home.

'Oh my love, how are you?' she said.

We chatted for a while about Mrs Christmas and work before Storm brought up a recent Tarot reading she'd done for me. I sighed. I still wasn't sure I believed in all that stuff, but sometimes when I was worried or confused, wondering which path to take, Storm's readings helped me sort stuff out in my head.

'Really?' This was interesting, even if it wasn't true I liked it.

'Oh... I have met someone actually, but I doubt it's...'

'Oops sorry, love,' she said, before I could finish. 'That was for June from the cake shop. I'm getting her by mistake. My chakras are everywhere at the moment.'

So are mine now,' I said. 'Storm, I just wondered if you're getting anything for me – it's just that this guy... I think he may be hiding something.'

'Oh that is a tricky one. . Mmmm okay... I did get something via Uncle Albert and the angels yesterday, but they can be a little sassy on a Friday.'

'Wouldn't you know it... What did they say?' I asked absently, sipping my hot chocolate with one hand and holding the phone with the other.

'Well... I won't repeat what Uncle Albert said because it was quite rude, but the cards that concerned me are the eight of wands and the hanged man.'

'Oh great, the hanged man... I'm going to be wiped out in a tragic tobogganing accident?'

'No. You are being told to pause and reflect, not to rush into anything. You're missing something... and Uncle Albert is telling me you're moving too fast. Stop talking and listen more – the clues are all there, he said. Perhaps that makes sense now?'

'No, not really, Storm.' I was by now heartily fed up of being told what to do: slow down, speed up, let go, enjoy the moment – and now Uncle Albert was sticking his nose in. Yet still, the idea that 'the clues are all there', and that little bit of curiosity... the constant optimist living in my head got the better of me, and I asked for more details.

'Oh, Jen, you know the cards – they're open to interpretation, but for you I'm getting the ace of wands, the page of cups... ooh and Albert's just reminded me – the high priestess made an appearance too.'

'Sounds like quite a party.'

'It was. She was flirting, Albert said – but I take him with a pinch of salt. But as I was working through the spread I saw something else...'

'What?'

'I don't quite understand what it means, nor is it my task to question – we have to trust the Goddess, Jen.'

'Okay, so what is she saying when she's not flirting with Albert?' Storm loved to build her part, hold you in suspense.

'Jen, I can see a baby coming into your life.'

I didn't know whether to laugh or cry; she'd clearly got her chakras confused again and I was beginning to lose faith in her.

'Well, a baby is highly unlikely. I'm on the brink of menopause, and any minute now my insides will dry up and hair will sprout from my chin.'

'Oh dear, in that case, given the presence of these cards, might I suggest that there's already been a pregnancy or a child?'

'Storm, I think I might have noticed if I'd been pregnant or had a child. But thanks anyway.'

'You know the rules – take what you need from the cards and ignore the rest. It may well be Albert and those sassy angels deliberately toying with us. Who knows, they might even be giving me June from the cake shop in your spread – she could be conceiving at this very moment.'

'Indeed,' I said, trying to push away the image of June being taken on a bed of fresh cream meringues.

'Let's talk when you get back,' she said. 'Mrs Christmas can't wait to see you.'

I came off the phone feeling rather bereft, and I sat gazing out at the snow and reflecting on the past twelve months, the way one has a tendency to do around Christmas time. Storm said I was going so fast with my holiday romance I was missing something. It felt like a riddle I had to solve, and the more I thought about it, the more I wondered what it was I wasn't seeing.

'Perhaps I'm so keen on Jon I've missed the fact my feelings aren't reciprocated?' I said to Jody when she made the mistake of stopping by to say hi between ski swoops (or whatever they call them). I'd wandered over to the café to get a drink, feeling restless alone in the chalet.

She stood at the table where I was sitting and fidgeted with her cuffs – which I took as body language for 'I refuse to listen to all your shit again'. She'd spent a year forensically dissecting my last relationship, so who could blame her for rejecting a sisterly dismembering of something that hadn't even started yet? But I just kept talking and didn't acknowledge the fact she was standing on one foot then the next, eager to get away.

'I'm disappointed in Storm's reading,' I sighed. 'I'm not even sure I believe it – but I was hoping I'd finally get the world card, the one with two naked people and lots of flowers on it. I've never had that card...'

'No, because you want it *so* much,' she said, finally speaking but sounding frustrated. 'You just want everything to fall into place, and when it doesn't, you try and shoehorn it until it does. Just enjoy this time with Jon, see it as a lovely Christmassy fling and don't worry about where it's going, what he's thinking or what's going to happen this time next week – because it probably isn't going anywhere, and that's okay, love.'

She said this last bit gently, like she was breaking it to me that the man I was falling for might just not be my happy ending, but I already knew that, didn't I?

'Jody, I'm not building this thing with Jon into something, honestly.'

'Mmmm, so why are you calling Storm and asking for a reading?'

'I called to find out how Mrs Christmas was... she had already done my reading. I simply asked if there was anything I should know... He might have a deep dark secret.'

'And did she tell you?'

'No.'

'Then forget it. Storm makes it all up as she goes along. She's as bad as you, both trying to make sense of the universe, turn it into a story with an ending and meaning – but real life doesn't always fit neatly into your narrative.'

'Don't I know it.'

'Stop trying so hard, Jen. Just because you want someone to fit into your world, it doesn't mean that they will. Don't make the same mistake you did with Tim and try and make things work with a guy you've just met – why not just enjoy Jon for a while?'

Oh God, Jody was right. She was sometimes brutally honest, but I needed to be told how obsessive and annoying I could be. This wasn't like being criticised by Tim – this was the truth told to me by someone who loved and cared about me.

'Oh hi, Jon,' Jody said, smiling as he appeared next to her at the table. 'I'll get off, leave you both to it.' And with that she set off up the mountain, leaving Jon standing there and me looking back at him.

'You okay, Jon?' I asked, shielding my eyes with my hand as I looked up at him. The sky was brilliant blue, and the sun was bouncing off the glowing white of the snow.

'I came to find you, Jen.'

I was delighted and patted the seat near me for him to sit down while we ordered drinks and sat huddled in the freezing bright day, chatting about the weather and the skiing. When our steaming mugs of chocolate arrived, towering with frothy cream and mallows, we laughed at the size of them and warmed our hands on the hot mugs, covering our faces in fresh cream and chewing on the mallows. I wanted to stop my life there and then, like a video, and just look at this perfect picture. Snow was falling, and Christmas was still around in the lights in the trees, the coloured bulbs dancing on a string around the café. There were children everywhere throwing snowballs, balancing precariously on snowboards, none of them thinking about tomorrow or the next day – just living for here and now. And if I could have stopped my life and savoured it just for a while it would have been then.

'There's something I need to tell you,' he suddenly said, putting down his mug, his face now serious, no smiles, no twinkly eyes.

I didn't say anything, but my mouth went dry.

'I haven't been honest with you Jenny. I like you and I never want to frighten you off... but I have something to tell you, and I don't think you will be liking it very much.'

I suddenly felt like I was going to have to go through some horrible betrayal all over again. I'd slept with Jon, and I knew people didn't see sex as the special, exclusive thing I always had, but I didn't sleep with people easily. I had to really like someone before I shared intimacy with them, and I'd believed Jon was perhaps like me and I could trust him – at least for the season. But here he was looking at me across a rickety coffee table, his beautiful face framed by the sparkly white mountains behind him and his eyes as blue as the sky above... about to break my heart into a million icy pieces.

'You don't have to tell me anything you don't want to,' I said slowly, trying to brace myself for his departure, not wanting to hear the excuses, the lies.

'I want to tell you... Jen, you know I have been married.'

I nodded, unable to speak.

'Well, I have to tell you, I see my wife every weekend...'

Oh God, it was worse than I'd even thought – so that's what 'busy' meant. He was still with his wife – at weekends!

'So you're still together...?' I gasped. How could he? Not only had he betrayed his wife, but me too. I got up to go. I didn't need this. I was destined to meet men who didn't care about me, men who didn't care about women.

'No, no,' he said, grabbing me by the wrist as I tried to leave. 'Jenny, she is living in another town forty kilometres from here...'

'So... you're not together?' I stood there, not wanting to go and not wanting to stay, confused and bewildered.

He was looking up at me, those blue eyes beseeching. 'No... but I have to see her... Please, Jenny, don't go... I have to tell you.'

I sat down slowly, perched on the edge of my seat, ready to go if anything arose in this conversation that made me unhappy or concerned. 'Do you still love her?' I almost croaked this last bit. I couldn't go through being dumped again, this time for an ex-wife. I was holding my handbag, mentally gathering my coat around me to leave. But he shook his head.

'Then why do you have to see her?'

'Because of Ella... our daughter.'

I was now staring at him, trying to take this all in. 'You have a daughter? Why didn't you tell me?'

'Because...' He shuffled his feet, moved in his chair. 'You talk so much about wanting the babies and your heart hurts because you can't have them, and you say you don't want the children luggage that comes with the boyfriends.'

I felt a pang of hurt thinking about a little girl whose father lived somewhere else and didn't come home every night after work any more.

'I said I didn't want the baggage because it's too painful, and I wouldn't choose to have a relationship with someone who already has a child... I grew up in a broken home – I'm not sure I could live through that.'

'And when I hear you say this I think... Oh no, she would never want to be with a man like me – a man with a child and all the luggage.'

'But sometimes if you like someone...' I stopped talking. It was far too early in our relationship for me to be declaring undying love and throwing all my principles out of the window. It wouldn't work for me – it would be too painful, a constant reminder of something I couldn't have... but then again... I may not like the idea of my boyfriend (if that's what he was) already having a child, but perhaps I needed to be open to the idea and at least allow the notion into my life.

'How old is your daughter?' I asked.

'Ella's twelve. She was nine when we parted. She is my angel.'

I nodded. 'How often do you get to see her?' I thought of my own father, who simply walked away one day and turned up several years later. I hoped things were different for Jon's daughter.

'I don't see her as much as I'd like,' he sighed. 'I see her some weekends, not every weekend... I wish it were all the time, but she has a new life and her mother, she says it upsets Ella to stay with me.'

I didn't understand. 'How could it upset a child to be with her father?'

'Ella has a stepfather,' he said. 'He takes her to school and he shows her how to do her homework, and he is with her so much of the time. He even took her to the slopes. I'm her father, I want to be the one who teaches her to ski... but I'm working and he's there with her.'

'So why don't you take some time off and teach your daughter to ski?' I asked. I was suddenly feeling a little prickly; I remembered my father making excuses about why he couldn't see me – work, his new wife, then his new baby. I hadn't cared about that – I just wanted my dad. 'What about this weekend? Is that why you were too busy to see me?'

'Yes, I take the weekend off work, but now my wife, she says Ella has the sleepover at hers this weekend with her friends... how can I say no to that?'

I nodded. I could see it was difficult from both sides in this kind of situation. It had never occurred to me that it may have been as difficult for my dad to see me as it was for me to see him. My mother had been bitter about the break-up and Jody had told me there were times when Dad had wanted me to stay with them, but Mum had told him I was busy with friends. This was true, and when you become a teenager your parents aren't the most important thing on your social calendar, but I didn't think about the impact this may have had on my father. Hearing Jon say this and seeing the sadness in his face made me realise how hard it was for everyone involved.

He was looking at me with some intensity and reaching for my hand. 'I wasn't going to tell you because I didn't want to put you off. Also... I wasn't sure if it was necessary. Were we together? Did you even like me or would you be happier with someone handsome and more confident like Hans?'

I had to laugh. 'No, I'm not interested in Hans, but I am interested in you.' I swallowed. It wasn't easy to say something like that, especially for me – I was rusty in the game of love and I'd been so determined not to come over as needy, but in doing this perhaps I had given off negative vibes?

'I'm interested in you too,' he said, 'but I wonder if you still want to see me now you know I have a child, Jenny?' I liked the way he said my name in his strong German accent laced with the softness in his voice that I'd noticed in Saas Fee. I looked into his eyes across the table. Our hands were touching and he seemed to be searching my face for an answer. Yes, I really, really liked him, but I was falling for the single man with no baggage. Now I had to see him as a father, and for me that changed things because someone else's happiness was now caught up in ours. He had responsibilities, a big life going on at the side of any romance he might embark on with some Englishwoman he'd met in the snow, and I couldn't bear to be the cause of another little girl losing her father. I recalled the way I felt about my stepmother, how I'd never allowed her an inch, despite her trying so hard to please me and be my friend. That's all she'd ever wanted, my friendship, a little warmth – but I couldn't. I was determined that if I were to meet Jon's daughter, things would be different. I would make sure she liked me – I would be everything she wanted in a friend, and if I tried hard enough, this could only strengthen mine and Jon's relationship. Couldn't it?

'I'd like to meet Ella,' I heard myself say.

Jon smiled. 'Yes? You don't mind that I have a child, and you still want us to be... together?'

'It isn't something I'd have chosen,' I said, finishing off my drink. 'But like I said... when you're interested in someone, you sometimes have to take the whole package.'

I thought again about Jody's criticism about my constant search for perfection. But what was perfection? I'd spent my life dreaming of the perfect partner and the perfect family, and my perception had been two parents and a child or two... or three. But families didn't always come in perfectly wrapped nuclear bundles – sometimes they were slightly different, flawed even – not perfect, but that didn't mean they weren't the right fit.

And as Jon continued to tell me about Ella and how hurt she'd been by the break-up, how clingy she could be when she came to stay, I saw another side to him. I knew he was kind and funny and knowledgeable, but here he was talking about his daughter, and he really seemed to want to be with her. He cared about her feelings, was sensitive and considerate – and it hurt him as much as it hurt her to be apart. Seeing this from Jon's point of view made me think again about my own father and my heart broke for both of them, but especially my dad – and what might have been.

Chapter 14

Nude Lipstick and a Filthy Mouth

Jon and I eventually said our goodbyes and this time we swapped phone numbers and planned to get together again.

'I'd really like to see you,' he said. 'But before we start anything I need you to be sure. This may last a week, it may last longer – but I come with the luggage. Are you sure you are okay with that?'

'Yes, I'm sure. Let's just go with it for now and see where it takes us,' I said, uttering a sentence I never thought I'd say to a man. But I had to embrace this and be more open to people and opportunities instead of prejudging and then dismissing things that didn't fit my idea of what life should be. This was real – messy, flawed, *real* life – and I had to embrace it, because if I didn't, I might lose out on something worthwhile.

'It isn't like he lied to you,' Jody said when I told her later about Jon's marriage and Ella. 'He just decided to tell you when he realised you might be staying around in his life,' she added. I liked the idea of staying around in Jon's life – at least while I was here in Switzerland – and as Kate pointed out, 'You wanted a child and here's one ready made, like a ready meal.'

I wasn't sure about that analogy, but I understood what she meant. It made sense in a weird way, didn't it? There's me pining for a child, and I meet Jon who has a daughter. She didn't need another mother, and that was okay because I wasn't her real mum, but maybe I could be a kind, fun, cool aunt. As I said to Lola, I could talk to teenagers on their own level; I had an iPhone, I was on Facebook, I Skyped and would start an Instagram account before I met Ella so I'd be up to the minute. We could share photos, do selfies or whatever young people did on Instagram, and she could come to me with her boyfriend problems and I'd be there for her. But more than this, I could relate to exactly how Ella was feeling because I'd been there at twelve years old too and could understand, and maybe I could gently bring her and Jon together. The more I thought about this, the more I realised it was meant to be, and when Jody reminded me of Storm's prediction about a child coming into my life, I just knew this was kismet.

So, as it was Jon's turn to have Ella, it was arranged that I would meet her for an afternoon before Christmas in Saas Fee and we set off in the snow in Jon's car.

We drove along mountain roads and through forests of high trees, their branches aching with snow, the roads cracking under the tyres, crispy with ice.

'I'm nervous about meeting Ella,' I said.

'Oh don't be nervous – she is very sweet,' he said.

As we had time before we were due to meet Ella, Jon wanted to show me some more of Saas Fee. 'This is a very special place,' he sighed. 'Ella always loved it here when she was little, always wanted to be the princess of this "kingdom".' He smiled at the memory.

We parked up and walked through rocks and snow, eventually coming to an opening by a huge, glacial lake. Standing silently together, his hand reached for mine and my heart tingled with cold and excitement. It would soon be Christmas and a wonderful magic and anticipation shimmered in the air – it wasn't something you could see or touch, but you just knew it was there. Jon pointed to something in the distance, a small castle standing on a mountain in the glittery white distance. It was like a film set and the most beautiful thing I'd ever seen.

'I can see why Ella loved it here as a little girl,' I said. 'This is like a fairy tale – I would love to recreate this in crystal icing... a glacial setting made from sparkly spun sugar and sweet crystals.'

'Yes, I can see it in the window of The Cake Café... We could have our own café and instead of gingerbread we could show the beauty of the glacier in sugar.'

I smiled and rested my head on his shoulder. 'What a lovely idea,' I said, as we gazed out onto this true winter wonderland. We had escaped to Narnia, stepped back in time into another world, another life. There was magic in the air, tangible and tantalising yet so tranquil, the frozen shades of white and silver and blue, a delicate veil of calmness wafting over and around us. 'Here is the most beautiful place on earth, and she's been here for hundreds of thousands of years, longer than all of us,' he said.

I just continued to stare, but what he said really spoke to me. Time here was meaningless, and the view of this pale, ceramic blue lake surrounded by mountains hadn't been changed by time – it was the same as it always had been. I looked at Jon and knew that I was right: somehow, some way, if we were meant to be together we would be – and if we weren't, that was okay, because there were bigger things in the world than us. I had to begin to loosen the ties that bound me to everything and let go.

Arriving at Saas Fee with its winding little traffic-free streets, the old buildings, the odd cowshed dotted here and there, I felt like I was coming home. We walked to The Cake Café, which was as welcoming and cosy as I'd remembered. The snow-encrusted windows glowed, drawing us in for Lebkuchen and steaming hot coffee. The warmth and the Christmassy aromas hit us as we stepped in from the cold, and we ate the crunchy, spicy biscuits hungrily as he filled me in on Ella's likes and dislikes.

'I know she'll love you,' he said. 'But when I told her I wanted her to meet someone special she was concerned I might spend less time with her.'

I understood that better than anyone; I'd shared the same fears when my parents had split up. Only in my case it had actually happened. I wasn't going to ever let this happen to another little girl.

The plan was that we would meet Ella in the café, and we'd spend some time getting to know each other. I had a coach booked for later when I would return to the resort and leave Jon and Ella to have the rest of the weekend together. I was determined this was going to work and I'd done my homework. I knew all about YouTube people with strange names who sang, talked fast and made up their faces listing every product they used, so I was up to the minute with beauty vloggers and lifestyle bloggers and everything in-between. I had a Facebook and Twitter account that I'd used daily at the library and I'd posted some lovely snowy scenes on my Instagram account – so I was 'good to go', as the kids say.

I'd also bought a couple of gifts for Ella – a lovely nude pink lipstick and a Justin Bieber album – something which, according to various teen websites, was what every twelve-year-old girl longed for, in the absence of the boy himself.

So Jon and I waited in the café for Ella to arrive, chatting, laughing easily and breathing in the cinnamon-and-gingerbread-laced air until Ella appeared in the doorway. She was half an hour late. Apparently her mother had set off late but had been too busy to call and let Jon know – or stop and say hi, but I tried not to judge. Besides, I wasn't in a rush to meet Martha the ex – meeting Ella was nerve-wracking enough.

I was well aware that life for a twelve-year-old girl these days was quite different than when I was twelve. Nowadays teenagers were very sophisticated: they had the internet at their fingertips and a global perspective, so I was ready for whatever issues Ella wanted to chat about. What I wasn't ready for was a twelve-year-old girl who looked eighteen, with backcombed hair, thick charcoal eyeliner and purple lipstick, chewing gum, who blanked me and rolled her eyes when I said hello.

She plonked herself down next to Jon, and I took a deep breath as he abandoned us to order some drinks.

'Do you speak English?' I asked. Jon told me she did – in fact she went to the international school, so many of her friends were British, and her English was excellent. But I asked hoping it might break the ice.

She looked at me for the first time, nodded and blew a huge bubble that popped before turning away to look at her phone. I didn't need a Tarot reading from Storm to tell me I'd just been dealt the hanged man and what I thought would be an afternoon of teenage banter and chocolate cake may not be quite what I'd expected.

Jon was, of course, delighted to see his daughter and when he came back to the table with hot drinks and a selection of cakes she suddenly seemed to perk up (though she didn't actually put her phone down for the whole hour we were in there). Jon asked her about school and she answered him in German even after he pointed out it would be 'nice for Jenny if we speak English'. I kind of understood and felt a little sad on her behalf – she wanted to share their first language between herself and her dad and not include this imposter. I'd have been just the same if I could have spoken to my dad in our own language. Ella's time with her dad was precious, and she wanted it entirely to herself. But in deference to Jon she spoke in English so that I would understand. However, it was an indecipherable mumble and she barely looked at me except to roll her eyes when I asked if she was on Facebook.

'Facebook? I'm not fifty!' she snapped. 'God, my mother's on Facebook and my shitting stepdad's on Instagram.'

'Ella…' Jon said in a reprimanding tone. This wasn't what I'd expected at all. I was suddenly doubtful that my gift of the nude pink lipstick would actually work with the charcoal eyes and the filthy mouth.

'It's fine,' I sighed, suddenly hearing the tone my stepmother had used when I'd been rude to her and my father had desperately tried to pour oil on troubled waters.

'I know Facebook's for old people.' (I didn't.) 'I get it… hey it's all about YouTube now, isn't it?' I smiled knowingly. Surely she'd see I was cool now.

'No.'

'Oh... really? I thought young people were all YouTubing?' I said, aware I sounded like I was about sixty-five. 'There's that one called "Zootopia", isn't there?'

At this she roared laughing, which I took to be a good sign until she stopped and scowled at me. 'Her name's Zoella,' she spat.

'Oh yes... I remember she brought out a book... I work in a library.'

'Oh wow, that must be as exciting as shit.'

'Ella! Really?' Jon was horrified and looked at me apologetically.

'It's fine.' I shook my head in an 'I've got this' gesture. 'Yes, it's bloody boring working in a library,' I said. 'But it means I can keep up to date with all the latest trends... I have a Twitter account.'

'Snapchat.'

'What?' I thought she was being rude again.

'Snapchat.' Without meeting my eyes she waved her phone at me, like this would explain everything.

Jon was obviously dying and tried to explain. 'It's an app... they take pictures of themselves and send them to each other.'

'Oh.' I just nodded like I understood, without having a clue, and Jon shuffled uncomfortably in his chair.

'Dude, you have no idea, do you?' she said, addressing Jon. Her voice was definitely less acidic when she spoke to her father – and 'dude' was definitely a softener. I recalled now how the teen club at the library often referred to each other as 'dude' and wondered if perhaps I should address her like this, but looking at her rolling eyes and curling lip, I feared that might just exacerbate the situation.

'I think you need to stop being so rude and remember we have a friend with us,' Jon was saying.

'She's not *my* friend,' I heard her mutter and my heart sank. Oh God, I'd done it again. I'd told myself not to imagine the perfect family – but what I did instead was imagine the perfect stepdaughter: a bright, shiny child in pigtails who smiled a lot and was looking for a librarian stepmother. When would I ever learn?

I felt somewhat defeated by this initial encounter, but at the same time I was determined this child would at least accept me, if not like me. I had to try and show her that I had her back, and I wasn't a threat, but I had no idea how I could do this. I wasn't completely sure if Jon and I were an item, but one thing I was sure of was I didn't want to be referred to in the same derogatory terms as her 'shitting' stepfather.

'Do you like Justin Bieber's latest?' I asked, thinking I was throwing a curve ball and she'd just be wowed by my knowledge of youth culture (told you I was an optimist).

'Justin Bieber?'

'Yeah, he's this young boy singer...'

'I know who he is. He's a tool.'

'Oh, is he?' My heart sank, and I tried to resist but knew there was a slight chance I may get desperate and address her as 'dude' any second now. 'He's just got a new album out...'

'What's an album?'

I didn't answer. How could you explain this to someone whose music was magically sent through space and 'landed' on their phone?

'It's a round disc...' I started.

'You mean vinyl?'

I nodded and made a mental note to dump Bieber and the nude lipstick, and next time I'd make sure I bought her something she'd like. If there was a next time.

After about an hour we decided to leave. The snow was now very deep and I was worried about getting back.

'I should go. I don't want to outstay my welcome. I can get an earlier coach,' I said when Ella had gone to the toilet with her phone.

'Oh don't go yet – let's do some Christmas shopping together, the three of us?' Jon said.

'No, this is the first time she's met me, and I don't want Ella to feel she has to share you all afternoon – her time with you is precious,' I said and smiled.

Jon reluctantly agreed and when she returned we stood up and gathered our coats.

'So aren't you eating your cake, Ella?' he asked as she wandered away from the table, leaving a beautiful chocolate cupcake untouched.

She shook her head. 'I'm vegan now.'

'Dude...' I started, and she whipped round, a half-smile on her face, but it wasn't affection – it was ridicule.

'Doo – do you not eat dairy then?' I recovered quickly and, looking disappointed, she shook her head. 'Hey, that's supposed to be the healthiest diet on the planet,' I said gushingly, as I followed her out of the café, hearing my stepmother's voice once more and seeing the look of disdain on Ella's face that I'd once worn so well... and so often at her age. I desperately wanted Ella to like me, but at the same time I felt her pain. I knew and understood only too well how she felt.

I longed for her to know that I too had been bruised by grown-ups falling out and leaving each other. I wanted to tell her I respected her veganism and would love to share her snapping chat and Zootopia YouTubing activities online. But I knew in my heart that, however hard I tried to make her like me, there was a strong possibility I could spend the rest of my life trying and it might never happen. My stepmother had wasted years of her life trying to reach me, but there'd been no way I was ever going to give in because I blamed her for everything that had happened to me and Mum. For Ella, her parents' marriage had already broken up – but now I wasn't just Dad's new girlfriend, I was another reason her parents would never get back together and someone who might take Dad away from her. That's why she had to start from a fighting position. It wasn't that she hated me, she just hated the fact that here was another competitor for her father's affection. And as Jon only seemed to see Ella when work and ex-wife permitted, his affection and attention was spread too thinly to begin with. And now there was me. I had to try and let Ella know I understood, because Jon was worth it – but then again, I wasn't going to be trampled on. I would have to give it time, this was early days, but I had to be strong with Ella *for* Ella – because if she wasn't stopped, she would just continue like this – the same way I had done.

We said our goodbyes at the bus station, where I would catch my coach back to the resort, and I watched as they both headed off down the road together. She linked arms with him, suddenly seeming less self-conscious, and he threw back his head and laughed at something she'd said. I was surprised to feel a tear spring from my eyes as I observed their easy closeness and realised they had something I couldn't be part of. I had no relationship with my father and I had no child – and here in front of me was a reminder of both those things. I thought of the Christmases without my dad, the longing for him to come home and for us to be a family again. This was later replaced by my longing to have a child – was it really so much to ask that I could share something like that one day I thought as they disappeared into the dusty white snow.

Before I climbed on the coach I dumped the Bieber album and the lipstick in a nearby shop doorway. Somebody might like them. Sadly, these would not be my weapons of choice in the quest for Ella's heart. Something else would be required, though God only knew what!

Arriving back at the chalet the girls were fascinated and amused to hear all about my afternoon. They gasped as I described the café, the depths of snow and the even deeper depths of Ella's frostiness, which I hoped, like the snow, might eventually thaw.

Meeting Ella had brought back all the pain of my own childhood, yet instinctively I felt I wanted to change things for her. I didn't know what would happen with Jon and me in the long run, but we were currently a couple and while we were together perhaps I could make things a little easier for Ella, cut through the teenage bravado and get her to talk about her real feelings?

I began to see that Ella was a gift – a strange one that may have been predicted in the hanged man in my Tarot, but a gift nonetheless. I had to see Ella in a positive light. Perhaps she was a Christmas gift in her own way – my opportunity to help another child while coming to terms with my own childhood.

Being here in this wonderful place with these great people I was gaining in confidence and self-esteem. I didn't let the small stuff get to me; I'd even slackened on the obsessive tidying and organising. I'd left a knife in the butter that morning, something I wouldn't have been able to do twelve months or even twelve weeks before. I was learning about what really mattered – and what didn't.

I was seeing myself through Jon's eyes. He'd told me I was beautiful and fun and though his daughter didn't feel quite the same yet (an understatement perhaps?) I was ever the optimist! Jon was spontaneous and saw me in the same light, not as the uptight and abandoned forty-year-old singleton I felt I'd become.

'I've been defining myself by my single status for the past twelve months – but being single doesn't mean I'm a failure,' I said to Jody the morning after I met Ella. 'Yesterday Jon and I had no time alone, yet I felt somehow closer to him through Ella – okay, Ella was being difficult, but that's what kids do. I love seeing him in the role of a parent, the way he asks her about her life and the way he smiles at her, that unconditional love that only a parent gives. I found him even more attractive, and my feelings for him are so much stronger now – he's a father, a caring one, and I love that about him as much as I love his big blue eyes.'

We were sitting by the window, drinking coffee. The view was amazing, the mountains covered in white, the sky a pale grey and the snowflakes flurrying past like a moving lace curtain.

Jody smiled. 'I'm happy for you, I don't envy you the uphill struggle of *The Omen* daughter, but it could be worse. Don't sweat it too much though, Jen. You're here to work and have a good time. You're not here to try and win over someone's stroppy kid – that's her parents' job.'

'I know, but if I want things to work with Jon then I have to get on with his daughter... she seems sad and a bit out of place. She doesn't know where she fits into this whole divorce thing.'

'That's life. I mean, who fits in anywhere? We're all just struggling to get through, Jen, but look after your own heart in all this and don't spend your time here taking on other people's problems.'

'You can't say that, Jody – you don't understand. You've never been part of a broken family, Dad living miles away, Mum crying every night, your only wish throughout your childhood that your parents get back together... so please don't tell me people don't fit in, because some do. You did.'

She looked shocked at my outburst. I suppose it's what was bubbling under the surface for me – it had been for years.

'I know you felt resentful at times... but I thought you accepted me.'

'I accepted you because I had to. If I had been as vile to you as I was to your mum then Dad would probably have avoided seeing me and, despite being stroppy and obnoxious and difficult, I wanted to see him. But sometimes when I left to go back to Mum I felt guilty, because I didn't want to leave you all, and there were times when I was just a phone call away from calling Mum and saying "I'm not coming back."'

'I understand that. Your mum was miserable, snappy – she never seemed happy.'

'Dad was the one who made her like that. He was different with her – you saw a happy, carefree guy who would come home

from work and swing you round the room. I never had that dad –
I had the one who didn't want to come home, who stayed late at
the office... probably seeing your mum.'

We didn't speak for a while. What could we say? We both just
sipped on our coffee and gazed out onto the white wilderness.
Eventually I spoke.

'I remember, I must have been about fourteen and I'd been at
yours for a couple of days with Dad and your mum, and it was
time for me to go back home. It was Christmas. I remember the
tree, beautiful it was – all gold and glitter, it took my breath away
every time I looked at it – but I never said anything, I kept all
my thoughts locked inside. My mum never bothered with a tree.
"Not worth it for two of us," she'd say, so yours was all the more
beautiful, unattainable. We were all in the living room. I was saying goodbye to you – you were asleep on your mum's knee, just
a baby. The lamps were lit, the fire was crackling and it felt warm
and cosy, and I was going out into the cold, to a grey, miserable
house with a woman who hated my dad and probably hated me
for spending time with him. That night, more than ever before, I
longed to be you, cuddled up on Claire's knee, the snow falling in
the dark outside but only warmth and light inside.'

Jody stood up from her seat and came to stand over me and,
putting her arms around me, she hugged me tight. 'I never realised, Jen... I never realised.'

Chapter 15

Bing Crosby and Bride of Chucky

I'd seen Jon most days after our trip to Saas Fee. He'd talk about Ella and how much he hoped we could become friends, and I tried to be positive, but on the few occasions he brought her along, I didn't feel any thawing of the ice. Once, when Jon had to work a little later than usual, he dropped her off at the coffee shop so I could keep an eye on her while I worked. I gave her hot chocolate and tried to talk to her about music and fashion, but she just basically laughed in my face.

'I'm not "on trend", am I?' I'd laugh along, thinking if you can't beat them, join them.

'It's phrases like "on trend" that make you look very stupid,' she'd monotoned from behind her phone. I decided to continue serving customers, but inside I was stinging, reminded of the time I'd laughed in Claire's face when she asked me if I liked 'that band The Oasis Brothers'.

So when, on Christmas Eve, Jon invited me to spend the evening with him and Ella, I wasn't exactly excited. I was keen to spend the evening with Jon and told myself this was a long-term project and wouldn't happen overnight – I had to keep chipping away and this was my chance to make Christmas special for all of us. Perhaps this could be an almost family Christmas, I thought as I packed my overnight bag to take to Saas Fee. But I had no illusions – I knew this wasn't going to be that Sunday-supplement Christmas filled with glitter and glad tidings. Knowing Ella, it would probably involve swearing, no eye contact and being permanently glued to her phone.

In Europe Christmas Eve is like Christmas Day in the UK – presents are exchanged and supper is a special family event. So on my day off I bought Christmas presents – a beautiful notebook for Jon to write his recipes in and a pair of black opal earrings for Ella. The earrings cost a lot more than the notebook, but they were slightly Gothic, which I felt she'd approve of, and as opals were her birthstone (October), I hoped they'd make her feel special, knowing I had thought about her when buying her gift.

I took the bus to Saas Fee and on arriving decided to walk out of the town towards Jon's flat. It was so Christmassy here with the snow-covered roofs. I walked past chalets, glimpsing candlelit tables, families warm inside their homes, while outside a wind was whipping up around me, and the snow was coming down much more heavily now. I pushed myself forward through the weather, just hoping I could find where he lived easily, before the snow became any thicker and deeper.

Eventually I arrived at Jon's home, a small, but lovely wooden chalet with a wreath on the door and fairy lights around the windows.

'Welcome,' he said, opening the door and letting me and the weather in. 'Wow, that feels like a snowstorm is coming,' he said, putting his arm protectively round me and guiding me into the warmth. Once inside, I looked up into his eyes and reached up to kiss him. He responded eagerly and his warmth took away all the cold in my bones.

'Oh God no,' a voice said from the sofa. I hadn't realised Ella was already there. She didn't look up from her phone. I wasn't sure whether the comment was about my arrival or not – but then that was the idea, to make me feel uncomfortable and if challenged say it was nothing to do with my arrival, and that she was referring to something on her phone. I knew all the tricks from long ago... I'd played a similar game with a copy of a magazine as a teenager.

'Oh, hi, Ella. Happy Christmas!' I said, walking into the room. She just grunted. It was going to be another one of those nights.

It was warm and snug and lamplit inside, and I could smell the delicious aroma of warm garlic and chicken coming from the oven. The chalet was two bedroomed, and downstairs was open plan, with the kitchen only feet away from the cosy living room and open fire. It was small and simple with a Scandinavian feel – all block shelving and straight lines, no frills, a real bachelor pad stacked with books, skis and snowboards leaning against the walls. Christmas music was coming from a little radio in the kitchen. It sounded tinny and fizzy, but I liked the old-school sound of it – like music from the past.

Ella immediately announced she was going to shower, which was her way of confirming I wasn't welcome, but I was determined to stick this out. Jon said she was likely to be 'several days' in the shower so not to take it personally if we didn't see her for some time. He was joking, but I knew he was trying to soften this for me – he'd picked up on her feelings too. I appreciated this and the fact he wanted to make things easier for me while trying not to antagonise and upset Ella. He was treading that tightrope and I could see the pain in his eyes – I recognised it as the pain in my father's eyes when I'd told Claire how much I hated her. I'd had no idea of the deep feelings, the complex layers of guilt and hurt, my treatment of Claire must have caused my dad.

'Your home is lovely and the food smells delicious,' I said, trying again to shake off the past and all the pain.

We wandered into the kitchen, where Jon put his arms around me and hugged me for a long time. 'I've missed you so much,' he sighed into my hair.

'You saw me yesterday,' I said, laughing.

'That's how it is. There is no rhyming and reason,' he sighed, as always getting the phrase a little wrong – which made me love him all the more. 'I miss you when you're not here, in my arms – I can't help it.'

I reached up and kissed him. This is how it should feel to love someone – that you can't leave their side. I felt the same way too.

'I hope this is going to be okay,' I sighed, gently pulling away from him.

'Why not?'

'Because it's Christmas, your special time with Ella. Perhaps I shouldn't have gatecrashed?'

'No, you're not crashing the gate, Jenny,' he said, pulling me back into his arms. 'I have never had a girlfriend since Martha and I parted. It's been a long time and it's new to Ella. When Martha left to be with her new husband, it hurt Ella so much I vowed I would never bring anyone into our lives... but just like you didn't want a man with a child, we can't help what our hearts do.'

I was touched by this lovely sentiment, and the fact that until now, he'd given up on the idea of a girlfriend or partner for his daughter. What a wonderful father was all I could think as we kissed and slowly danced to Bing Crosby now singing on the tinny little radio.

Eventually we pulled apart and Jon poured us both a glass of wine before we sat on the sofa together. 'I want you both to be friends more than anything I've ever wanted,' he suddenly said.

'Me too,' I sighed.

'And you can... if anyone can reach out to Ella, you can.'

'I'm not so sure, Jon.' I almost rolled my eyes Ella style at this. In the first few encounters I'd hoped we might have a breakthrough, but the longer I was with Jon and the more I saw Ella, the more it felt like we'd made no progress at all. The idea that she would ever even make eye contact with me was still a stretch of the imagination.

Jon stood up and wandered into the kitchen area where I instinctively followed him. We stood together as he stirred the chicken casserole. It was unspoken, but we both knew we had to be discreet and neither of us felt comfortable showing affection in front of Ella. She would be out of the shower soon – even Ella could only string it out so long – but we took a chance and kissed again. I longed for him to lift me up and throw me on his bed and make love to me, but the slamming of the bathroom door was a reminder that we weren't alone and we sprang apart as Ella appeared.

'That was a quick shower, for you,' Jon said.

'I changed my mind,' she snapped. In her efforts to avoid me, she'd obviously realised it would make it easier for Jon and I to chat or kiss or do any of the other things couples were supposed to do. I knew what she was doing, I'd done it all myself, but I had to let her believe she had the upper hand. She needed to exercise what little control she had, because throughout everything that had happened to her, she'd had no voice.

'Dad, shall we do presents?' she said, like I wasn't even there.

'Yes, let's.' He smiled, clapping his hands together like an excited child. I loved this about Jon. He could be serious and strong, which I found very attractive – yet he could also be childish and spontaneous and fun.

Jon picked up an armful of gifts from under the little pine Christmas tree. It was quite bare, with only a few baubles and a wooden train decorating it – and there was little colour coordination. I had to smile – if there was such a thing as a bachelor tree, this was it. Jon took the presents to the sofa and plonked himself down, where Ella joined him, while I put my presents on the coffee table and sat down in the nearby bucket chair.

The present giving was fun, though it felt rather naughty opening them on Christmas Eve. I've always been a stickler for waiting until the day, but this was how they did it here. Jon gave me a beautifully wrapped robe. It was long and thick and cherry red, and I held it to my face, feeling the soft warmth.

'I wanted to get you something because of your suitcase mishappiness,' he said and Ella smirked at his language mix-up.

'Oh and this is from Ella,' he said, handing me a small parcel. I opened it and inside was a bauble, a beautiful white glass bauble that glimmered and glittered under the light.

'Oh, Ella, it's so beautiful. Thank you,' I said.

She shrugged, a little shimmer of embarrassment crossing her face. 'Dad chose it, I didn't.'

'Well, it's lovely,' I said, putting it carefully back in its packaging so it wouldn't break in transit. I glanced at Jon and Ella, sitting expectantly together on the sofa, his arm around her, unopened gifts waiting to be discovered, a funny little Christmas tree in the corner – and I felt a tingle of happiness. Was it possible that one day Ella would let me in and we could become a kind of family?

It was my turn to hand out gifts, so I plucked Ella's from the little pile first. 'I hope you like them,' I said, holding the beribboned gift out to her.

She waited a few agonising seconds before she took it and glanced from me to Jon as she opened it.

'I thought they were your style – I hope so...' I started as she undid the wrapping and opened the box.

'My ears aren't pierced,' she said and, unsmiling, she closed the box and put it on the table.

What an idiot I was. I felt so stupid and I'd been so desperate to give her something special I hadn't even checked that her ears were pierced. So much for being caring and showing her some support.

I smiled, embarrassed, looking at Jon for reassurance and he looked as lost as I was.

'You don't have to be so rude, Ella.' Jon said this gently, but my heart lurched. I didn't want Ella to react to this by creating a big row on Christmas Eve. This was a special time and I didn't want to live through another awful Christmas.

'Perhaps you could have your ears pierced?' I suggested.

'Mum won't let me,' she said.

'Oh. Well, you don't have to wear the earrings,' I said, imagining this gift could open a whole new can of worms. Ella could easily translate this to her mother as 'Dad's new girlfriend says I have to get my ears pierced'. 'I just wanted you to know I was thinking about you,' I said, smiling broadly, braced for what she'd say next.

'I thought you'd bought me the new Bieber vinyl,' she said and looked disappointed.

'Er, no... why?'

'Well, you kept going on about him when we went to the café the other week.'

'I just thought you... might like him, but you said he was a... tool.'

'He is. But I would have liked the vinyl.'

I thought about the vinyl and the lipstick I'd bought for our first 'encounter' abandoned in a shop doorway because I thought she'd hate it. I sighed. I couldn't win this one.

Once the presents were exchanged, Ella was immediately back on her phone and Jon, who was now tending to the Christmas Eve casserole, had given up on any kind of Christmas ceasefire tonight and was losing himself in chicken and garlic.

'What time is supper?' Ella said, putting the earring box on a shelf without acknowledging it and now addressing Jon. I felt a pang of hurt, but I also felt a little bit angry. It didn't matter what my reason for being here, I was a friend of her father's and she was being rude. I considered saying something but decided to leave it – I had to hold back and hope she'd come round.

'Supper is... now!' Jon said and she giggled at the sudden way he said it. I giggled too and looked around to see if she would grant me this, but she didn't catch my eye, just opened the drawers and took out cutlery. Two of everything.

I stood in the kitchen hoping Jon would realise and say something, but he just kept stirring his bloody stew and smiling inanely.

'Take a seat,' he said to me and I sat at a place with cutlery, much to Ella's annoyance.

'Ella, you silly billy, you forgot my knife and fork,' he said, not missing a beat as he placed the bowl of steaming chicken stew in the middle of the table and winked at me. Oh he was good. He'd managed this whole situation without offending or hurting either of us – and I know perfect doesn't exist, but in that moment he came pretty close.

Ella didn't say anything. She just walked back to the cutlery drawer like a robot and took out the necessary fork, knife and spoon. I pretended not to notice; again this was her way of exercising her voice and I must let her do this. Claire would sometimes comment on my rudeness or reprimand me – and as gentle as it was, it gave me the glorious opportunity of saying those words stepchildren love to keep in their armoury and use to wound: 'You're not my mother.'

I was thinking about this as we all sat down and ate in silence, the wind howling outside and the snow on the window ledges growing higher and higher.

'I think you have more books than me,' I said to Jon, seeing some titles and authors I recognised among the mainly Swiss-German novels along the shelves.

'I have the cookery books too,' he said, gesturing towards a shelf in the kitchen with several large books. He got up from the table and opened a cupboard – inside were jars filled with flour and sugar, molasses, candy canes and brightly coloured sugar strands.

'Wow, is that all your baking equipment?' I said, as he proffered an open jar for me to smell the divine aroma of sugar infused with cloves, the most beautiful Christmassy fragrance. I just wanted to breathe it in for ever.

'I was going to make topping for cakes – the café in the village said they would buy them from me – but I haven't had the time.'

'Oh you must. I bake most weekends when I'm at home, but I can never eat them all so take them to our neighbours,' I said. 'There are quite a lot of families with children who can't afford luxuries like cake, so I have a weekend of baking therapy and they get to enjoy the results.'

'That's what you call "winning-winning",' he said, pleased with his mastery of the English language.

I smiled. 'Win-win.'

'Yeah, win-win, Dad.' Ella smiled and rolled her eyes, and I didn't know if it was with me or at me, but I took it.

After supper, Jon asked Ella to help him clear the table and she grudgingly asked me if I'd like some coffee. I said that would be lovely, and Jon washed the crockery as I opened a curtain to peep out at the snow.

'It's coming down pretty fast,' I said, a little concerned at how much the snow had risen since I'd arrived. Jon leaned over and looked through the window, our heads touching. 'Oh dear, it's bad – it looks like a snowstorm out there.' Ella joined us at the window. 'Bloody, shitting hell!' she said and glanced at me to see if I was going to react. I didn't. I presumed Jon was too worried about the weather to reprimand her, and then someone knocked on the door and Jon went to answer.

'It's a neighbour,' he said, wandering back in and putting on his coat. 'He needs help moving his car from a snowdrift. You ladies will be okay for a little while, won't you? I won't be long.'

'We'll be fine,' I said and smiled as he left. 'I hope your neighbour's okay,' I said to Ella. 'I'm not used to snow like this... I had planned to go home to the resort tomorrow. I hope it clears so I can get back.'

Ella shrugged and lay on the sofa, engrossed in her phone.

I continued to dry the crockery and wipe down the kitchen units, and when it was all sparkly clean I turned round to see Ella was still on her phone.

'How long has your dad been out?' I asked, beginning to feel a little concerned. He'd only gone out in a coat and it was minus twenty degrees.

Again she shrugged, but then I saw her glance at her watch.

'I reckon he's been gone about forty-five minutes now,' I said, trying not to sound worried. I didn't want to alarm her.

She again didn't answer me, just shuffled her bum further into the sofa and continued to gaze at her phone.

I swept the floor and leafed through some recipe books and then went to the bathroom, by which time another forty-five minutes had gone by. Jon had said he wouldn't be long, and now I wished I'd asked him how long that meant. He hadn't even taken his phone, and I didn't know what to do, so I just kept going to the window to look for him.

Ella hadn't moved or spoken throughout this time but, as I turned from the window, she finally looked up from her phone and made eye contact with me.

'Are you looking for Dad?'

I nodded, still trying to hide my concern. 'I don't know how long it takes to get a car out of snow, do you?' I asked.

'No.' She put down her phone and stood up. I expected her to announce she was going to bed or the bathroom, but she walked over to the window where I was standing.

'I'm a bit worried,' she said, almost to herself.

'Me too,' I admitted, as we both looked out into the snowy darkness, joined briefly and awkwardly by our love for one person.

'I'm scared,' she suddenly said. 'I don't want anything to happen to my dad.'

At this my heart swelled and I put my arm around her, fully expecting a rebuff, but for once, she allowed me this. 'Don't worry – I'm sure he'll be fine. Nothing will happen to your dad. He knows his way around here, doesn't he?'

She nodded slowly, and I pulled away slightly to look at her face and reassure her, but I could see indents on her chin that suggested she might be about to cry and I knew just how she felt. She'd lost her dad once when he and her mum divorced – she couldn't go through it again.

'It's okay, he'll be fine,' I repeated, guiding her away from the frightening blizzard at the window. We sat next to each other on the sofa, and I reached my arm out tentatively again to comfort her as one would a touchy cat.

'How do you know he'll be fine? You don't know what it's like here. People get killed from falling snow, it happens – people just disappear!'

'I know they do... I know they do...' I said gently. 'But your dad has lived here all his life – he knows what he's doing and he wouldn't leave you, Ella. Your dad will never leave you, I promise.'

'Promise?' She looked up at me, a frightened little girl in clown eye make-up, silent tears running down her face, and she seemed so vulnerable. And then she started to cry in earnest, huge sobbing tears, unable to get her breath as she dropped her phone onto the carpet and put her head on my shoulder. She collapsed into me, and we stayed like that for some time, me and the little girl with all her sass and pseudo-sophistication wiped away along with the charcoal eyes.

If we'd been at home I'd have put on my wellies and gone on a search, but I didn't know where I was, there were now weather warnings on the TV and there was nothing we could do but just sit and wait it out.

Ella couldn't stop crying, and I realised that sitting here with the TV showing images of people stuck in the snow wasn't helping either of us. I had to be positive. There was nothing I could do physically, but the longer time went on, the more concerned I was that Ella might decide to go and look for him. Jon in a blizzard was one thing, but his twelve-year-old daughter out there exposed to the cold and the danger was quite another.

'Do you know what I do when I'm upset or worried?' I suddenly said.

She shook her head.

'I bake a cake... or two... or three.'

'That's what Dad does,' she said, a half-smile emerging through the tears.

'Does he really? Well then, he'll understand when he walks in to find several cakes in the oven,' I said and laughed. It was a hollow laugh, but I think I got away with it. 'Thing is, Ella, I don't know where the ingredients and the pots and pans are – could you, would you mind... helping me?' This was a long shot. Yes, I did use baking as therapy, but I was doing it on this occasion to take Ella's mind off the fact her father had gone out of the house two hours ago and hadn't come back.

'I'm not baking a stupid cake with my dad out there,' she snapped, now back to her old self. I could see where she was coming from though, so I abandoned the flour and the whole pretence of making a jolly cake to cheer us up and called Jody from the bedroom.

'I'm just ringing to say Happy Christmas and carry on without me tomorrow because the roads are blocked and Jon's missing – so I could be here until Boxing Day, or worse still, the rest of my life,' I said.

'Oh my God, Jon's missing? And you're snowbound with the evil munchkin,' she gasped.

'Yes, but I'm hoping Jon's just doing his Good Samaritan act in the snow, and I hate to tempt fate, but a few minutes ago I'm sure I felt a slight thawing regarding the daughter from Hell.'

'Really? Or is it perhaps that your expectations are so low even if she catches your eye by mistake, you think she's calling you "Mummy",' she said.

'Mmmm, probably.'

'Well, if you ask me, you needed a dose of reality with Hell Girl. Most of the time kids just aren't that cute – and it's about time you realised that motherhood isn't all about girls in blue dresses and whiskers on kittens.'

'Nice analogy – I agree, it is less *Sound of Music*, more *Bride of Chucky*. She keeps rolling her eyes and giving me filthy looks. I suggested baking a cake, but she looked at me like I'd just urinated on the carpet.'

'I thought you'd done your research. You said you knew everything about teenagers,' she said, laughing.

'I did – but she's so difficult! I daren't mention Facebook, which apparently is only acceptable in old people's care homes these days – it's all about snappychat and "what's up" or something.'

'It's called Snapchat and WhatsApp, and you're trying too hard again, Jen. Stop jacking her style, girl...'

'I don't even know what that means.'

'Exactly, just be yourself and stop trying to force entry into her world. That's the point of being a teenager, remember – no adults allowed.'

As always, Jody amazed me with her knowledge of people and life, and I put the phone down realising that I had to just get on with it and hope Ella would climb aboard when she was ready. And the words 'snappychat' and 'Justin Bieber' weren't going to leave my lips.

I went back into the room and tried to think of something real to say that was relevant.

'Look, Ella, it's a bad night. But your dad's probably helping other people too. He saved me when I'd been out in the snow and collapsed...' I started.

'Did he?' She seemed vaguely interested. I'd never told her how I met her dad; perhaps just by being natural and saying what I was thinking rather than trying to second-guess her, I could reach her. That's what my little sis reckoned anyway – so it was worth a try.

'Yes, it was awful, I was so embarrassed.' I told her all about my suitcase issues and my outfit and how I'd chatted with him outside the nightclub and the minute I'd walked back in I'd collapsed in front of everyone. I told the story with feeling, and she gasped in all the right places, even giggling a little at my humiliation.

'So even in my advanced years I can still manage to make an idiot of myself in front of the opposite sex,' I said, laughing.

She smiled at this and then told me how she liked a boy at school and she'd fallen over in front of him and was mortified. 'He'll never like me now,' she said.

'Well, your dad still likes me and I was face down in a night-club, so don't give up... You should tell your dad about the boy you like, get the man's view.'

'No... Dad's always too busy to talk to me about stuff like that. He's not interested.' And there it was, crystallised in a few words – the problem.

'He is interested in you. I know that might be how it feels, Ella, but your dad thinks about you all the time. He never stops talking about you – you're everything to him.'

She didn't answer me, but I just kept talking. 'My mum and dad were divorced too. I lived in another house in another town from my dad like you do. And it's taken me a long time to realise that even though he wasn't with me every day, I was with him. I was his child and he carried me in his heart – I just wish I'd realised it when he was alive. Your dad carries you with him too, Ella, and it doesn't matter how many people he rescues from the snow or falls in love with – you will always be special.'

Tears filled her eyes and she suddenly put her arms around my waist and clung to me. 'I'm scared, Jenny.'

I hugged her and thought about how Dad had described me as 'the clever one', something I'd never been aware of until Jody told me recently. How I'd longed to fit into his new family but had felt so betrayed when he'd left. How he'd called me 'the most important girl in the world' but had gone on to have another little girl. I'd felt like I had no place in his life, so I'd fought him, permanently pushing barriers, defensive just like Ella. But all that time, I did have a place in his family. It wasn't a traditional family unit, but that didn't mean I didn't belong, and it had taken me until now to realise my dad did care.

'I understand how you feel, Ella. And I want to make you feel better. No one really explained it to me, and I just think you should know that parents are sometimes so wrapped up in their own lives they forget to tell their daughters what's going on. They love us so much they assume we know and we don't always, do we?'

She shook her head.

'And if me being in your dad's life and yours is a problem, then I will go. I won't make a fuss – I'll just go. But me going away won't make things change between your mum and him. You know that, don't you?'

She nodded sadly. 'I know, and you don't have to go, Jenny.'

'Really?'

'No, you can hang out a bit, but just stop being silly.'

'You mean I can't tag you on Facebook and talk about Justin Bieber too much...'

'Don't ever tag me on Facebook and as for Justin Bieber? Shitting hell, you're obsessed,' she said.

I looked at her and saw the twinkle in her eye – she was teasing me. I laughed and she smiled a lopsided 'I don't want to smile but my mouth is doing it anyway' smile.

❄ ❄ ❄

A few minutes later the phone rang. 'Jon,' I said, waving at Ella on the sofa. 'He's fine, your dad's fine,' I said, and she sat up suddenly, hair on end, beaming. Jon quickly explained that he was now helping another neighbour to clear the snow from his front door. 'I'm so sorry, I would have called you, but I didn't take my phone. I had to borrow this from a stranger. It's really bad out here, people need help. I may be another hour. I won't be able to take you back tomorrow, Jenny – the roads are all blocked.'

'That's fine – I'm sure Ella will be delighted I'm staying for Christmas Day,' I said, winking at her. She rolled her eyes, but this time it felt more good-humoured.

'Are you and Ella okay?'

'Yes, we're fine. Do you want to speak to her?'

'No, I'm too busy...'

'You do? Yes, she wants to speak with you too... she's been worried.'

'Oh, of course, yes – I'm sorry, sometimes I forget.'

'I know,' I said, handing Ella the phone and going to the bedroom so she could have her dad to herself.

❅ ❅ ❅

'So... baking... let's bake a cake for when your dad gets back,' I said, walking back into the living room.

'I'm not baking – that won't get Dad home any quicker.'

'You're so right – baking a cake won't do that, but it will provide him with cake when he gets home – and he loves cake, doesn't he?'

She shrugged and picked up her phone, lost again to the world of snappychat and texting and doing whatever you were supposed to do on Instagram.

I wandered into the kitchen, which was filled with a mix of old-fashioned and ultra-modern crockery, and enjoyed the sense of being surrounded by all the wonderful baking paraphernalia. I felt like I'd died and gone to heaven. This was the kind of kitchen I would have loved to bake in, but unfortunately I had to make do with a corner of Storm's kitchen, which was often taken up with magic teas and strange herbs.

I felt like Nigella as I started to take ingredients from the cupboard and describe them, hoping to engage Ella. 'Ooh, just smell this cinnamon,' I sighed. 'Oh and what's this?' I took a jar out of the cupboard and unscrewed the lid, oohing and ahhing about the smell and the texture and just what I was going to bake. But nada. 'I wonder if you could help me with the weighing?' I asked, in a final act of desperation. 'You need to be a space scientist to work out how to use these scales.'

She tutted as she stood up from the sofa and skulked into the kitchen. 'It's not difficult, Jenny, you just put the flour in there and the numbers are here – it's digital, anyone can use one... even you.'

With that she wandered back into the living area, and I continued to weigh and mix ingredients and start baking, feeling rather foolish because I was only doing this because I thought she'd join me and it would stop her worrying. I couldn't help thinking if Jon walked in now he'd think I was mad. His daughter was lying there upset on the sofa while I was baking a bloody cake like a Stepford Wife whose wiring was loose. So I tried one last time to engage her.

'If you help me I won't mention Justin Bieber.'

'Promise?' she said with her lopsided smile.

'I can try... but let's do some snappychatting anyway.'

'God you're annoying,' she sighed, taking an apron down from the kitchen hook and throwing it at me. She found another one in the coat cupboard, and we both started to gather together the ingredients.

And at precisely 10.15 p.m., having been gone for over three hours, Jon pushed his way into the chalet, covered in snow, to see us just about to whip up a cake storm. He was cold and exhausted, but the smile on his face at seeing us together in the kitchen said it all.

'Daddy, we've been so worried!' Ella yelled and ran towards him, hugging him hard and gently guiding him to the sofa like he was an injured bird. Tears sprang to my eyes – for someone who seemed so disagreeable on first meeting, she was actually very caring.

Jon and Ella sat on the sofa, her arms wrapped around him, and as I walked towards them I felt a barrier go up and I flinched. He reached out his arm to bring me into the hug, but I understood and offered to make him a hot drink instead while he told us all about the car stuck in the snow. 'So have you girls been baking?' he said.

'Yes, we're thinking cinnamon spice cake with citrus buttercream – it's perfect, sharp yet light to cut through the richness,' I said.

'Ah no, no, no – she needs the Christmas gingerbread base, rich and chewing.' Jon was now standing up and walking into the kitchen area.

'Chewy,' I said, laughing, 'not chewing.'

Jon laughed too... and God bless her, Ella laughed and caught my eye conspiratorially.

'Dad, the lemon buttercream will be perfect, Jenny and I already decided.' I glowed. She had brought me into her world, if only in a sentence, but I felt a warmth in my tummy.

This was followed by some good-natured arguing over cake flavours, where Ella and I disagreed with Jon and laughed at some of his mispronunciations, which I'd realised he did deliberately for Ella to enjoy.

'Okay, I know a way we can prove we're right.' I winked at her. 'Let's have a competition – Ella and I will make our cake and you can make your "chewing ginger" cake. What do you think, Ella, does that sound like a plan?' I held my breath, ready for a deflating shrug or creative use of the word 'shitting' as an adjective.

'Okay,' she said, 'but we'll win.'

'No, you won't,' Jon said.

'Oh yes we will,' Ella and I answered at the same time, just like in panto. We laughed at this and as she lifted her hand to give me a high five I flinched. I was still slightly unsure of her – but she and Jon laughed at my reaction.

'Jenny, you are just so uncool,' she said.

'Yeah and you're a bit scary,' I said, laughing. She giggled and lifted my hand to meet hers, showing me just how to do it, which of course I did know, but I let her show me.

'I love baking late at night,' Jon said as he began pouring syrup into a bowl. 'I come home sometimes after night-shifting and bake bread and cake for breakfast,' he said, his eyes glittery.

I never saw him quite as animated as when he was talking about recipes and flavours, and I found his enthusiasm quite infectious.

'Pass me the fresh ginger, Ella,' he said, grating it into black treacle, adding baking powder and turning the mixture with an old whisk. It went from yellow marbled with black treacle to a deep, dark brown batter that smelled (and tasted) divine. Ella poked her finger in for a taste and he slapped it playfully, making us giggle. 'It's almost midnight and we're baking cakes,' I said. 'Could this night get any crazier?'

Once the gingerbread cupcake bases were in the oven, we started on the citrus buttercream, and this time it was his turn to sample. I told him off playfully, but when he put a blob on the end of my nose, Ella retaliated with a handful of flour. This escalated and before any of the cakes were finished we were all laughing and covered in cake ingredients. We couldn't do anything for laughing.

Later, when Ella went to put on her night things, Jon and I were finally alone. Jon pulled me towards him gently and licked some of the sweet, sugary batter off my upper lip as I melted in his arms. We kissed. His mouth was warm and he tasted sweet, like Christmas, and my heart was all wrapped up in gingerbread and squishy buttercream.

'Get a room, you two,' Ella groaned and we both went red with embarrassment, not realising she was back.

Jon set to work whisking up the topping, all three of us sampling every now and then and making suggestions. 'More cinnamon?' Ella said, and I nodded. 'More rum?' I asked and Jon obliged. Once the buttercream was adorning the cakes, they didn't stick around for long, and we ate them with gusto. 'These are almost the Glühwein cakes you talked about creating,' I said, eating a ginger cupcake covered in Christmassy cream.

'Yes, the citrus are light and not too sweet – I like them with the topping,' he said, offering me a bite of his cake. I took a large bite and licked my lips, and then I offered him my ginger cake. I'd never realised cupcakes could be so erotic.

'Let's take these into the living area,' Jon said, filling a plate with the delicious cakes and grabbing a bottle of wine.

He added some logs to the fire and I lit some candles as he opened the wine, and we sat in front of the fire on a squishy sofa eating, drinking and discussing our baking creations.

'I think Dad's gingerbread "chewing cake" is excellent,' Ella said, 'but mine and Jenny's cake was just dope.'

'Is that good?' I asked.

'Oh yes,' Jon said. 'I reckon you two have won.'

'Fair enough, the judge has spoken.' I smiled.

We finished off the cakes and then Jon suggested Ella should really be in bed. 'Your mother would be cross with me if she knew.'

'Then don't tell her,' she said and winked, taking a sip of her dad's wine and saying a final goodnight. Then she kissed her dad and I felt a slight hesitation about whether she was about to come towards me and perhaps hug me too. But she didn't, and I just blew her a kiss, which caused the eyes to roll, but I detected it was slightly more good-humoured than before. Ella still needed time. She had to do what she was comfortable with when she felt like it. She'd already had so much taken out of her hands – she had to make her own decisions about some things.

Jon and I continued to sit by the fire and talk quietly.

'Until I came here I thought my life was over,' I sighed. 'I've always seen it as this great tragedy that I left it too late for children, and I suppose it's something I will never quite come to terms with. But I'm enjoying spending time with Ella...'

'Yes, I felt the difference tonight – I think you may have won her over.'

'Oh, I don't think it will all happen so quickly. There will still be some challenges ahead, but I think I'm beginning to understand her better.'

He looked into the fire, watching the flames. His eyes were glassy, wet, like he was about to cry.

'My own parents stayed together – they were happy for ever. I tried to stop the divorce, begged her not to leave – I didn't want this half-life for Ella.'

'It's only a half-life if you keep her in the dark, Jon,' I said. 'Look, I know it's none of my business, but Ella's been lost in the middle of the grown-up war, and you and your ex have always loved her, made sure she's warm and safe and has everything she needs. But perhaps no one has really talked to her about how she feels. And I understand why – it's because neither of you want to know.'

He looked uncomfortable and sat up from his recumbent position by the fire. 'I'm not criticising the way you've handled it, just observing, from an objective position as someone new in your lives, and also from the perspective of the child. I lived through this, like Ella is now, and I think she feels like she doesn't have a voice. I know she's only twelve, but she needs to feel empowered, her feelings and opinions respected – and as a parent that will hurt because no one wants to think their child is hurting because of them. But trust me, it will be good for all of you if you just allow her an opinion, allow her to make the decisions sometimes about where and how she spends the weekend. Ask her what she wants instead of you telling your ex and her telling you what you both want and how many days and what time for pickup and collection. She's not a parcel, Jon.'

I hadn't meant to be quite so honest. I'd intended to be more tactful, more sensitive and he would have had every right to say, 'Mind your own business.' But he didn't.

'Jenny, I think I'm falling in love with you,' was what he said.

'Oh.'

'Tonight when I rang and you gently reminded me I had a daughter who loves me and worries about me and you gave her the phone, I just felt such powerful emotion. You've stuck around, you haven't been scared off by the luggage... I worried you might be.'

'I wasn't sure how I would be with all this,' I said, meaning the Ella situation. 'But I'm beginning to care about you too... and

Ella... you come as a package. It's not always the prettiest package, but I care about you enough to see if we can make it a little easier, for all of us. I don't know the answers – who am I to tell you, a real parent, how to treat your daughter? And I'm sorry – I shouldn't have been so direct on the phone.'

'No, you should. Her mother and I have been blind; as you say, it's always the fighting over Ella, about the time and place, and I think we lost what it's all about. You have helped me understand that now. Do you think we have some kind of a future?' he asked suddenly.

'You mean more than just a working holiday romance?'

'Yes.'

'I don't know, Jon. We live so far apart, but I could go home after the season, make some changes and come back here. You know I was thinking of taking classes in cake decoration. It's something I've always wanted to do.'

'You could come back and get work in a bakery – better still, one day we could run our own business making amazing cakes,' he said, excitement flashing in his eyes. 'We could do this together, Jenny. We both want the same things, and you *can* have a family – me, you and Ella. You don't have to live your life without a child after all...' he started.

I smiled and sipped my wine. I was not yet ready to dwell too much on my childless status – I was still coming to terms with it myself. 'When you put it like that, it sounds very tempting. I may never have my own wedding or my own baby, but I could make cakes for other people's special days, birthdays, wedding, christenings... God, I need to stop talking and thinking about babies.' I laughed. 'But more than any of that... I could be around for Ella... and for you.'

'I would like that,' he said.

And as the snow came down outside we kissed, and taking my hand he led me to his bedroom where we took off our clothes and lay together on the bed. For a long time we held hands, just talking, and as daylight broke over the mountains we made love. This time it was slow; we took our time, kissing, caressing quietly until he moved into me and I wrapped myself around him. I'd never felt so close, or so in tune, with anyone in my life before, and when it was over we lay there, hand in hand again – and now it felt different.

I looked over at him, this handsome man who I'd known only a few weeks, yet he felt so familiar, so right for me. Until Jon I'd been trying to make everything perfect, in its place, no surprises – but now I knew you couldn't catalogue love like a book. He had a child already, not something I'd ever wanted from a man, but I could imagine loving Ella like my own child one day. I had a lot to learn about motherhood that Ella could teach me. And in all the madness I was slowly learning to enjoy the moment – and despite all the hurdles I would still have to encounter, thinking about Ella made me feel warm inside. She didn't have a new family or a new baby to compete with as I had, but Ella had her own uncertainties – where did she fit in with Dad's new relationship? I didn't have any answers for her, and I knew as long as I was with Jon there would be ups and downs with Ella, but perhaps if we stayed together we could create a niche in our relationship for her. And just as importantly, perhaps she and Jon could create one for me, because along with Ella I was a lost girl and always had been. Until now.

Chapter 16

Christmas Gingerbread and Birthday Champagne

On Christmas morning Ella came running into Jon's room and though initially she looked a little surprised to see me there in his bed, she took it in her stride.

'Let's have croissants for breakfast,' she said and left us to get up.

'That went surprisingly well,' I said quietly in Jon's ear.

He smiled. 'I think she's starting to realise that you are as wonderful as I know you are.'

I forced myself to leave him in bed and joined Ella in the kitchen, where we made breakfast together and behaved like we were almost friends. I say 'friends' as she didn't roll her eyes once – which given our history to date was bordering on besties! Jon appeared in the kitchen and made his special hot chocolate (with melted chocolate chunks), and we all spent the morning eating croissants, watching TV and laughing together.

At one point, Jon went to check on the neighbour from the previous evening and it gave me chance to talk to Ella.

'You're okay, aren't you... about me ... staying overnight with your dad?' I asked as we sat together on the sofa. As usual she was on her phone, but she looked up at this.

'You mean do I mind you and Dad having sex?'

I was a little taken aback. 'Well, I wasn't going to put it quite like that.'

'Ha, well I suppose it's better than what Mum said the first time she had sex with Paul at our house. "We're having a sleepover," she said. I'll tell you what I told her: it's gross, and I don't want to know about old people doing it. Anyway, enough of all that disgusting stuff – we have a surprise for you. Don't get too excited, it's a bit crap, but the best we could do given that it's Christmas Day and we're snowed in,' she said, clearly wanting to move on. This was good. I'd been worried about how she'd feel when she saw us together, but it seemed she had taken it in her stride... and I dared to hope it was because she actually liked me.

Then she got up off the sofa, turned down the lights and Jon came into the living-room area carrying half of one of the cakes we'd made on Christmas Eve. They sang 'Happy Birthday' and I was urged to make a wish before blowing out the mismatched candles pushed into the icing. The cake was slightly stale, the tree was wonky, and no one (Jon) had thought to buy a turkey, so we ate chocolates and cake – and it was the best Christmas birthday of my life.

By Boxing Day the snow had cleared enough for Jon and Ella to drive me back to the resort, and Jon to then take Ella to her mother's.

'Can we go to the kingdom on the way to Jenny's resort?' Ella asked.

'What's that?'

'It's the most beautiful place, Jenny – it's very special. Only Dad and I know about it, but we can show you. When I was younger, I used to say I was the princess there, but I'm not a baby any more.'

'You can still be the princess,' I said. 'You can be princess of anywhere you like.'

'Yeah, I can. Dad, please can we show Jenny my kingdom?'

Jon gave me a thank-you glance for not telling Ella I'd already been. She wanted to show me this special place, and I wasn't taking that from her.

Once outside I couldn't believe how thick the snow was still. At home we'd have just stayed in for weeks, but they were used to it here and if Jon said it had stopped snowing, then it had stopped snowing.

'But that's a snow elephant, not a car,' I said, laughing as we emerged into the brilliant white, brittle cold day. The snowfall overnight and through the morning had completely covered it, something Jon and Ella were obviously used to because they ran towards the small hillock of snow and began clearing it – with their hands. I was just imagining how long it would take them to get to the car underneath when he hurled a giant snowball at me.

'Oh how very childish,' I said and, throwing myself onto the car, began clearing huge armfuls of snow and flinging them at him and Ella, which provoked squeals of joy and more snowball action from Ella. We ended up wrestling in the snow, me screaming and Jon trying to overpower me to stop me landing a huge snowball in his face like a giant cream pie. Then he started on Ella, who was screaming like something from a horror film. God only knows what the neighbours thought – then again, who cared?

Once he'd grappled the snowball from Ella, I lay exhausted and giggling in the snow while he marched off to get a spade to help free the car from its white blanket.

I lay alone, looking up at the white sky, snowflakes falling thick and heavy on my face, melting on impact and cooling and calming me after the frenzied snowball wrestle. This had been my happiest Christmas, my best birthday and I was looking forward to a future, a different one than perhaps I'd envisaged. Was I really brave enough to come back here and make a life? Only time would tell. I didn't know what I would do next – and I liked how that felt.

I'd spent my life wanting it all, always worried about time slipping away, about being too late for everything, but in trying so damn hard to capture it, I never achieved it. Time was like another lover, always leaving me behind, making me feel like everything was too late – but here I felt I was in control and was beginning to feel like I knew what I wanted, what would make me happy. And if I came back here, I thought I could make Jon and Ella happy too.

On the way back to the resort we stopped off at 'Ella's Kingdom', and I marvelled again at the glacial beauty, the icy shards hanging like diamonds from the trees and the smooth ceramic blue lake.

'Yeah well, I guess I don't mind you seeing it... just don't tell anyone else. It's a secret place.'

I caught Jon's eye and we smiled at each other, and I imagined how we must seem, the three of us together, a sort of family standing in our own perfect little world.

Eventually we dragged ourselves from the wonderful wintery setting and walked away from the greys and silvers and blues and the deep, deep silence. The heater and the engine and the radio all came on at once, and I felt like I was back in my life again, but this time I felt different, better, more accepting. And more accepted.

❄ ❄ ❄

When I arrived back at the resort, the girls were delighted to see me, and I was touched that they'd waited to share Christmas with me.

'I know it's Boxing Day, but we couldn't have your Christmas birthday without you,' Jody said, mixing Christmas cocktails, George Michael on full blast.

'This is great,' I said, 'I'm having two Christmas birthdays this year – one with Jon and Ella and now one with the girls!'

I was soon shaken from my thoughts by Jody hurling herself onto the balcony shouting; 'Iiiit's Chriiiiistmaaaaaas!' She was carrying gifts for everyone, and I felt bad as my gifts for her were still in my suitcase, which still hadn't arrived, but I promised she would get her real gifts when we returned home, or whenever my case turned up. I gave them the little gingerbreads from the village, which they seemed delighted with, and Lola ate hers hungrily, dunking it in her champagne, exclaiming, 'I've never had anything quite so tasty on my tongue.'

'I bet you have,' Kate said and rolled her eyes, which made us all laugh.

Jody, who'd already bought me the cow suit, gave me some nice soaps and a lovely candle, and the girls had all clubbed together to give me a beautiful cashmere jumper in the palest pink.

'This is so beautiful,' I said, holding it to my cheek. 'How did you know this is just what I wanted?'

'You liked my merino-wool jumper the other day, but you said you wouldn't enjoy wearing it in case you spilled something on it,' Kate said.

'So while you were tasting Jon's gingerbread... and yes, that *is* a euphemism,' Lola added, 'we went shopping. It had to be something to wear, because let's face it you have a limited wardrobe. So now you have a jumper like Kate's and you can spill as much coffee as you like on it because it's all yours.'

Later Jody brought the champagne in an ice bucket into the living room and we ate gingerbread and drank fizz. 'I can't believe I'm doing this,' I sighed. 'This time last year I was alone in bed, sobbing, with just Mrs Christmas for company.'

'I know. What a difference a year makes,' Jody said.

'Yeah, I'm so glad I'm out of it – I'm so much happier. I just wish I hadn't left all my crockery at Tim's. The tosser, he never gave any of it back.'

Jody nodded. 'Seriously, ladies – get a ring on it and a wedding list written. My friend was down to John Lewis as soon as he said "Will you..." He'd barely got the words out and she was there checking out the fondue sets and the oven to tableware.'

'My mum says no one should get married without at least one piece of Le Creuset,' Kate sighed.

'It doesn't matter what you ask for, Le Creuset, fine china, whatever, they all last longer than men. Love will die, but a beautiful Versace tea set would keep me warm long after he'd gone. No... better still, get a boob job! If you ever get married, you should make the wedding list a "bride's boobs" gift and everyone can contribute to your lovely new breasts. Then when it comes to splitting up he can't get his hands on any of it.'

'You old romantic,' I said, laughing. 'But that's the trouble with never actually being married. I contributed to that home for ten years and what am I left with? A bloody hostess trolley,' I sighed.

'Count yourself lucky. When Darren and I split up, him and his new boyfriend flogged all the furniture and blew the lot on a holiday of a lifetime in Thailand.'

'I'm sorry, Kate. I knew you were divorced, but I didn't realise he was gay.'

'Yeah. He was lovely, but he took me to see Take That for my birthday, and while I was screaming for Jason Orange, he was crying for Gary Barlow. When we split I didn't even get the dog, because Darren said he would be traumatised without two parents. I told him I was the dog's mother, and he said I was discriminating against same-sex families – I wasn't.'

'Did you ever wonder about Darren, before you found out?' Lola asked.

'No... not at the time, but then again, as my mother pointed out at the wedding – for a straight man, he was very involved with the table decorations...'

'He sewed the bloody crystals on your dress,' Jody sighed. 'I didn't want to say anything but it was a bit of a red flag... You met him in a fashion chat room and your first date was a yoga class.'

'Well yes, but it was a blind date and I was concerned about safety. There's never been a serial killer who enjoyed yoga – I did my research.'

'It must have been awful for you, to find out the man you loved was gay,' I said.

'He'd been living a lie,' Jody added.

'Yes, but I wasn't going to. When he told me he fancied men, my mother was furious. "Get him drunk and dress up like Antonio Banderas," she said. "You have to make this marriage work, our Kate... but I said no."'

'So what happened about your dog?' I asked; macabre fascination had kicked in now.

'Well, I told him that as far as I was concerned, she was my dog and could only ever be Robin's stepdog... but now we have joint custody.'

Lola was gazing into her phone, probably sexting again.

'Lola, do you have a dog?' I asked.

'I've had a few,' she muttered absently. I don't think she meant the furry kind. 'Jeez, you would not believe what this guy is suggesting... and at Christmas too.'

❄ ❄ ❄

Apart from the snow and the music and the Glühwein, one of the main reasons that particular Christmas was so special to me was the rediscovery of female friendship. I was getting to know my sister properly, but more than this I had made new friends too. Despite our differences, I was becoming very fond of Kate and Lola. Their hearts were in the right place and they were on my side – they were rooting for me. And being with them made me realise that their kindness and loyalty was a stark contrast to anything Tim had ever shown me.

That night, as we all sat together by the log fire, drinking and chatting, we grew even closer, sharing secrets and stories with each other. I'd learned so much about them, and in doing this I was learning all about myself, discovering who I was and what made me happy. And I had never been happier.

Chapter 17

Under the Stars, on the Piste

It was a few weeks after Christmas and time to leave the resort, and I couldn't believe the time had flown by so quickly. I also couldn't believe how much my life had changed. Ella and I were becoming firm friends, and Jon and I were talking seriously about me returning to live there, with him. As much as I adored Jon, I was also glad to be around for Ella, because her mum had recently announced she was pregnant, which had sent Ella into a tailspin. 'I want to come and live with you and Dad,' she'd said. 'It's all about baby, baby, baby. My mother hates me – she wants the shiny new baby now.'

I'd reassured Ella as much as I could but longed to be here per-manently so I could be there for both her and Jon. But our time in Switzerland was limited, and before long we all had to return to our lives back in the UK, and I had some decisions to make about my future. It was a no-brainer: I had to come back here – but I just had to make everything good back home first.

On our last night at the resort, Jon and I joined the girls in the nightclub for a final celebration. Jon was friends with some of the men the girls were meeting up with, and it was a lovely crowd of people, sad but happy, who walked under the stars to On the Piste, a far more welcoming sight than it had been when I'd first arrived. So much had happened since then, and I marvelled to myself how wonderful life could be as I linked arms with Jon along the pathway. The snow had been cleared, so there was no chance of any repeat performances of me in a miniskirt, raging through the snow like a weirdo.

I was really taking to life here and harbouring my little secret about coming back on my own. I hadn't told Jody because she'd said she worried I was spending too much time with Jon as it was. 'I hope you're not just a babysitter,' she'd once said. 'I hope he's looking for a lover and not just a mother for his child.'

I knew Jon and I was sure of him, but Jody had had her fingers burned and was overprotective of me and my feelings – especially after Tim.

Once in the nightclub I was swept up in the music and the drinking, and not only did I dance on the tables, Jon, his friends and the girls joined me. I was drinking cocktails and shots like a party girl, loving every moment, and despite the freezing temperatures I was described as 'hot' by a man at the bar.

As dawn broke, we all meandered wearily back to the chalet, Jon and I leaning on each other, Lola being carried by Hans and Jody holding hands with the Canadian guy she'd met earlier in the holiday.

'Where's Kate?' I asked.

'Oh, she's with her ski instructor,' Jody said.

'Yeah she's gone back to his chalet for some après ski,' Lola guffawed through a drunken haze.

'She's got this crazy idea about coming back and getting a job here,' Jody sighed.

'Why is that crazy?' Jon said.

My heart leaped slightly at this.

'Because it's just a holiday romance. These things never translate into real life.'

I glanced at Jon, and he smiled reassuringly, but for a moment I wondered if she was right. Would we forget about each other once I was home?

'I'll talk to Jody, she'll understand,' I said to Jon later. 'I can't believe I will ever feel any different.'

'You won't. You will always want to come and live here, she is so beautiful.'

'She's even better with you... and Ella.'

'You will come and live with me, yes?' he asked.

I nodded. We had something special and yes, it was early days, and Jody might be angry that I was even entertaining the idea of throwing myself into another man's life, but I'd grown – I knew what I was doing. I'd learned that life was for living, and I was determined to do just that.

'I don't want to take you out of your life, but if we are to be together... I can't come to England. I can't leave Ella. It might be a little difficult... there isn't much room at my flat and...'

'It will be fine. I used to worry about every little thing – let's not spoil this by looking for problems. Let's just enjoy the moment and I'll come back in the spring. I could get work in the coffee shop until something else comes along. And, besides, I would love to live here. I'm not the stressed, obsessed woman I was, I'm learning to be "going with the flowing" as you taught me, and I'd rather spend our last night talking about the possibilities of an exciting future – and not the possibilities of any problems.'

He agreed, and we walked back to the chalet and I led him to my bedroom. I tingled as his beautiful hands ran all over me, teasing me, seducing me, reminding me how it felt to make love, and I ached for him. I was racing through a wonderful glittering snowstorm, my heart in my mouth – I couldn't get enough of him as we moved gently, then more urgently together. He was ardent but tender, and as I felt myself explode, a million snowflakes filled my head, falling like confetti, covering me, folding me into him. This was what I'd been waiting for, and when we came together it was passionate, hands and lips and bodies entwined, and we held onto each other like we'd never let go.

Waking the next morning it was wonderful to see Jon's dark curly hair on the pillow next to mine. And when he turned his head, opened his eyes and saw me, his face lit up with a huge smile and without words, we just reached for each other and kissed for a long time. And then he left me, disappearing into the bleak, beautiful whiteness while I vowed to myself I'd return. If only I'd known what fate had in store for me.

Chapter 18

Mind over Menopause – the Sequel

Going back home to the house I shared with Storm was comforting, but it felt like I was going backwards instead of forwards. I'd had a glimpse of what my life could be and I wasn't going to stay here.

I had to work three months' notice at the library, which felt like an eternity. I got through this by speaking to Jon every day either on the phone or on Skype, and I began a course in cake icing, which happened every Tuesday night. I was also allowed to become Ella's friend on Facebook, which was a huge honour, and she messaged me most days, usually upset about her mum's pregnancy and how it was impacting her. I talked her down a lot, sometimes sitting on the phone for hours on end. When I wasn't Skyping Jon, counselling Ella, working at the library or practising for cake icing exams, I spent many nights reading lovely romances about women swept off their feet and loved until their bodices ripped. But instead of making me happy, they made me cry. What was wrong with me? I was in love, I'd see him soon, and I couldn't understand why I was suddenly so tearful and helpless all the time.

'Why are you so bloody miserable and moany?' Jody said when I met her and the girls for a few drinks at her flat. I'd finally told her of my plans to return to Switzerland, and she'd taken it surprisingly well. In fact she said she'd toyed with the same thoughts and might even follow me there.

'I'm just hot and uncomfortable. I don't know why you have to have your heating on full blast, Jody.' It was like the bloody tropics in her flat.

'I don't even have the heating on... I can't afford it. But, Jen, it's February, it's bloody freezing. What's wrong with you? You're complaining about the heat all the time.'

'I don't know, must be menopausal, but the sooner I get back to chilly Switzerland the better,' I sighed. 'I just feel so lethargic, no energy. It's not like me.'

'Issues, shrinking hormones... you've got the lot,' Kate sighed.

'I reckon your middle-aged juices are crying out for a final fling,' Lola said, momentarily distracted by a photo of a topless Gerard Butler on her phone.

'Jon is my final fling,' I said, 'and only just in time the way this menopause is raging through my body.'

It didn't take a nurse to spot the wild hormones and rampant emotions of menopause. I'd broken down several times in 'Romantic Fiction', where the tables were turned and customers had to shush me. By mid-February I felt so out of sorts I turned to Storm for help. As she had prophetically predicted the presence of a child in my last relationship (Jon's daughter), I hadn't quite given up on her talents, and I asked her to read the cards for me. But through a haze of patchouli oil and steaming green tea, we would hold our collective breaths, only to sigh as Storm turned over that hanged man and swords. This was always followed by cards with people being crushed by brick walls and screaming faces, and she'd try desperately to convince me this wasn't all bad.

'Your immediate future is suggesting rough storms and swirling tempests,' she said, gazing at the picture of a man upside down and dead with a noose round his neck. 'But it's not all bad... there's either a birth... oops or... or is that a death?' She rolled her eyes. 'Sorry.'

'So am I... if it's a death,' I sighed.

'I know, I know... but birth and death are the same, aren't they really?'

'No.'

'Well, would you rather I lied about what the cards tell me?'

'Frankly yes. Or at least pretend you got mixed up again and these gothic images of death, destruction and falling walls are June's.'

'No... they're not June's, quite the opposite – June went on a cruise and met an exotic male dancer from Buenos Aires... I read her cards last week. She got the world card.' And she smiled, like I should be pleased.

'Lucky June,' I sighed, deeply and irrationally envious of a woman whose holiday romance was in full swing, while I had to wait for mine while working notice at the library.

My moods were all over the place, I kept forgetting things and, as Jody said, this was proving to be one hell of an early menopause. My tropical moments were more like the swirling tempests the cards had predicted, and when one evening I spent a whole evening at Jody's being sick, she did a nursey thing and checked my blood pressure.

'It's pretty high,' she said. 'And this sickness bug combined with your hot sweats is a little worrying. I think you should see a doctor.'

I almost collapsed. 'Really? Oh no, Storm predicted a child and now she's predicted my death! Oh my God, the woman is a shaman,' I said, collapsing in floods of tears on Jody's sofa. 'Give all my jewellery to Ella when I'm gone.'

'You haven't got any jewellery.' Jody was, as always, quite calm; she didn't believe in Tarot cards and as she'd recently done a stint in A&E, the sights and sounds of me vomiting, sweating and swearing was just like another day at work to her.

'Look, Jen, get a grip. You're not dying, but if it is the menopause, then your doctor will be able to at least give you something so you can function – every time I've seen you in the past few weeks you've been crying or sweating. And trust me, it isn't cute.'

She had a point, but I was scared of my GP. She was tall and thin and seemed to be looking down on me, literally and metaphorically. She had no facial expressions as such and had been last in the queue when they were giving out sympathy. I decided if I was going to be told devastating, life-changing news about my health, I didn't want it delivered by a robot. So I ignored Jody's advice to call my GP and instead I started to write a will, which worryingly Storm said was a good idea.

However, on realising that Mrs Christmas and my first edition of *The Christmas Cake Café* were my only earthly possessions, I decided to do what I always did in times of stress – bake a cake. I was all over the place, but a couple of hours and a few tears later I was eating a big slice of coffee cake and feeling much better, convinced I would live forever.

The sugar rush must have been the reason I called the girls that afternoon and invited them over for the evening. I was missing Jon and Ella and wanted to remember Switzerland so I hosted a Christmas dinner in spring. I made Christmas cocktails and to remind us of Christmas in Switzerland, I sprinkled fake snow everywhere, baked fresh gingerbread and a proper German Christmas cake.

'Ooh, Christmas is great any time of year – and I think from now on we should always have two Christmases. The queen has two birthdays, so why not?'

'Yes, let's make it a girls' tradition that every March we revisit Christmas and remember Switzerland,' Lola sighed, no doubt thinking of Hands-on Hans, who she still spoke to on Facebook. He was even planning to come over to the UK later in the year. Who'd have thought it? It seemed like we'd all left our hearts in Saas Fee.

'This is delicious,' Jody said, taking a huge bite of chocolate cake between sips of her Christmas Orgasm. 'What's the secret ingredient, Jen?'

'The salt from my sweat and tears,' I joked. 'It's Jon's recipe and it's just like the one we ate at The Cake Café in Saas Fee.'

Kate put her hand on my arm. 'You miss him, don't you?'

'You could say that... This is good,' I said, nursing the non-alcoholic cocktail I'd christened 'Hormones in the Snow'. I hadn't felt like drinking since that alcohol binge in Switzerland. At my age I couldn't take it any more.

My spring Christmas with the girls empowered me, and I spent the next few days determined to shake off this malaise before I embarked on the serious stuff like leaving work and booking my flight. So I armed myself with luxury scented wipes, Evening Primrose oil and a tub of floral remedy donated by Storm. I'd bought a book called *Mind over Menopause* that basically said the condition didn't exist and if you denied it long enough it would go away. I liked this philosophy – I didn't have time for hormones and I had to live my life, buy stuff to take to Switzerland and have a new passport picture taken as mine had run out. So I approached these tasks like a post 9/11 New Yorker in defiance of the terrorist hormones rampaging my body. *I will go about my business, and you won't stop me*, I thought, wiping my forehead and sipping tea at Costa. *Oh no, mister, you will not win*! I smiled as I handed over my credit card for some delicious new pastel winter wear to take away. 'You will not destroy me,' I mantra'd at the Vista Print shop while a nervous man took my passport picture and I dripped sweat all over the seat. And for the next few weeks this is how I soldiered on – until April when a worried Jody physically dragged me to see scary Dr Boyle.

I envied people who had a doctor who didn't look at her watch as you walked in and even gave you a few seconds above the allotted time. I dreamed of a GP who engaged in small talk – a 'How are you?' would have been nice – but I was convinced she hated her patients, begrudging even the most poorly specimen. The day Jody made the appointment and forced me there was no different, and I knew if Dr Boyle had bad news it would be delivered like the evening news, emotionless, unbiased and with no feeling. I was

glad Jody was with me, and I tried to take my mind off my immi-
nent death in the waiting room by flicking through *Woman's Own*
and gasping at the so-not-beach-ready bodies of diet-lapsed celeb-
rities. I looked up from the body-shaming pull-out and glanced at
my sister. She was looking right back at me, concern all over her
face, and in that moment I felt loved. Here she was, the only relative I had left, holding my hand and helping me to face whatever
was ailing me, and she was doing this totally for me. I smiled at
her, knowing that whatever news the doctor had to tell me, my
little half-sister, the one I'd resented for most of my childhood,
would be there for me.

Little did I know how big the bombshell would be that day in
the doctor's surgery, and how much I would come to rely on Jody
– how I'd need her like I'd never needed her before.

Chapter 19

Sick, Dope and Very Gassed!

As soon as I was before Dr Boyle I began to tell her all about my ravaged and unpredictable emotions, my inability to keep food down (including my beloved doughnuts) and my permanent, tropical sweat.

When I'd finished, she looked at me for too long without speaking. I was used to this, but Jody wasn't and stirred uncomfortably in her seat. The only reason I knew Dr Boyle was still with us was a slight curl of the lip at the very mention of doughnuts – which had the opposite effect on me and made me hungry. I was in a constant state of flux.

'Pee in this,' she suddenly said, thrusting a tube at me and returning to her computer screen.

I did what was asked, then Dr Boyle sucked some blood from me and told me to wait in the waiting room and she'd let me know what my urine results were. 'The bloods will take a couple of days, but I'm ruling nothing out,' she said. 'Nothing.'

❄ ❄ ❄

Twenty minutes and three *Hello!* magazines later, we were tannoyed in the waiting room and asked to return to the surgery.

We both sat down together, Jody holding my hand, both thinking we were ready for the worst but not ready for what we were told.

'Lie down,' Dr Boyle barked. I looked around the room, saw the bed behind the curtains and climbed up.

'Baby's due around the end of September,' was Dr Boyle's sensitive way of announcing the cause of my nausea, and the hormone imbalance creating night sweats and emotional upheaval.

'I told you I wasn't ruling anything out,' she barked without waiting for my response as she hoisted up my top and began kneading my stomach like dough. I felt like I was being assaulted, emotionally and physically.

I couldn't speak. I was in shock – and Jody, who was also in shock, just kept murmuring things like, 'Is she okay?' and, 'What happens now?' I nodded, my head moving almost involuntarily like a ventriloquist's dummy.

'But I was having a... the menopause... I didn't take precautions because I haven't had a proper period for a year. It was Christmas...'

'Well, it must have been an immaculate conception then,' she said, and without looking at me, she pulled down my top and whizzed back on her wheeled chair to consult something far more urgent on her computer.

I sat up, and Jody helped me off the bed. My legs were shaky and it wasn't the most elegant dismount. I'm not exactly sure what was said after that; despite desperately trying to listen and understand what was happening, I felt like I was trying to wake from a dream, but the more I pushed, the more I remained locked inside it, at the mercy of whatever happened next. The room was swimming, Jody was speaking but I heard nothing, just watched her mouth moving. I was aware Dr Boyle had dismissed us, and when I climbed into Jody's car, I still hadn't spoken.

'You weren't having an early menopause,' Jody said finally as we pulled up outside hers. 'You were so upset about everything with Tim it had probably affected your periods... but not, it seems, your fertility.'

'I just hadn't even considered this... not for a moment.'

'Do you think, subconsciously, you wanted this – you made it happen?'

Jody was right, I had wanted this to happen, but I couldn't make it happen – this was wonderful, glorious fate and I was delighted, if shocked and scared by the news.

I spent the next couple of days with Jody, trying to get my head round the situation. I desperately wanted this baby of course, but I wasn't sure how Jon would feel. And there was Ella to consider.

'I'm going to love this baby so much,' I said, through tears.

'I know, love. You'll be a brilliant mother – and I'll be the perfect auntie,' Jody said, hugging me. 'But when are you going to tell Jon? You've known two days now and you still haven't told him.'

'It will break Ella's heart. I just feel so awful – the timing is terrible.'

'The timing might not be good for Ella, but at forty-one you're very, very lucky to get pregnant,' she reminded me. 'Look, I know how you feel. You're worried about Ella going through the same stuff you went through. I get that – but you have to put you and Jon in here somewhere. He has a right to know and once you've told him, you can talk about how you break it to Ella.'

I took Jody's advice and that evening I Skyped Jon.

'I don't know how to start this...' I said. 'But I have something I have to tell you, and I really wish it wasn't on Skype... It's something I should tell you in person. I don't know what you're going to say...'

'Jenny, tell me,' he said, unsmiling. 'My heart she is beating and I'm thinking you've met another man.'

'No, no, it's nothing like that.' I almost laughed and the relief on his face was clear even through fuzzy Skype. 'Jon, I'm pregnant – I'm pregnant, Jon.'

'Oh my darling... my darling.' He was shouting this and jumping up and down, and before I could say anything he was calling, 'Ella, Ella, it's Jenny – she has some news.'

I almost stopped breathing. This wasn't how I wanted her to hear about this. Her heart would break in two, and I was here and she was there, and I wouldn't be able to comfort her. She appeared in front of the webcam dressed in her towelling robe, looking puzzled at Jon and then sitting down and adjusting the camera to her own height.

'Jen, Jenny, are you okay?' she was saying.

'Darling, I am – I'm great.'

'You're still coming back, aren't you? Dad and I have just decorated the bedroom. I don't want to see you two kissing so you can do it in there,' she said and giggled.

'Lovely... that sounds lovely... Ella...'

'It's lavender... yes?'

I couldn't speak. After all the building bridges and bonding, all the hurt we'd helped to ease, I was now going to hurt her all over again with this news. I remembered how I'd felt about Jody, the baby who stayed full-time at my dad's house, the baby who took my place as 'the most important girl in the world'.

'I'm going to tell you something now, but before I do I want you to know that you are the special one. You will always be your father's first child, his eldest child and...'

I held my breath. I had to go for it, just tell her – yet I knew the impact this news could have and I felt it so keenly for her.

'I want you to know how much I love you, Ella. I know we haven't known each other very long, but I feel like you belong to me, that we're family... and even if... a baby were to come into that family, those feelings, that love, will never change.'

'I know, I know. Everyone keeps telling me and at first I was upset but Mum and Paul have wanted one together for ages. The baby's due 23 August and today they found out it's going to be a boy, did you know?'

'Yes, a boy...' I'd been trying to gently broach the idea of another baby – mine and Jon's, but of course Ella had immediately assumed I'd been referring to her mum's pregnancy.

'I heard you were a bit upset Ella, but everyone still loves you just as much and it's... lovely to have a new baby in the family,' I said hopefully, still trying to prepare her for my news.'

'No, it's not. It sucks.'

'Oh, Ella, I'm so sorry.' This was the reaction I was dreading, if she thought her mother's pregnancy 'sucked' then I could only imagine the expletives she'd use to describe mine.

'Does the idea a new baby make you really unhappy?' I asked tentatively, almost scared of what she might say.

'Yes, it does.'

Oh God.

'… because I wanted it to be a girl,' she said. 'I don't want some snotty little bro… but Mum says I'll love him when he comes out.'

I sank back in my chair with relief. 'So you're okay now about your mum having a baby?'

'Yeah… but I'd bought it some really dope little pink skis and Dad says he won't be able to wear pink.'

'Well, first of all there's nothing wrong with boys and pink. Your dad needs to chill and stop gender stereotyping colours,' I said.

'Whoa yay, you go, Jen,' she said and laughed as Jon pulled up a chair.

'And secondly, some time around late September, you'll be having another baby sister or brother.'

'Oh my shitting God!'

I heard Jon's gentle reprimand in the background.

She screamed a blood-curdling scream, and for a second I wasn't sure how she was taking it, then I saw her and Jon hugging each other and crying before she put her face back in the camera.

'Jenny, what the shitting hell are you doing sitting there telling me about my baby sis? Get over here so I can rub your feet and get talking to that girl… I rub Mum's feet and talk to my little bro all the time. But this is my sis… It had better be a sis – that would be soooo sick. Man, I am gassed!'

I smiled with relief. 'I guess *sick* and *dope* are good… and *gassed* means you're pleased?'

'Yessss! In fact I am *very* gassed!'

I could have cried with relief. 'I don't know if she's a girl yet...' I said, 'but I just wish I could hug you and your dad right now.'

'So what are you waiting for? Hurry up, we want you back. Come home now.'

At these words my chin began to tremble and I burst into floods of tears. The noise I was making brought Jody running into my room.

'What on earth... Oh no, the bastard...' she said, pushing her face into the camera, about to give Jon a piece of her mind.

'No, no... it's okay, Jody, look,' and we both looked together into the camera as Jon and Ella looked back – all four of us crying with happiness. Here we were, three people, hundreds of miles apart in so many ways, yet brought together by love – and now there was a baby who would tie this ragtag bunch into the imperfect, perfect family I'd always dreamed of.

Chapter 20

My Sister, My Friend

A week later, Jody was helping me pack for Switzerland and a new life. I was five months pregnant and didn't want to leave the travelling too late; besides, we now had lots to do at home in Saas Fee. Jon was talking about buying a three-bedroomed chalet, but Ella was insisting her sister share the room with her. I didn't mind; I was just happy that Jon was happy – and Ella of course. I was excited and a little frightened about the birth and the future and how I was going to cope, but Jody was there for me, as she had been for some time now, and I knew I would explain all this 'half-sister magic' to Ella one day.

'I'm so happy, Jody. I just hope Ella will be okay when both babies are born.'

'She'll be fine, love – I promise. Ella's situation's different to yours. She has four parents who pretty much manage to get along – and she belongs to two families, not just one. You see, as much as you felt you didn't fit into our family, I always thought you did – and when you didn't want to go home to your mum, I always envied you having two homes, two bedrooms, two sets of toys.'

She was carefully folding a towel and holding it to her chest, looking into the distance. 'Dad was so upset about your mum never allowing him to see you he actually went to court one Christmas to try and force your mum to send you to spend Christmas with us. He had legal permission and your mum was told she had to let you go – but at the very last minute your mum sobbed and begged him, saying she'd be alone at Christmas if you weren't there. I remember him telling my mum he couldn't hurt her any more – he said he'd already ruined her life. It was on his conscience, and the irony was he never really embraced true happiness with Mum because of the terrible guilt he felt at what he'd done. And all he did was fall in love.'

'I never realised Mum had kept us apart so much,' I said. 'I once found a Christmas card on the mat and I saw the postmark was Warrington, where you lived – and I was excited, thinking he'd sent us a card. But Mum said she knew lots of people who lived there and it wasn't from Dad – it was from an old friend. I think even then I guessed she wasn't telling the truth – but I felt her pain.'

'Yes, but by telling you that Dad hadn't turned up, or hadn't sent a card for Christmas, she was making you believe he didn't love you – and he did. All the time you were thinking he had this new family and we were perfect, I was listening to him talk about "my Jen", as he'd call you, and his eyes would go all misty, and I used to wonder if he loved me that much,' she said and smiled sadly.

I was surprised and happy to hear this. Jody was right, I'd always imagined this perfect family, their perfect Christmases (often described with relish and venom by my mother), filled with laughter and plenty. But nothing was perfect, and Dad had lived with the guilt, and Mum had lived with the betrayal, and it had tainted all their lives.

'Going away last Christmas was one of the best times in my life,' Jody suddenly said, clamping down my suitcase. 'I spent time getting to know my sister, and now... we're having a baby,' she said, putting her hands on my stomach, glowing as much as I was apparently supposed to be doing.

My pregnancy had brought out the nurse and the carer in Jody, a side I hadn't seen before – one probably saved only for patients and people she loved.

'I always wanted us to be friends,' she said, 'then after last Christmas I felt like you were a friend who's my sister... but now you feel like my sister who's my friend.'

I couldn't have put it better myself.

Epilogue

New Beginnings and Happy Endings

Christmas, a year on

I'm sitting alone by a log fire, the snow is softly falling outside, the tree is twinkling and I'm enjoying the peace. Mrs Christmas is washing her face in front of the fire, Dora is sleeping and 'White Christmas' is playing in the background. I'm a little unnerved, because this is beginning to feel a lot like the perfect Christmas, and they don't exist – do they?

My baby daughter is now almost four months old and she's quite delicious in her red velvet onesie trimmed with fur. It's a gift from Jody, and it takes me back to my cow onesie from last year – and trust me, Dora's working hers far better than I did mine.

Jody came over for the birth, shouting like a personal trainer to 'push hard' and 'dig deep'. I screamed back at her, hurling all the profanities that are apparently usually delivered to the partner at high-hormone times like that. But Jon was lovely and calm and mopped my brow and continued to tell me I was beautiful, despite the literal blood, sweat and tears.

After a while I hear the door open. It's Jon – he's home with Ella, who's with us for Christmas. I can't wait to get to know Ella in the way I was never allowed to with my father's 'other' family. I want her to feel like she's part of the family, and I'm keen to welcome her and let her know she's still her daddy's little girl, the most important little girl in the world. The new baby isn't a threat to the special relationship she has with her dad, and neither am I, and we will be a happy, blended family forever. But I needn't worry. We eat chocolate cake and Ella talks excitedly about Father Christmas and hugs her new baby sister with such love that it brings tears to my eyes.

When I arrived here, Jon had a surprise for me: he'd rented The Cake Café in Saas Fee. The old lady who owned it said she'd rather rent it to someone she knows than sell it to some corporate chain, and she knew Jon would maintain the traditional baking and keep the magic. After Christmas we reopen as The Christmas Cake Café. We're going to recreate our glacier kingdom in spun sugar as a window display. I've already started work on the most important piece – a sugar-crystal Princess Ella, who will rule the kingdom. We have a lot of work ahead and with a baby and a new home I know it won't be easy – but life isn't easy. Life is tough and it can be messy and sad and absolutely wonderful and exhilarating too. I thought I had my life mapped out until Jon appeared in the snow, but he gave me back my dreams and he gave me the best gift of all – Dora. When I look back over the past two Christmases I can't believe how much my life has been transformed – and how much I have too.

Meanwhile, we're recreating a little bit of home here in Saas Fee this year as Storm, Jody and the girls arrive tonight to spend

Christmas with us. Jody says one day she'll move here and get married in the snow. I really hope so. I just know if Jody moves here my life really would be perfect... yes, perfect, because she's my sister, who also happens to be my best friend.

And that's what Christmas is all about: family and friends being together, and it doesn't matter that there's no champagne, no expensive Christmas gifts and no surprise engagement ring in the bottom of the glass. I want to be here, with Jon, forever, but my Christmases have taught me that true love isn't about the music, the posh restaurants and candlelit proposals – and being in love doesn't mean you have to sit under mistletoe all night ... or put a ring on it.

I've brought my childhood book *The Christmas Cake Café* back to Switzerland with me. I want to read it to Dora when she's big enough. I want her to share my love of books and escape into that wonderful world of imagination. In the meantime I'm reading it to Ella, who I refer to as 'my teenager', and she seems to like it. I love her as much as Dora, and what's more, I even like her now – a lot!

Our own café is remarkably similar to the one in the book and when I reread it I could see what I'd been looking for all these years. The final picture in the book is two pages wide and filled with the windows of the café. The Christmas cakes are covered in swirly icing, like snow, and the biscuits are heart shaped and buttery. There are clouds of icing sugar and snow, and sparkles of spun sugar catch the shards of light, and The Christmas Cake Café is glowing in the snow... And just behind the window is the heroine. She's holding a baby and her new husband is by her side. All my life I've been trying to write this happy ending for myself.

I never had the perfect family, yet I believed it existed for everyone else. But having spent time with Ella and Jon, I can see now that there isn't a cookie-cutter family life to live. There are no rules, and sometimes square pegs have to fit in round holes, and lives and families aren't perfect, but the secret is to open up your heart and love will find you.

It may not be what you thought you were looking for – it may be different, unusual, even slightly flawed – but to you it will be perfect, and that's all that matters.

Happy Christmas.

Acknowledgements

Thank you to Bookouture, who always make my books sparkle! Christmas kisses to Oliver Rhodes, Claire Bord, Kim Nash, Emily Ruston and the rest of the wonderful team who guided me down the slippery slopes and helped me to create *The Christmas Cake Café*.

To Nick and Eve Watson, thank you for putting up with my 'Christmas stress' in July, and as always thanks to my lovely family and friends for their love, support and laughter.

A special thank you to my author and blogger friends for their retweets, likes, shares and friendship, and for inspiring me in so many different and delicious ways.

And last but definitely not least – thank you to my lovely readers for reading my books, staying in touch and making it all worthwhile.

Happy Christmas!

Letter from Sue

Thank you so much for reading *The Christmas Cake Café*. I do hope you enjoyed the snowy scenery of Jen's seasonal journey. And who knows? We may one day revisit her, Jon, Ella and Dora in their wonderful café. In the meantime I'll keep in touch with Storm – I'm sure she knows what will happen next!

Anyway, if you liked the taste of *The Christmas Cake Café* and would like to know when my next book is released, you can sign up at the address below. I promise I won't share your email address with anyone, and I'll only send you an email when I have a new book out.

I would love for you to follow me on Facebook and please join me for a chat on Twitter.

In the meantime, thanks again for reading, and have a fabulous Christmas!

www.suewatsonbooks.com/

www.facebook.com/pages/Sue-Watson-Books/201121939909514

Twitter @suewatsonwriter

Made in the USA
Middletown, DE
03 December 2017